THE GEMINI PARADOX

BOOK 3 OF THE ZODIAC

PAUL SATING

PAUL SATING

Editor: Cindy Niespodzianski

Cover Design: Jake at jcalebdesign.com

ISBN-13: 978-1-7322617-6-1

To Adam Burke. You are a warrior. Never forget. Thank you for helping me believe in me!

To Adam Burke. You are a warrior. Never forget. Thank you for helping me believe in me!

GRAB THREE FREE NOVELLAS

Free Fantasy!

Sign up for Paul Sating's newsletter
at paulsating.com and receive
THREE novellas for free!

THE ZODIAC SERIES

UNDERWORLD, FIFTH CIRCLE

One Month after Taurus

I WAS OUT OF SHAPE. Overindulgence will do that, even to an immortal.

"Come on!" Ralrek shouted over his shoulder.

Of course, good looking and strong in his Fire magic, Ralrek was also now in far better shape. I ignored the fact that he was probably making better lifestyle decisions for himself than I was.

Than I had been.

"I am," I said, snapping in the same ugly tone he used for everyone below him, which I think included everyone not named Lucifer.

That thought led to another incubus, my hefty best friend and just how far behind he would be if he were here instead of back in the Eighth Circle. I missed Bilba and wondered how he was doing. After I caught the criminal we were chasing, maybe I would talk to the Council about allowing me a few days to go back to the Eighth and check on him. If his mother was mistreating him, I'd ...

"Hurry then!"

Ralrek's long legs, courtesy of his nearly six and a half foot frame, stretched and he pulled away.

Selth Thulmox rounded the building at the next intersection, into a narrow alley that dead-ended at a monstrous trash heap hiding a forty-foot fence. He wouldn't know that, since he wasn't from the Fifth Circle. This was perfect, because I was so tired of chasing him through our streets and parks. Daily sessions at the gym were in my immediate future, starting tomorrow.

"I'm right behind you," I shouted between my heavy breaths. Ralrek was never going to let me live this down.

Selth Thulmox was a demon from the Ninth Circle of the Underworld—which I prefer to call Hell, because it is less cumbersome and I'm lazy—who had somehow slipped through an open gateway into our own Fifth Circle. The Third Council tasked Ralrek and me to find, retrieve, and return Selth to his home because, Lucifer knew, traveling to other Circles was such an egregious crime in the eyes of our rulers —easily rivaling theft and murder, I guess, because they'd never shown a repugnance to those types of actions.

At least this most recent task was a distraction from the joyful tedium of my routine at *The Book Abyss*, my full-time job. Unlike that job, this one, like all Council work, paid well and coin talks in the Underworld. Yes, I feel dirty depriving demons of things like freedom of movement, but I'm only one demon in an Underworld full of them. I cannot change any policies, no matter how strict they are. No matter how I wished I could.

Ralrek was around the corner first because he hadn't spent the last month of his life drinking too much and shoving crap food and treats into his mouth-hole. I tried to shout a warning, but I was lucky to be breathing right now. Very soon, he'd find out this alleyway would pen in Selth, and a cornered animal was always dangerous.

I chose not to activate Creed until I was in the alley. The mysterious halberd, gifted to me by Aries the First during my first mission from the Council, still freaked out those who saw it in action. In its normal state, which it was now, it appeared to be nothing more than a thick stick hanging from a loop at my waist, four inches in circumference and made of petrified dark cherry. Sort of like a baton, just way cooler. It earns me odd looks from time to time, but not as odd as when I activate it. But to be fair, no one should expect such an unexceptional stick to grow to six feet in length and sprout two ax heads from its top and a long dagger at its bottom with the simple flick of the wrist. Guess you could say that I'm considerate like that.

When I rounded the corner, Selth was already facing Ralrek, the realization he was trapped plain on his face. That's when I pulled the halberd out and activated it with a quick shake. It shot open.

A sensation like sandpaper rubbing across my neck was the first sign that Ralrek was casting a Fire spell. I don't know where it came from, but I think I have always been able to sense when someone was casting a spell if they were close enough. That ability though, my only one worth speaking of, was heightened when Aries gifted Creed to me.

A chill accompanied the rough sensation. The surrounding air grew colder and the impression of smooth ice ran the length of my exposed skin. Selth was using Water magic, his Ability—one I'd just recently learned about from an Eighth Circle succubus who was on my naughty list.

As the only demon without magical Abilities in the history of our species, I didn't have to worry about what my conjuring felt like to them. That gave me the upper hand in my fights because I did not waste time running through an incantation before getting into the fray. Selth didn't know that, but Ralrek did. And in our eight months of working together doing the Council's bidding, he had seen me do some strange things. Though I couldn't stand him as an incubus, we did work well as a team. Our combined skills only improved in the past month since we'd returned from a mission in the Eighth because we had to work through our differences and difficulties without Bilba around.

This was our third mission this month, all minor needs of the Council. And in that time Ralrek and I had gotten better and better, nearing a level where we didn't have to verbalize anything in order to get the job done.

"Leave me alone," Selth screeched, his voice wavering. He held up a single hand. "I—I don't want to have to hurt you."

I jammed the dagger end of Creed into the brimstone, which split open with ease. I have learned that making a big scene with the halberd intimidated demons before they had a chance to process what they were seeing, giving me an additional advantage. Sensing magic before a spell was cast was great, but I was still susceptible to its effects. After spending the first six thousand years of my life getting my ass kicked by bullies and my best friend in training sessions, the last thing I wanted was to be someone's victim.

"Cut off your spell and we'll take you back unharmed," I said firmly.

His eyes switched between Ralrek and me, measuring us. No one released their spell, so I still had time to find a peaceful resolution.

"You're trying to trick me," he said, but still held his spell. "I won't fall for it."

Ralrek snorted. "Cut off your spell or I'll obliterate you."

I groaned. First, it wasn't accurate. Demons could only injure each other while in the Underworld. Well, there was one exception I didn't want to think about at the moment. Second, I was struggling to de-escalate the situation and Ralrek was doing what he always did, acting arrogantly and trying to intimidate. It was almost as if he enjoyed confrontation. I guess that came naturally for a tall, dark, and handsome incubus who had life lay at their feet on a daily basis.

"No one will obliterate anyone," I said, assuring Selth he would be allowed to walk out of this alley in one piece.

He shifted his weight from foot to foot, his arm beginning to shake, from exertion or anxiety, I couldn't tell. "I don't want to go back. It's ... a miserable place. Hopeless. I ... I can't go back."

"You can, and you will," Ralrek said, holding a growing fireball between his hands.

I wished he held his tongue as much as his spell.

"Let's all calm down, and talk this through," I said, eyeing Ralrek, who didn't even look my way. His eyes were locked on the demon at the end of the alley.

I would have moved closer to Ralrek to afford me an opportunity to whisper my message, but that would give Selth an easier target too, to take both of us out with a single attack. If Water magic was good for anything, it was subduing your enemy. A treacherous succubus named Marijon—the one I didn't want to think about—taught me that a month ago. At the thought, an image of the beautiful brown skinned, hazel eyed traitor filled my mind. The aching in my chest had subdued a little. It wasn't like I had time to fall in love with her—that was ridiculous—but her betrayal hurt. Had I not— well, nevermind—but she was the cause behind Bilba and Ralrek nearly being seriously injured.

Marijon used her Water magic more than once to encase our enemies in blocks of ice. That was all Selth had to do if I drifted too close to Ralrek. He wouldn't even need to injure us, he could stop us from interfering and be well away before the ice melted.

"There's nothing to talk through," Selth responded, shaking his head. "I'm not going back."

"Yes, you are!" Ralrek spent no more time with the situation after he spat his comment. His fireball roared to life, now bigger than his stupid head and crackling with heat.

"No!" I yanked Creed's blade out of the brimstone and raced toward the end of the alley.

In the blink of an eye, Ralrek had undone everything. A battle would start, one I didn't want. Fighting sucks. There are no winners in skirmishes, only lesser victims.

I was halfway down the alley before Ralrek's fireball raced past me. Normally quick when I'm not out of shape, my ability to sense magic being heightened by Creed still gave me an extra burst. Normally I would be ahead of any spell. But Ralrek had already conjured. The distance between us and Selth was too far and did not help, nor did Ralrek's temperament and my inattentiveness. That gave the two casters an advantage.

Even as the fireball raced down the alley, Selth countered it with a thick spray of water. The opposing spells collided a few feet in front of me. Water struck fire in a violent collision, shooting a massive cloud of steam into the sky.

Ralrek was beginning a new spell and Selth was readying his own as they held their equal initial attacks. Exactly what I needed.

I closed the final twenty feet well before either of these idiots got off their next spells. Tucking into a roll, I gripped Creed by the haft at the blade end as I came out of it. Careful to not slice his ankles with the double ax head, I swung. The petrified wood haft connected, swiping his legs from underneath him with a crack of wood on bone. Selth yelped as he fell. I was on him.

"Don't move," I said, collapsing my halberd and shoving it back in the loop.

"My ankles," Selth cried.

He tried to wiggle free, and I pinned his arms to his side with my knees. "I said, don't move. We'll get you to the Council and they'll heal them. Let's just end this."

He went limp. And then he cried. At first it was soft, restricted. As I tied his hands behind his back, it grew until he shook.

"I don't want to go back. Please. Please don't make me."

I finished tying him, full of regret at the ache in his voice. That ache didn't come from injured ankles, but from the prospects of his future. It was not hard to empathize with his plight. For nearly a year now, I'd been doing things I didn't want to do either, including this. Because living a life of mandatory service demanded it. His life might not be all that great in his own Circle and I hated the thought of being responsible for forcing him back to it, but I was also being paid handsomely to do this. I felt dirty. But if I didn't, I would have troubles of my own with the Council that would compound the public humiliation, travel restrictions, and stalking I already suffered through. Not abiding by their commands was not an option until I could make it one. That time was not now, unfortunately for Selth.

Before Ralrek joined us, I lowered my head to Selth's ear. "I don't know what happened to you or why you don't want to go back, but you can't change this. Don't fight it."

Selth cut off his crying, gulping down his sobs, and looked at me through watery eyes as if I'd spawned fourteen heads. "You have no idea what it's like, man ... what will happen to me back there."

My lips pinched together. "No, I don't. And I'm sorry. But it gets a lot easier if you don't fight the Council. Let us take you, get home, and then figure out what you change."

Selth looked away, hatred burning in his eyes.

I was getting used to feeling gross.

2

UNDERWORLD, FIFTH CIRCLE

THREE DAYS after Ralrek and I turned Selth Thulmox over to the Council, I did not feel any better about my actions. It was as slimy as selling an Underworld time share to a mortal. Looking in the mirror at the demon staring back at me caused serious questioning. They remained unanswered.

Hell was a lot less fun when you couldn't stand your place in it. Old Towne, my new neighborhood, used to be a light in my life, especially on dark days. For the past few, even it and all its excellent drinking spots, lost their luster. I was grateful to be heading back to *The Book Abyss* to work a shift for the first time since arresting Selth. Dialphio, my boss and owner of the shop, would be the kick in the ass I needed.

I hoped.

Like the saying goes, shit in one hand and crush angels in the other, and see which one fills up first.

Old Towne was quiet now because it was late and none of the restaurants were open. Even the most depressed demons, the ones who made me look like a ray of Hellfire, were not out on the streets after late-night martinis. The only movement at this point of the morning centered around the coffee stands. I stopped at my favorite one to get a double caramel latte—demons have a heavy-carb diet and no, it has nothing to do with the fact that it's a bikini barista, and more to do with its proximity to the bookstore. Hell's temperatures make iced coffee a necessity and I don't like my coffee warming up even before I get to work. And the double shot was because food and drinks in Hell are bland—something I only noticed after the fine experiences of eating in Seattle.

Chilly Willy's was a shack of a building with one way in and out, and two windows on each side from which customers walked up and ordered. It was on the main pedestrian zone of the shopping district, blocked off to wagons and carriages by thick metal pillars at each end. When the restaurants and shops are open, the stand is busy, usually packed with incubi posing as coffee-thirsty patrons. But now, only employees walked the block and most didn't give the stand a second glance. The coffee is expensive, and they probably had grown numb to the nearly nude baristas who worked it after seeing them day after day. I understood; I wouldn't support a business that had incubi who looked like Ralrek walking around in bikini briefs either. The image of that alone sent shivers through me.

Thankfully, few incubi worked this stand. The staff was almost all succubi. Some gorgeous, some not so gorgeous, but friendly as heaven. And some right in the middle of them all, the sweet spot. That's where Gigaa Detrial fell.

"Good morning, Zeke," Gigaa smiled. I tried not to look at her breasts, encased in a small bikini top. Everyone calls her Gigi. Sometimes I forget her name.

I was thrilled to see her working; from the tip of her blond hair to the pumps she wore, Gigi was as visually sweet as her personality.

"Hey, how are you doing?"

She smiled like she'd just gotten away with something and

shrugged nonchalantly. "Can't complain," she said as she made the drinks for a customer at the opposite window. She turned to hand him his coffee. Her butt, encased in a black bikini bottom, was harder to ignore than her top until I remembered this was Gigi.

I smiled. Not in a creepy way, but in a way of relief, feeling partially like myself again. Those times were rare ever since I became Hell's first murderer.

When Gigi served him and took his payment she asked me, "The normal?"

"You got it. Thanks."

She made my drink, and we chatted. Halfway through, she stopped and stared at me. "You okay?"

"Yeah, why?" It was becoming far too easy to lie.

Her thin shoulders slumped as she blew a wisp of blond away from her face. Her pale skin rivaled Bilba's in its pastiness, now coloring slightly. "I've been making your coffees since you moved to Old Towne, haven't I?"

"Yes."

"And in that time, you've been one of my nicest customers."

"Not *the* nicest?"

Her eyes twinkled. "Some demons know how to tip. Besides that, you're near the top of the list."

"Just under the tippers?"

Her smiled brightened the day. "Just under the tippers."

"Touche," I responded, looking away at the menu prices and trying to do fast math to determine the level of gratuity for a barista. Who knew tipping was an expectations with something as simple as coffee?

Gigi leaned down to whisper. Her pronounced cleavage nearly blotted out her words. "That's what I'm talking about, right there. You're not yourself, Zeke. You haven't been for a while. I don't want to be nosy, but I hope everything is okay. If you need anything, promise me you'll let me know."

She laid a hand on top of mine that held my coin. Hers was warm and soft. I tingled in places I didn't need to be tingling this early in the morning. "I appreciate that, Gigi. I really do. Everything is fine, and even if it wasn't, I wouldn't bother you with it. You're always so busy."

"I'm never too busy for you, Zeke." Gigi smiled and went back to making my coffee. Three incubi appeared in the opposite window, as if on cue to disprove her sentiment. While she finished my drink, two more walked up behind me. "Be right with you," she said cheerily to the new customers.

She swiped the five coppers from the counter and gave me a sad smile—whether it was that her customers proved me correct or for my miscalculation, they were indistinguishable. She raised an eyebrow when she saw the extra coin. "Whoa, Mr. Big Spender." Her laugh was light enough to tell me I hadn't insulted her. "See you again tomorrow?"

"You got it," I said into my drink.

I made it to work on time.

"Good morning!" Dialphio shouted from her desk at the far end of the bookstore, hidden by a towering stacks of books, at least ten columns across.

I closed the door and wished her a good morning, lacking my boss's enthusiasm. I didn't dare fake it with her because I respected Dialphio too much for that.

She came out from around the stacks, waving at them. "Got a new shipment last night."

Dialphio Tywald was a short and round bundle of joy. The perfect balance to my recent moods. A book nerd through and through, I think she owned the shop her entire adult life—I never asked. Today she wasn't wearing her typical green eyeshadow that complimented her emerald eyes, making the contrast between her eyes and her auburn hair even more pronounced.

"I see," I said. "Now we just have to find a place for them."

"Don't be silly, we have plenty of room."

I looked around, wondering if Dialphio had bought neighboring properties and planned to knock out a wall or conjure an extra dimension in space and time. She hadn't done either. "Uh, where?"

"I'm sure you'll figure it out, Ezekial. You're so smart. My best employee!"

"You and I both know I'm your only employee."

Dialphio winked. "Still number one in my book."

Now, I had to laugh. "Thanks. At least I'm at the top of someone's list."

Dialphio's eyes twitched in confusion.

I let it go.

Before I got to work on making miracles happen, I set my coffee and Creed on my desk, which sat parallel to hers, behind the counter that separated the office space from the store. Each passing day, Dialphio was growing more comfortable with the collapsed halberd sitting on my desk. In the early days, I did not think she would survive to see the end of the workday, exhausted by her paranoia of Creed. But now, the stick—thank Lucifer Creed wasn't sentient; my intuition tells me he would hate that moniker as much as I hated mine—was as much a part of the store as we were.

When I first received it, Creed wouldn't allow separation, and I had old injuries to prove it. The first sign that I had a needy magical item was when I was mowing the lawn and had left the halberd in the front yard. The welt on my forehead from its speedy reconnection stayed for days. If I left it on my bed when I took a shower, it would fly into the bathroom and clatter against the glass. If I tried to walk downstairs without it, I'd get a nasty surprise—and bruise—in the middle of my back as it flew at me to reconnect. I even tried in the bookstore, leaving it on my desk and going to clean the front, only to spend part of the day re-stacking towers of books it knocked over.

Once I realized what was happening, I tested how far away I could move, which was never very far until I tried calling to it. I started small, walking a step or two away and calling Creed to me. The going was rough for a while, but over time my ability to connect, to feel the halberd and call it to me, improved. It became more responsive and I could move further and further away from it. Though I had yet to try it, I bet I could walk a few blocks and still call it, so strong was the connection.

Like I said, Creed is needy.

At least my boss wasn't.

"You look tired," Dialphio said after I put my things away and set about my tasks.

"That last mission exhausted me," I said, avoiding eye contact.

"Still?" Dialphio's tone wasn't accusatory, but it wasn't light either. The single word was a slicing analysis of my recent life. It's so annoying when demons wanted the best for you so much that they try to help out. "That was a few days ago; I hope you haven't been skipping out on me. You still owe me time."

"Skipping out? I love being here, why would I miss a single day?"

Dialphio crossed the store. Silently, she grabbed the book from my hands I was trying to shove in a tightly packed shelf. She set it on the table behind her, completely out of genre, something that would assuredly bother her until one of us fixed it. When she turned and grabbed both my hands, bobbing them slowly between us, I knew playtime was over.

"You're in a bad spot, Ezekial. Anyone who knows you can tell. Plus, you're absolutely horrendous at hiding these things." She looked over her shoulder, back toward the store's door. When she faced me again, her tone had turned dark, heavy. "Listen, I know you're not happy about what you are being made to do. And I wish I had something better to say. I wish beyond all wishes you were happy. You're a good demon, and I hate seeing you like this. I don't have an answer about how to get out of the situation. But I have ideas and as I'm standing here today, I'm telling you, resilience and patience are the keys. Wait for your opportunity and it will come. But," Dialphio said, holding up a chubby finger, "until that time, stay strong and focused. Stop letting them get the better of you."

I was speechless. Dialphio was a succubus of few words unless she was talking about books. I'm not the smartest demon in all of Hell, but I'm aware enough to know that when several demons make the same comments about you, it might be a good idea to pay attention.

"It's hard," I said, the words coming slowly. Vulnerability, especially as an incubus, wasn't allowed. Kanthor Sunstone drilled that message in my head a hundred thousand times over the past four or five thousand years. With Bilba, I could open up. But with anyone else, including this wonderful succubus, I had a lot of subliminal crap that made it difficult to open up in this way. "I don't like it. I feel dirty. The demon I arrested this week was scared, Dialphio. Scared to death to be sent back to his Circle. But they still made him go back!"

Dialphio took a moment to respond. When she spoke, I saw her in a new light. "We're in the dark about the Council's business because that's how they want it. They have their reasons and it's not the reason we're given on the news every single night."

She so got me. "I don't like what I'm involved in."

"And you still must do it."

It wasn't a question. I gave her a slow nod. "But I don't know how long I can do it. Each time they call, I feel myself falling further into their crap. I'm expected to be part of … whatever they're after, as if I don't have a mind of my own to think about what I'm doing."

She still refused to relinquish her hold on my hands. "Oh, Ezekial, if I could take this away from you, remove this burden from your shoulders. You're too young to have dilemmas such as these. It's unfair, but it's not going to change either. The sooner you realize that, the better off you'll be. Better to be prepared because preparation is everything. How are you doing that?"

The last of her words came out strong. Dialphio was saying something without saying something.

When I didn't respond, she broke the handhold and moved to the front door, doing something I never thought my boss would ever do, no matter how desperate. She locked *The Book Abyss* during normal business hours.

"What's going on?"

She moved to the back of the store, behind the half-wall and towers of books we never sold stocked atop it, leaving me alone on the floor.

"Dialphio?" I asked. Books shuffled, bags dropped to the floor, and frustrated grunts floated out from behind her hiding space.

"One moment."

When she reappeared, Dialphio held a rolled scroll in her hands. It was a grayish-white hide, and round copper capped each end. The copper had etched designs that might be lettering. After the Taurus mission, her revelation about Creed's inscription left me apprehensive about what she had planned.

Dialphio handed it over.

"And this is?" I eyed the scroll. The exposed hide was rough, hundreds, thousands of tiny ridges and lumps against the skin of my palms. Shades of green corrosion darkened the channels etched out of the copper caps. Millenia had passed since this thing's creation. Knowing that Dialphio possessed Construction magic, I asked, "Did you make this? It's awesome."

She only shook her head.

"I rarely use my Abilities, Ezekial," she said. "Not that I have any worth speaking of. They're weak. Besides, if I did, I'd use it to keep a leash on you before wasting it by attempting to build something like that. No, it's old, created long before my father's father. I want you to read it. But go home and do it. Take the rest of the day off."

"Dialphio, I need the money to make rent." I didn't, but I also didn't want her to know the actual reason I needed to be in the store and out of my own head.

But she wouldn't have any of it. "I'm going to pay you for the full day. No questions. Do as I said. Oh, and I don't know a thing about that scroll or where you got it."

"Something's up. What is this? Why are you giving it to me?"

Dialphio wagged her finger. "No questions. Go home and read. Think. You need to be prepared and the only way I can help is by informing." She clasped her hands like she was trying to imprison an annoying Hellfirefly in them. "You didn't get that here. I've never seen it before and have no idea how you obtained it. And I'll tell anyone that very thing. However you came by it, you did so on your own. Go, Ezekial. Go find your answers. With those answers will come happiness. I expect to see you first thing tomorrow morning."

I numbly nodded and made my way to the back of the store to collect my coffee and Creed. It was the most awkward departure from the job I've ever had. "Okay, I guess I'll see you tomorrow."

My hand was on the door handle when Dialphio made her last comment of the day. "And be sure to stop by that coffee stand you like to patron and tip that young incubus something fair. Just because she doesn't look like she fell out of one of those magazines young incubi like to look at doesn't mean she isn't deserving of at least a standard tip. She works hard and word is you're incredibly cheap. Five coppers is standard."

I started to say that's exactly what I paid when she cut me off.

"On top of the price of your coffee, Ezekial. Now, go."

———————

I STOPPED BY THE CHILLY WILLY AND SLIPPED EXTRA COPPERS into the collection jug Gigi kept on the ledge of her window. She was busy with three incubi at the other window and I didn't want to interrupt. Plus, I didn't need to celebrate overcoming my embarrassing frugality. One day, we might laugh about my ignorance. But today wouldn't be it. Nothing could delay me getting back to my apartment. Including Gigi.

My mind burned with the possible contents of the scroll just as my legs burned with the effort to get back to the apartment. As I strode through the pedestrian zone, to the side streets and narrow sidewalks, I thought about how Dialphio had been so unlike herself. At least it kept my hand from unfurling the scroll, which I really wanted to do. Curiosity itched. She had just done something significant, possibly dangerous. I didn't want to abuse her kindness or put her at unnecessary risk by disrespecting her by prying.

I climbed the narrow stairs of my apartment building, which was really just extra space at the top floor of a building that housed a coffee shop, its owner and her home on the second floor. I don't think she enjoyed climbing the stairs this high, so she rented out the space to make a little extra coin each month. Who could blame her? Old Towne was the posh part of the Fifth, and her mortgage had to be steep.

Being on the top floor of a three-story building gave me a decent view, but I'd had my living room drapes closed for weeks now, cutting out the blue light of the Hellfire during the day and the prying eyes of my neighbors across the street at night. It also gave me quiet, since my landlord and coffee shop owner, Manes Mezess, spent all day in her shop on the bottom floor.

I flicked on the light and squinted. Even with the curtains drawn, the blasted white walls radiated with the daylight bulbs Manes used. I planned on replacing them with soft blue bulbs but still hadn't bothered to get to a hardware store. One of these days. After I was done being a donkey to the Council.

Throwing my keys on the white table in the hall, I made my way to the living room two doors down, past the bathroom and small kitchen. Pushing everything off of my coffee table, I carefully unrolled the scroll.

Cracked open, the hide smelled of an old hellhound. I winced before returning my attention to its contents.

The face of the scroll was covered in thin lettering that was a challenge to read. The handwriting was the type you'd see in museums, swirling letters that found loops joyous. Each melded into the next. Fluid elegance, as if the demon who wrote it took great care with each letter, knowing even the slightest mistake would ruin the entire contents.

Over the course of the morning and into the afternoon, I read and reread the scroll. Over and over again. The message it contained was short, barely over two dozen words, but the implied meaning was profound. A meaning I did not want to understand.

Not in the fires, but of the One, the mastery of the arms, the protector of the Balance; its creation, a tool of necessity, for who wields, liberates.

"Who wields, liberates," I read aloud for probably the fiftieth time today.

The inscription on the haft of Creed. This scroll, as ancient as Hell and Heaven, was about the creation of my halberd.

If Dialphio had given me the scroll to relieve me of my stress, she'd failed. Now, more than ever before, questions dominated the answers, and I did not have a single idea where to begin.

One thing was for sure, Hell's Segregate was deeper into this mess than he wanted to be.

3

UNDERWORLD, FIFTH CIRCLE

ONE OF THE most difficult things about being the Segregate is that, by default, you're rejected by everyone in the Underworld—do you know how many succubi refused my request for a dance at school dances because I was supposedly a freak because I could not cast spells and their fathers would have disapproved? The public relations campaign—okay, I'm being hyperbolic because I was an impling and have no actual recollection of what the Council did to ostracize me and my parents when it was apparent I had no Abilities—was effective. A pariah because I could not cast like every other member of my species, I was always on the outside of Hell, looking in at all the opportunities others received. The same opportunities they denied me.

All because of something beyond my control.

Starting and continuing life as a default outsider left me with one source of acceptance. My parents.

In my case, a not-so-reliable source.

"This is great, Mother," I said, spooning another mouthful of her concoction into my pie hole. It was my second helping, and I still wasn't sure what I was eating. Mother is hardly a good cook, but she manages, which is more than I can say

about my own skills. As a young bachelor, my culinary reper-
toire wasn't exactly robust, so home cooking made me a very
happy incubus.

"Why thank you, Ezekial. It's nice to have my meals
appreciated." Mother looked down the length of the table at
Father, her square jaw set in playful determination.

"Dear, I completely appreciate your cooking," he paused, a
smile spreading on his lips as the crow's feet stretched from
his eyes. Kanthor Sunstone is tall, so tall many of his friends
joke that he can't be my father. So tall, he had to hunker down
over his bowl so not to spill Mother's … food—stew?—on the
table. "Almost as much as I appreciate having a break
from it."

"Oh, you!" Mother said playfully, picking up a roll from
the basket at the side of the sink and tossing it at him. He
tried to catch it, but it crumbled when it struck his palm.

"Mmm, as moist as ever," he laughed.

I rolled my eyes. "You two are so gross."

Father dipped his head, trying to hide a mouthful of food,
pointing the handle end of his spoon at his wife. "You should
be so lucky to find a love like this. We pray to Lucifer you do."

"Soon, too," Mother added with a smile before blowing a
stray strand of dark hair from her eyes. Her brown eyes,
never a pair to sparkle, turned to me at her comment,
shooting a lifetime of unspoken wishes my way. She'd have
me married off tomorrow if she could.

"Whoa, can we slow down? I just moved out. I still don't
even have furniture in most of the rooms. Heavens, if it
wasn't for Manes I wouldn't have any."

"Please don't curse, Ezekial," Lilith Sunstone shook her
head, her bob-hairstyle swaying as if it were a single piece.
"You know I don't like that."

"You should by now," Kanthor Sunstone said over top his
bowl. He looked healthier somehow. The crow's feet were still
prominent and his pure white hair was just as full as the last

time I'd seen him, but something was different. He looked more ... alive. Maybe my moving out had relieved him of a couple stresses. "The way I understand it, you've been making good money with the Council."

"Kanthor," Mother chided, the same way she had one million times during my lifetime. He twitched his mouth before spooning more soup—stew? I'm still not sure—in. "Don't listen to him. Take your time. Plus, I would rather have you decorate your home with a nice, young succubus's input. I remember how you kept your bedroom and wouldn't wish that on any apartment."

"Ha ha. Very funny." I glanced at the far wall, lined with towering boxes of moisturizing balms that promised to counter the damaging effects of exposure to the Hellfire. Mother's side hustle that still hadn't shown a profit. How she hadn't been accidentally buried under an avalanche of them was a minor curse from Lucifer.

I wouldn't say anything about the boxes cluttering their home, but I also would not bite on their push to find succubi interested in a relationship. Relatively speaking, I'd just gained independence, and I wasn't about to give that up.

"Is it true, Ezekial? Are you doing well ... financially?" she asked.

A carriage rolled by outside, the passenger's voices drifting in through the open window. I wondered if the day would come where I could afford to move my parents out of this place, away from the crowded neighborhood and the Angel Tree home that was clinging to life. Even with a renter, they couldn't afford to upgrade it or modernize it like their neighbors, converting the natural structure to a demon-made home. If things went well, if I could tolerate the Council and avoid unscrupulous assignments, maybe I'd earn enough to raise the entire family to Floater status. Imagine that. Living above the Fifth in a floating island home, the realm of privilege. A mansion or palace, like so many of the Floaters, was not on the cards, but a modest floating home would be just desserts for them. Especially for Mother.

"I'm getting more and more work from them," I answered. "They seem to be happy, at least enough to continue giving me jobs. Not that I'm crazy about it."

"How so?" she asked.

I swirled Mother's concoction with the spoon. "I'd rather just work in the bookstore. I'm happier there. It's good, fun work. I'm reading a lot now and learning all the time." I kept my experience deliberately ambiguous. "And I don't feel dirty about collecting my coin at the end of the week from Dialphio like I do from the Council."

Father's spoon handle pointed in my direction. "But you're doing Lucifer's work. Important stuff. You should be proud. Don't forget that."

"I guess so," I said, not meaning it.

A brief silence fell around the table, the three of us moving the contents of our bowls with the spoons clinking against the ceramic. It was an improvement. Not that I didn't enjoy talking to my parents. Since moving out, my visits were far more enjoyable than the days of Father making an inflammatory comment followed by me unable to resist fighting back while Mother played peacemaker. It was a sign of their growing respect of my independence that we now had these moments of quiet reflection instead, even though I imagined we all struggled with what lay underneath the silence.

Then Father threw the first punch—because he always did. "Well, you could be grateful. I've said it until I'm pale in the face, but you've been given an opportunity very few ever get. Something you should be thankful for."

"Don't you start, dear."

Mother was trying to steal glances at me as she chastised him. Have you ever had a time when you wanted to fight your parents' stubbornness, their refusal to see you as an adult, growing and maturing into your own role in life, but then realized it was not worth your effort? This moment, spoon stuck in swirling gruel, was that for me. I did not have the energy for anything that wouldn't change for another century or two under the best of conditions.

"It's fine, Mother."

I jumped when she slapped the table. Lilith Sunstone, usually wound as tightly as a ball of yarn, rarely lost control of her emotions. But right now, a fire burned behind her intense gaze. "No, it's not fine. Kanthor Sunstone," she said, using a harsh tone while using his full name was a sure sign that he was on the brink of spending the night on the couch. "Your son is very much aware of the curses Lucifer bestowed upon him. But look at him. Look at him," she repeated with emphasis when he didn't, pausing until he did as she bid. "He's your son, and he's not the same. He hasn't been the same the last few visits. For five seconds, can you stop pushing him?"

Father was smart enough to not respond.

Mother reached across the table, extending her arm, her fingers searching out mine. I wrapped mine in hers, sensing her strength. "Are you okay?"

"I have a lot on my mind," I let my gaze slip from her invasive one.

"Don't lie to your mother," she said, a tenderness encasing her brusque statement. This was her true ability, not Manipulative magic. Mother made a Heavenly tempest feel like a safe place.

The same could not be said about the incubi at the head of the table. All of existence was objectively good or bad in his eyes. Kanthor Sunstone didn't recognize the middle ground. Throughout my life, watching him come home from working the Hellfire all day, hearing his stories about that experience, I was acutely aware of his opinions on the unfairness of life. His job was never something he aspired to. Instead, he once had dreams and aspirations. But fate demanded something different, preventing him from achieving that which he dreamed to do. And somewhere along the line, those dreams were lost, and he gave up. At least that is what it looked like from the outside.

I drew a deep breath. Taking the next step was apropos to stepping off a cliff. If I admitted my depression and burgeoning career as an alcoholic, Mother would stick to me like a wet cloth.

"What is it? Go on."

The word quit wasn't in Lilith Sunstone's vocabulary. A glance at the boxes along the wall, her chain to a pyramid scheme reminded me of her determined nature. She would keep pushing until I finally broke, whether that was now, at their table, or a month from now in the middle of *The Book Abyss*. Mother cared enough to not let anything slip by, and I didn't know how long I could fake happiness.

"I'm going through some stuff," I started. "I've been a little depressed since the mission to the Eighth. It threw me off my game to see how those demons live; how they struggle to survive each day. Honestly, I wasn't ready for it."

"You're pouting because other demons have it tough?" Father said with a bite.

"Kanthor!"

I was exhausted. "Not just that. No."

"Then what?"

Could I do it? Could I tell them about what happened? Would they understand? Would they care? Would they believe? Mother might; in fact I was confident she would, but I wasn't so sure I could say the same about Father. And if he didn't, then why did any of this matter? I could tell the one person who always understood me, Bilba, and save myself a parent-sized headache.

But my best friend wasn't, and hadn't been around, and I had no idea when he would return from trying to salvage his relationship with his own mother. Thinking of him reminded me of how alone I was, sitting at my parents' table, realizing the only demons I could share my most vulnerable secrets with were the ones who brought me into this plane of existence as its only magicless being.

Depression compounding depression. Good stuff, right there, let me tell you.

"There's something more, isn't there?" Mother squeezed my hand. "And it breaks my heart to think you can't share it with us."

"You wouldn't understand," I mumbled into the tabletop. Mother's grip loosened slightly.

"You wouldn't understand," Father scoffed, repeating my words verbatim. "The boy is so smart he knows what we can understand or not." His voice rose through the sentence. "In case this is news to you, we've lived full lives, and have a pretty good idea of what it holds for each of us. I'm confident I can guess why you're feeling down."

"I'm not feeling down," I said, my head snapping up to glare at him. "Give me a break and stop treating me like a child. You think my life is so simple, that you have all the answers to what I'm going through. But you don't have the slightest clue or any idea what it's like to work for the Council, to do the things they make us do. You sit here in this house. Then you go to work, only to come home and do it all over again. If you had any idea how involved in our lives the Council is ... and you sure as heaven don't know what they're willing to do to ensure they get their way."

I realized I was huffing, and that they had fallen silent. My mother pulled back from the table, letting go of my hand and placing hers against her chest. My father was staring at me, as he ground his teeth with sickening scrapes.

I lowered my head and voice. "I'm sorry." I wasn't, but if I admitted my actual reasons for the outburst, they might truly lose the sense of who their son was—as being the parents of Hell's only murderer would do to demons.

"Don't you dare ever take that tone with me again."

For the second time during this meal, my mother slapped the table. "You did this. You pushed him because you don't listen. He's an adult with adult responsibilities. And he's right. How can we be sure our perspective is the right one? We don't even know what it's like outside this zone. He does."

"Because we haven't requested travel permissions," he replied with an undeserved aloofness.

"Exactly to Ezekial's point," she said, tearing a corner off her dry bun. "So maybe we should stop talking over him and actually listen. Then we can understand what his experiences are." Mother sat up straighter, her chest swelling with a deep breath. "Ezekial, I'm sorry I haven't treated you as an adult. I need to remember that you are. I'll work on that, I swear. But right now, please tell me what's going on. Something is different. Are you in trouble?"

"Thank you," I said, stirring the thickening sauce in my bowl. My mother had given so much. It was time for me to invest back in the conversation, regardless of my father's preconceived notions. "Ever since I came back from the Eighth, things haven't been good."

"I noticed," she said, softly.

"They should be," my father said somewhat under his breath, receiving a stared down from Mother.

The only way to get him to cease his insistence might be to proverbially punch him between the eyes with facts. But doing that would mean pulling back the lid on something I'd carefully kept under wraps. Still, at this point what did I have to lose?

When I started, the words came out mechanically. "Something happened there. Our assignment was to retrieve a magical item for the Council. We had to take it from someone."

Mother put a hand to her mouth. "You stole?"

I tilted my head and shrugged. "I guess you could call it

that, yeah. That's the stuff the Council expects us to do, what you don't hear about in the news because it doesn't set the best impression, does it? But it's the truth. And it's also not the worst of it."

Father wore a disgusted look, his eyes scrunched together in judgment and examination, looking at me as if I just accused my mother of being an angel. "What's worse than stealing something that belongs to another demon?"

I couldn't meet his eyes. "Killing that demon?"

Mother gasped.

Father spat. "Heresy."

Our eyes locked. "Truth. See, you think you understand everything that happens because you believe in the Council. It's a choice to ignore facts that conflict with what you want to see as true when you automatically believe they have our best interests in mind. And I'm telling you that isn't correct at all. Especially if you and your interests interfere with theirs."

"Please tell me this isn't so," Lilith said, once again reaching across the table.

"Where did this happen? In the Eighth?" my father asked.

I nodded, drawing a bark of disbelief from him.

"There you have it then," he said. "I don't know what your aim is, Ezekial. It's like you enjoy upsetting your mother, but I won't have you telling lies and disparaging the name of the Council."

"Kanthor!"

"They're not lies," I said, feeling myself regressed three thousand years in the span of a single conversation. He was treating me as if I was a impling who got caught pulling a fae's wings off. "It's the absolute truth."

Father closed his eyes and shook his head. "It's impossible. Demons can't die in the Underworld. That's a fact. Even the Founders can't kill someone here. Only Lucifer's Will brings about our end. So you didn't kill another demon, Ezekial." He stopped, biting his bottom lip. "I don't know what's going on with you, but I won't stand for such disgusting lies. Whatever is happening, just tell us so we can help."

I rocketed to my feet. "You can't help me because you don't want to. The truth is too hard for you. I *did* kill a demon, and it's screwing with my head. His name was Taurus Hammerwulf, and he had a powerful artifact, and the Council didn't want that. That was our mission, and we did it. We broke into his home and took it from him. Seraph was with us. One of your precious Council members was part of a theft."

Mother's eyes were watering. "Is that … is that when you killed him?"

My shoulders slumped. "No. When we were escaping, he and his bodyguards attacked us. Another succubus betrayed us and they outnumbered us." Again, thinking of Marijon brought pangs of pain. "Bilba and Ralrek were … they were hurting them. Bad. Taurus was trying to put a gauntlet on my wrist. He didn't say why, but it was obvious it had some properties that would have made me too weak to resist him. He kept saying something about losing the Horn was a fair trade for making me work for him. I think he was going to enslave me."

"Enslave you?" Mother repeated the words as if they were foreign to her.

"You? Why you?" Father's question was less harsh now, like my comments seeded doubt. That, or I was absolutely harpy-shit crazy. If there were some seedlings, though, now was the time to water them.

Even after all this time of running through the events that led to Taurus's death, I had no clearer idea why he thought I was something special. "He seemed happy to have lost this Horn, something important to a family member who once sat on the Council. Happy, if it meant he had me."

"How … how did you get away?" With each word, my

mother sounded like she was losing another small piece of herself.

"I killed him," I said. Truth. They needed the truth. I slipped my hand to Creed and pulled it out. "With this."

When I activated it, Mother screeched, and Father jumped back, nearly toppling out of his chair. The clink of the three blades popping from the haft drew a curse from him.

"Wha—what is that?" He was squatted slightly as if he was ready to dodge an attack from my magical halberd.

My parents had never seen Creed in its full glory, only ever noticing it hanging at my hip around the house. I said it was a truncheon I used for sparring with Bilba. But it was time for them to know. I would pay any consequences later, if I ever saw the Council again, since they seemed to have major magical weapon envy over it.

"Mother. Father. Meet Creed. Aries the First gifted it to me in the Overworld. He said he had been holding it for me ... well, he wasn't sure it was for me until I proved it."

"What? How? You? Why?" my mother asked, her questions nearly drawing a laugh from me.

I shrugged. "Whatever his reason, he was adamant." I rotated Creed one hundred and eighty degrees, careful not to hit the table. The waving dagger now pointed at the ceiling. Father flinched. "I shoved this into Taurus's chest as he was about to slap that gauntlet on me. It was an accident, but that doesn't matter. That's how I killed him."

"But ... it's impossible. We ... we can't kill each other," my father sounded less sure than he had ever in his life.

I took in Creed's length, feeling its power surge through me. Every time I held it, my confidence surged, each time growing stronger. Then I spoke, my voice sounding hard to even my ears. "I don't know about anyone else, but I can kill demons."

He visibly shook.

I gave Creed another shake, deactivating it and placing it

back in the loop on my belt. "I'm going to go. I don't feel so good."

Mother was on her feet, wearing a sad smile that hinted of begging. "Please. Stay."

"No, I need some quiet." When she approached, it was my turn to take her hand. "Now you understand, and I hope that helps you see why I'm not myself. Why I haven't been myself. I took someone's life, Mother. And I can't let go of that. It haunts me, in my dreams and when I'm awake. The memory is always there."

As I moved to the door, Father joined her. "I know it's tough, Ezekial. But it's all for the Balance. One day, that will become clear."

"Thanks," I said, flatly. "I love you guys."

I kissed my mother on the cheek and gave my father a quick hug, leaving at a brisk pace.

"All for the Balance," my father had said. For what Balance though? For whose benefit, was more like it.

It was a long walk home.

4

UNDERWORLD, FIFTH CIRCLE

I UNLOCKED my apartment door and stepped in, dead bolting it behind me.

"So nice of you to have finally joined me," a voice hissed from the darkness.

I jumped and spun, snagging Creed from my belt and activating it.

From somewhere in my dark living room, my unwelcomed company laughed, a distinct hiss accompanying their expression of joy.

"Apopis?"

He clicked the lamp on, casting a bright blue light across my sparsely decorated space and his grotesquely tattooed face. "Welcome home."

I remembered to breathe, deactivating Creed and slipping it back in the loop. As my heart thumped, my anger surged to life. "What are you doing here? And more importantly, what's he doing here?"

Apopis wasn't alone. Seated next to the vegan-thin, tattooed-faced Council member was Ralrek, on my couch —*my couch*—with his elbows on his knees and his hands draped between them. He wore a cocky smirk.

The Founder kicked back, crossing a slender leg over his other. He didn't even look at Ralrek when he spoke. "You two have a new mission and he needs the briefing as well."

"I figured he'd already know."

Apopis raised an eyebrow, stretching the left side tattoos into a comical semblance of ancient characters. Wondering what demon lacked the good judgment to not tattoo their face, I promised myself to one day get him drunk and fill in the stupid design with a marker when he was passed out.

"Is that jealousy I hear?"

"Not at all. I just figured the two of you didn't sit here waiting for me in the dark without exchanging notes. To that point, how long have you been in my apartment?"

"Long enough to know you need to clean up," Ralrek said with a grimace like he'd sucked down an entire lemon.

"Not one of my top priorities," I said, leaning against the wall and popping my shoes off since I didn't have a place to sit except the couch they now occupied. As fun as it would be to make them both uncomfortable, joining them was not worth it. Laughing had become so difficult.

I grunted as the last shoe came off. "I hope you don't mind, but I've had a killer day and I'm kinda just looking forward to getting to bed early."

Ralrek made a sound somewhere between a grunt and a snort.

Apopis rolled his fingers on the arm of the couch, his gaze never wavering. "How are your parents?"

I shook my head and thought about going to the kitchen to grab a drink. A strong one. But someone had gotten into my vodka. A bottle of Blue Sky vodka sat on my coffee table. An inch of clear glory filled the bottom. Nearly empty. On each end table sat a martini glass. Both bastards were enjoying my booze. I wondered how awkward it would be to have a drink or two with one of the Founders, then I remembered I didn't care. The loss of vodka caused me to groan as I went to the kitchen and poured myself a bourbon instead. Rejoining them was only easier after I downed the first glass. When I returned, it was with a nastier mood, inspired by my loss.

"That's expensive," I said, pointing to my nearly empty bottle in front of Apopis.

"It was good." He sucked through his teeth and lifted the martini glass, which held a breath of clear alcohol. "To alcohol. May it always lift our troubles."

Ralrek joined him. "Interesting glassware, Zeke. These were all I could find."

I hesitated, noticing them waiting on me, before finally joining. "Ezekial. And all of my highball glasses are in the sink."

Apopis hissed. "I noticed."

Since they didn't appear to be in a hurry, I set my glass on the coffee table and took a seat on the floor. "I'm exhausted. What does the Council need?"

It was amazing how far I'd come with Lucifer's leaders in a relatively short time. They were major demons, ancients who'd lived dozens of lifetimes more than me, and the first time they called me I was so intimidated I couldn't think straight. As I approached my first year under their employ, I was sitting in my living room, having drinks and chatting with one of them as if we were casual acquaintances. It was strange, but the lack of default reverence was exquisite and I wondered why I hadn't attempted it before.

Apopis changed his hairstyle since I'd last seen him. Gone was the slicked back style he previously wore, replaced with a haphazard design that included the right side peacocking up, while the left side was greased forward. His thick eyebrows highlighted the oddity of his short, multidirectional hair.

"I see you grew an earring," I said, looking beyond the tattoos and the new, obnoxious hair. I just couldn't trust someone with the pain tolerance to tattoo their face and do that to their hair.

Apopis continued to roll his fingers on the couch's arm, watching me.

Ralrek slurped his drink. Who slurped vodka? "Despite his ... coolness, I'm very interested to know what the Council has for us, sir."

"And so am I. I don't imagine this is another minor side job since you're here at this hour, in my home. That alone, combined with your presence instead of some errand incubus, tells me you've got something bigger for us. Am I right?"

Apopis raised a thin hand over his—my—glass, long fingers hovering as if he suddenly possessed telekinesis. The fingers finally dipped down, barely grasping the glass by its lip. He swirled the tiny bit of vodka he had left.

Bless it, so expensive.

"You would be, Sunstone," he replied. "In fact, this one might be more challenging than the other missions we've sent you on."

Internally, I groaned. "You've got something bigger for us then going to the Overworld to chase a first of his name or stealing an ancient and mysterious artifact from the richest demon in a Circle? Do I want to hear the rest of this?"

Apopis stared at his glass, then at me. I hated when he did that because his flattened vertical pupils unnerved me, making me feel like he always knew a secret. "You don't have a choice," he said.

Swirling, swirling, swirling.

"Not even a night to sleep on it?"

Ralrek huffed. "Don't be an ass."

I was about to open my mouth when Apopis cut me off. "You'd think someone of your station would be more appreciative of the work the Council has for you. I mean," he gestured at my living room with the glass containing my alcohol. "Before we required your services, you were living with your parents in that decrepit tree house. What were your prospects then, Sunstone? You needn't answer that; everyone is aware of the options you had available. As pathetic as you have now, what would you be without us? So, when the Council has need of you, it would behoove you to express appreciation."

"Oh, I'm appreciative. I totally appreciate how the Council constantly puts me in harm's way and threatens me with a promise of eternity in slavery if I fail you. Since Ralrek is so hot for your work, let him run it. He loves being in charge, even when he's not."

Apopis slithered forward, the glass he held clinking on the coffee table hard enough to make me wince and search for a crack. "You are a miserable flea. Ungrateful."

"Ungrateful? Exactly what should I be grateful for?"

"He already told us," Ralrek said, stepping into a conversation I hadn't invited him into.

But my fixation was with Apopis. "The way I see it, all I have I've earned. You had a job for me. I did it, you paid me. End of story. Why would I express gratitude for that?"

I didn't think it was possible, but Apopis's eyes narrowed further. "Millions in Lucifer's domain would trade positions with you in an instant."

I could have argued there weren't millions who could. A dozen like me didn't exist in the entire Underworld. I was the only demon in the history of Hell without an Ability, providing me, according to the Council, immunity against Aries's magic in the Overworld. I was also the only demon who possessed Creed, which Aries gave to me because 'I was the one' apparently. But none of those legitimate points would have made a difference with him. From the first time I stood in front of the Council to tonight, watching him drink my expensive vodka, I'd never been a fan of Apopis. He was combative and antagonistic, qualities without redeeming value and completely unhealthy when dealing with an unwilling gofer such as me. He would never listen to my justifications.

I smiled the way a rebellious impling does when going through puberty. "Let them."

Apopis's eyes flickered, his tongue shot to the corner of his lips. My comment had caught him off-guard.

"The Council chose you to execute these duties," he said instead of putting voice to what was probably on his mind. "So it is you who will see them through. I'm not going to argue with you about this."

"So I am a slave?"

Ralrek groaned. "You're hopeless."

But Apopis seemed happy to cede the point. I tried to not let that distract me from avoiding whatever task he had. I was just trying to get him off my case because he loved to bully me. I hadn't expected him to agree. "If that is how you choose to see it, Sunstone. I am not going to waste my energy convincing you or dealing with your meandering."

"Thank you?"

His head swiveled quickly. "It was not a compliment."

Outside, the clear, high-pitched voice of the sector's Caller, the living—sort of—breathing—I think—magical purple creatures created to help keep time for the Underworld's residents who do not live near our clock towers, rose into the quiet night, signaling the official end of the day. "It's getting late. Do you feel like telling me what I need to know or do we carry this conversation into another day?"

Apopis didn't take a moment to consider any alternatives. "No, we do this now."

"That's what I figured. So what do you have for me?"

The Founder leaned forward and reached into the satchel between his feet. Pulling out a now–familiar brief, he slapped it on the table with disregard. What was it with demons abusing my coffee table tonight? I mean, it wasn't the finest table you would ever see, but it wasn't mine either and I didn't feel like paying Manes for any damages when I moved out. "The details are in there and the pair of you can read about it after I take my leave."

"Want to at least give us the rundown?"

Apopis mumbled the spell I already sensed coming, his hands slithering in the air. The listening ward was set, the first one in my new apartment. "Two weeks ago we had an operative disappear. We can't be sure if he disappeared here or in the Overworld."

"You're not sure where your operatives are?"

"You can't possibly understand the complexities of our operations." He squinted. "That matters not. The point is, an operative, one of your peers, was conducting an operation and we believe a squad of angels detected his activities and that he may be in their hands ... if they haven't killed him. We've got very little else to go on."

Ralrek had turned in Apopis's direction, his vodka forgotten. I cringed seeing it go to waste. Over the last few weeks, it had become my best friend, replacing the one stuck in the Eighth Circle dealing with his mommy issues. "Angels abducted one of us?"

Apopis flicked the corner of his mouth with his slender tongue. "It's hardly an anomaly. The sneaky bastards have been doing it for millennia. We need to find him. He holds ... vital information."

"All joking aside, a demon being abducted or killed by a gang of angels sounds way above my pay grade."

"Normally, Sunstone, I would agree about your lack of qualifications to handle Council business. But as unfortunate as it is, you and Ralrek are our best options for finding what happened."

"You don't have any details beyond what is in the brief, sir?" Ralrek asked.

"None. And it's extremely frustrating."

"So what do you need from us?" I finished off my second bourbon, trying to dull the recognition of being sucked into another big mission.

Have you ever had one of those situations where you seek answers to questions you didn't necessarily want answered? That's what was happening in my nondescript and expensive apartment in downtown Old Towne between me, Hell's asshole, a Founder, and a rapidly emptying bottle of vodka.

If we were getting involved with angels, the game had changed. Aries, we had handled in part because we didn't know what the heaven we were doing, and because Beelzebub turned the tables using treachery against a pretty cool and kind demon. With Taurus, we stayed in the Under-world and Seraph's talents and abilities had come in handy more than once. Messing around with angels wasn't at the top of my priority list, and neither was my inference that such a high–level mission would require babysitting by another Council member. If Apopis's presence meant that he would be the one supervising us, all of this was less attractive by the moment.

"We're tasking you to head to the Second Circle and see what you can find out about him," Apopis answered. "That brief has enough to get you started."

The Second Circle of Hell, the second I would visit on Lucifer's coin. I wondered how it would compare to the previous one. Soon enough, I would find out.

"And I imagine we are to start pretty soon?"

It was a question with an expected answer. So I wasn't all that bothered when he said, "Refill your glass and get pack-ing. You're leaving at First Call."

5

UNDERWORLD, SECOND CIRCLE

"You're welcome to go first," I told Ralrek, staring through the sliver of the gateway that gave us a watery view of the Second Circle. He hung back, looking apprehensive. Easily justified since the little I could make out of the weather on the other side of the divide was less than enticing.

I finally understood what the term 'pissing rain' meant.

"The two of you will absolutely love this Circle," Apopis hissed. "Have fun."

I turned away from the gateway and faced him, hope springing in my voice. "You're not coming?"

He tilted his head to the side to look beyond me, before standing erect again. "I have too much to do here to follow the pair of you stumbling your way through the Circle. I'll join you if you need my guidance ... or supervision. You know how to use sanctuaries now."

"You could always give the mission to another operative," I offered.

"This one is all yours, Sunstone," he said. "Get going. I have other things to attend to. And we do not have much time."

Summarily dismissed by Apopis, I faced the gateway, still

holding back from stepping through. "I didn't even bring a damn rain jacket," I grumbled and led Ralrek into the Second Circle.

The familiar flash of blinding light no longer disoriented me. I moved through the darkness that followed without a misstep and touched down on the sleek, uneven cobblestone and into the storm.

The first thing that stood out about this Circle was the rain. It was cold, big, and wet. I realize all rain is wet, but this was a different level, the kind that soaked through your clothes and made you shiver with each impact. Without a doubt, I swear, it was raining sideways, drenching us and our bags within seconds. The day was so gray I couldn't see a hint of the Hellfire's blue light.

I had to shield my eyes to look for cover. Spotting a ragged and faded awning that stretched over a storefront, I shouted over the rain to Ralrek. "Let's go over there. Get our bearings."

We didn't delay, sprinting down the street, careful to not bust our asses on the wet stone. We pulled up underneath the cover, the sideways rain invading even this place.

"Lucifer," Ralrek said, shaking his head and splattering me with droplets.

I laughed. His hair, normally a bulb of thick, immaculate blackness, was now flattened, falling in jagged clumps around his forehead.

"What?" he looked at me askance, but a smile etched his expression.

"Nothing, I've just never seen you out in public looking less than perfect," I said.

Ralrek pulled his hair up and tried his best to get it to hold in its previous style. "No one is perfect, Zeke."

"Ezekial," I corrected, looking at the shop. "Want to head in and see if the owner can help us find our apartment?"

"Sure."

Done with his primping session, Ralrek's hair was nearly perfect again, even after being doused. I had no idea how he did it. Some demons have all the luck.

The store belonged to an elderly succubus who looked tired from life. Her hair was white as the pictures of snow in the Overworld. She shot us an untrusting glance as we hovered in the door before making our way inside, like she expected us to act no better than her grand-implings in this shop filled with precious trinkets.

We left our bags at the front because a diverse range of knick knacks covered every square inch of floor space and wall. Ceramic forest scenes, grandfather clocks, miniature farm equipment made of black metal, brimstone animal figurines, and more than I could describe in a day, cluttered the shelves. The store couldn't have been more than thirty feet across, and yet the owner still thought it was a good idea to put so many displays on the floor that we had to weave around the haphazard design. I was dealing with the Second Circle's version of Dialphio. I feared bumping into anything lest it create a domino effect that took down the entire store with one misstep.

The shop keep sat behind an L–shape glass case filled with more valuable knick knacks of emerald and jade. The large case even held an assortment of watches from every age— ours, not you short-lived mortals. Truly, no rhyme or reason explained the layout. Somehow, we made it to the counter without upsetting the Balance—don't ever let it be said that I'm hyperbolic.

A floral pattern of obnoxious reds and yellows populated the shop keep's blouse, which was as chaotic as her store. "How can I help you?" her voice cracked, like old paper ripped slowly.

"Hi, we're looking for this place," I said, sliding the address of our temporary home across the counter. "Do you know where that is?"

She confirmed that the Council had opened the gateway in the right neighborhood by nodding as soon as she read the address. "You're very close. Once you leave the shop, take a left and walk two blocks down. Make a right at the storm flood canal and follow it for another three. I'm not sure which building, but that will get you close."

"Thank you very much," I said, looking around to see if there was anything I could pick up as a gift for my mother. Even she would not want this stuff.

"Have a wonderful day," the shop keep said, saving me from a quick bout of guilt that was not alleviated as we left the shop.

Out underneath the shop's awning again, we collected our bags and looked out at the sideways rain. "Do you think it will lighten up?"

Ralrek ducked, glancing up toward the dark gray sky. "Doesn't look like it will quit ... ever."

"Yeah."

Our mission brief explained that the Second Circle was an island, battered by weather. But I didn't realize what that meant until I was standing in it. As restrictive as the other Circles felt, I was trapped on an island now. There was nowhere else to go if we stumbled into something bad here. Having the skill to open a gateway would be a real nice attribute, I suddenly realized. Especially since I could not trust Apopis to open one for us, should we need rescuing or an escape. Lucifer knew, I would not risk swimming the Acheron Ocean that surrounded this place if I needed to get away. Demons and water don't mix.

If this Circle's purpose was to provide the Underworld with enough rainfall to sustain the other Circles, it was doing an amazing job.

Hopefully, our first day here was just a bad day for Mother Nature—she's real, by the way—not a trend.

"What do you think about making a run for it?"

Ralrek raised an eyebrow. "For five blocks?"

I pointed up and down the street. "I don't see any carriages, so it's either that or we wait out the storm, and I don't imagine the shop keep would be thrilled with the two of us standing in front of her store, scaring away business."

For a second, Ralrek looked as if he would argue, before huffing. "Fine. Let's go." He sprinted off.

The rain pelted my face the moment I stepped from underneath the awning. By the time we'd reached the second block, I was already shivering.

I caught up to Ralrek, and we dashed between the rain and awnings when they made their appearance from buildings along the broad street. The sidewalk was narrow, like a thin, black liner bordering the buildings instead of something that was supposed to serve pedestrians, of which I saw a few strolling from the shops that populated the bottom floors of the buildings up and down the street. Everyone was dressed in black. Black pants, whether slacks or jeans, sweatpants or trousers were the fashion of the day in the Second Circle, it seemed. Rain jackets, coats, ponchos too; all in black. Hats? You guessed it. With the monochrome dress and the way the low, gray clouds suffocated the Hellfire, one could not be faulted for thinking this Circle was allergic to color.

A carriage, black—did you have to ask?—passed. Even the chimera pulling it was draped in a black rain sheet.

This place was going to do wonders for my depression.

The flood canal stretched from my left to right. Twenty feet across, the water moved swiftly through its depths. I feared for anyone who fell into it. At my thought, a huge carriage tire floated past, bobbing up and down in the rushing water. I reminded myself to not get lazy near it, thinking of what lay beyond an ocean's barrier in the Underworld—these are things they never teach you in school that would come in handy.

That when I started shivering uncontrollably against the

wind-blown rain. The Second Circle might as well have been Seattle.

We raced the final blocks to a building that should have been our apartment if our directions were correct. This time though, there was no shop awning to protect us. I pulled out the paper to double check and the rain instantly soaked it, bleeding through the ink and obscuring the address within seconds.

Thankfully, Ralrek had it memorized, for which I was grateful since Bilba was not with us. Who knew Ralrek would come in handy during this mission if it did not involve using his Fire Abilities?

"This is it," he said, pointing to the street number etched in the stone facade.

The run wasn't too long, at least it was a step toward getting back into better shape, but my feet were soaked through. My shoes squished with each step, so I couldn't be happier about reaching our destination and getting the heaven out of the downpour. My toes had rubbed together during the run, becoming raw. I hoped this place had a bath, because I planned on soaking in it to remove the chill. It was almost as cold as the Overworld here! Ridiculous.

We climbed the stairs to the fourth floor and found the apartment. Ralrek tried his key, and the door opened to our newest temporary home.

"Looks like we got a promotion," I said once we entered.

This apartment was newer and roomier than any the Council had given us before. The hallway floor was highly polished bamboo. Instead of a living room in the front, we were greeted by a sitting room, with white overstuffed chairs and a bookcase that ran the length of the wall, filled with books. Maybe Hell's leaders wanted to make me feel at home, like I was back in *The Book Abyss*. I stepped through the doorway into a dining room and almost ran into the eight–

chair dining table. The kitchen was off to the side, each appliance stainless steel.

"You should see these bedrooms," Ralrek said from down the hall, his voice echoing slightly in the spacious apartment. "I call dibs on this one."

"Bless it," I said, cursing myself for choosing the wrong priority. Without Bilba around, I imagined I would spend a lot of time in my room when we weren't out on the mission, especially if the alternative was sitting in the same room as the tall demon. No matter how spacious the apartment was, no realm could provide enough distance between him and me. I should have been thinking about grabbing the best bedroom like I did when we went to the Eighth, before Ralrek could beat me to it.

He was in his room, the biggest one, lying on the bed with a broad smile on his face and his bags on the floor at his feet. Large windows let in as much of the gray sky as possible. Ralrek wiggled his fingers, teasing me in his comfort.

Moving down the hall, I was pleased to see mine wasn't much smaller than has, larger than what I had back home, but windowless. I don't know if that was a curse or a blessing. My bag hit the floor with a gross squish.

The room was clean and smartly decorated, the wide bed centered on the back wall. The huge television hung from the opposite wall. The dresser was six feet long, wide and made of walnut. I ran my hand along its smooth polished surface.

"Nice."

"I have a bathroom in my room. Do you?" The question echoed down the hallway.

I turned around and saw a door in the corner and went to it, letting out a whistle when I peeked inside. "Yep. A big one too."

It was. Tan, tiled floors, a glass bowl sink, and a stand/sit shower that could fit five demons. Each fixture gleamed like new, as if the apartment had just been built for our arrival.

As lousy as the weather was outside, I was in no hurry to get back to the Fifth if this was going to be my life in this Circle. Now I just had to figure out how to accomplish the mission from in here.

Of course, that changed once we unpacked and readied ourselves to hit the streets again. By that time, the gray sky had darkened toward night, the wet streets growing eerie as fire lamps struggled to stay alight against the constant assault of rain, which was now only a downpour instead of a deluge. Either the Council or the landlord for the apartment had left rain jackets in each of our closets, and we gladly donned them, making the walk much more tolerable. Yes, they were black.

"What was the name of the club where we were supposed to find him?" Ralrek asked.

"Shady's," I answered. "Supposedly, it's around the corner."

And it was. Without the jackets, we might not have gotten to the club—I could only take so much rain to the face—because even with them I was miserable. As it was, we strolled into the club as dry as anyone in the Second Circle. High quality stuff, let me tell you.

As we stood in the dark hallway, illuminated by a single blue bulb hanging in the far corner, we both stripped out of the rain jackets. The attendant looked at them, then us, and then the jackets again.

"Do we have somewhere to hang these?" I asked awkwardly.

The young incubus, barely old enough to have shaved, rolled his eyes before flopping both hands out to us. "I'll take them," he said, as if we were reminding him of a family favor he had to repay.

Freed of our rain jackets, we entered the club. The narrow hallway betrayed the impressive size of the bar and dance floor. Even at this relatively early hour, demons filled the floor, dancing along to the music with bass so deep it seemed to reset my heartbeat with each downbeat. Strobe lights gave the mass of bodies a jerky effect, disorienting me. The bar stretched along an entire wall, every square inch crammed with thirsty demons. If they weren't dancing or drinking, they huddled around in tight circles.

What I needed now was a drink. I tried to ask Ralrek if he wanted one before we looked for the Council's source but had to repeat my question three times, my lips uncomfortably close to his ear. When he could finally make out what I was saying he nodded his response. He's smarter than me like that.

We waited for a hole to open at the bar and only after we secured our location did I scan for the demon we were supposed to find. The strobe lights and swirling bodies constantly churning made distinguishing one demon from another nearly impossible. As soon as I locked eyes on one incubus who might be the one, the crowd swallowed him, and another replaced him.

By a miracle of Lucifer, we accurately ordered our drinks over the cacophony of club music. Ralrek, first to get served, of course, looked out for himself, getting a martini. I got the biggest screwdriver they had, not wanting to fight for a bar spot again.

"Want to split up? Might go quicker," I shouted to Ralrek.

He nodded. "Remember what he looks like?"

The mission brief contained twenty different pictures of our source, in all situations and spaces. It was creepy how many the Council had of him, and that made me wonder if they were stalking me just as much.

His name was Maelstrom, though I doubted that. It was likely a stage name, something he probably thought made him sound cooler than his actual name. I based this determination solely on the pictures. He had a frail build for someone who was

only twenty thousand years old, the type of incubus succubi snickered at even as they avoided them. The type I almost felt sorry for, and I'd never be on the cover of some magazine. Part of me understood why he would do it then. Fabricating a name to sound more intimidating happens in the Underworld. A lot.

Maelstrom had wispy hair and squinty eyes that spoke of dishonesty. His hooked nose was unique, dipping at the point. He should be easy enough to find if not for the swirling, undulating mass of bodies.

"Let's do it."

Ralrek nodded again. "Meet back at the coat check in an hour."

I appreciated his bluntness. The loud club music made it exhausting to hold this conversation. The more succinct we were, the better.

He went his way, and I went mine, the both of us starting on the periphery and working inward.

Moving around the floor, I searched the crowd for the hooked nose incubi, even taking a few opportunities to step onto the floor and peer in toward the middle. It was the last place I expected him to be. The brief said he worked the music scene as a DJ.

I kept track of time by paying attention to how many songs the DJ—not Maelstrom, like we thought—played. Close to the hour mark, I made my way to the entrance, and hung out with the jacket checker with a poor attitude.

"Just waiting on a friend," I told him, as if he cared.

He grunted in response.

Within a few moments, Ralrek joined me.

"Anything?" I asked.

Ralrek shook his head. "It's like a sea of bodies out there. It's going to be impossible to find him in here."

I shook my head. "Don't tell me you're thinking what I think you're thinking?"

"Outside is our best chance, Zeke. If we try to find him in this mess, we might search all night and totally miss him."

"Ezekial," I said, but conceded. Ralrek had a point, a precise one, but one I didn't have to like. "It makes sense," I said begrudgingly.

Snagging our jackets from the miserable attendant, we stepped back into the rain, but only after handing over my empty glass to the bouncer who eyed us as if we were trying to get away with something.

Over the hours that followed, more and more demons stepped out of the club as I shivered closer to mortality. "Does it ever stop raining here?" I asked the bouncer, who blinked without moving a muscle, and looked at me out of the corner of his eye, blinked again, and went back to his gargoyle impersonation.

"Don't freak everyone out," Ralrek said, gesturing at the bouncer with a thumb. "He doesn't know we're not from here, so he probably thinks you're an oddball."

"Good, then I'll fit in with everything I just saw in there," I said, jerking a thumb at the nightclub door.

Ralrek smiled. "They were pretty strange, weren't they? What was up with their clothes?"

"And the dancing? Jumping up and down? Constantly?"

We shared a quick laugh then, simultaneously, recognized what we were doing and stopped, turning away and focusing on anyone coming out of the door rather than our own discomfort.

We tried to outlast the storm—and lost—as patrons trickled out of the club. As the rain pounded my protective layer, the trickle became a steady flow, for which I was grateful since I was sure I would never be warm again.

"You look miserable," Ralrek said in a deadpan.

"That accurately describes my current situation," I replied, clenching my teeth to stop them from chattering.

A solo incubus exited the club, lifting my spirits. It wasn't Maelstrom. My spirits dropped.

"He better be in there," Ralrek said, wrapping his arms around his elbows. "It's cold as heaven out here. If we're suffering for nothing, I'm going to be pissed."

"Whoa, slow down, rebel," I said, teasing. But on a serious note, I'd never heard Ralrek ever disparage the Council. Was there hope for him?

"Whatever," he said. I could almost hear the eye roll in his tone.

The flood from the club increased as night turned to early morning and the Hellfire's light began its ascent from the Grand Chamber, revealing a cloud-covered sky. From the middle of the new jumble of bodies, Maelstrom strode out of the club, as if he owned it.

Ralrek saw him about the same time I did. We both lunged, grabbing separate arms and yanking in opposite directions. Maelstrom screeched, and at first, I thought we'd accidentally grabbed one of the succubi. Seconds later, we wordlessly agreed which direction to pull him and moved away before the bouncer cared to intervene. No one else bothered.

This might not be so different from the Eighth after all?

"Who—who are you?" Maelstrom whined as we pulled him down the street and around the corner. "What do you want?"

Ralrek slammed him against the wall, eliciting an *ooof* from the smaller demon.

I scanned the alley for witnesses. "Careful," I said, staying alert. The first sign I had Maelstrom was conjuring, and I'd make him swallow his teeth. I had no idea who this demon was and if he was dangerous or not, and I wasn't about to put my own safety at risk. Maybe not even Ralrek's.

"This is me being careful," Ralrek said through gritted teeth.

Maelstrom was spitting and sputtering. "I don't—I don't have any money. Please—please leave me alone."

I snagged his collar, pressing my face close to his. "Quiet. We're not going to hurt you."

He looked from me to Ralrek. "Then—then what do you want? Please ... if I was hitting on your old succubus, I'm sorry."

Old succubus? Who said that anymore? Old-school demons did in days long-gone. That colloquialism predated Maelstrom by at least ten thousand years.

"We need information, that's all."

"About what? I don't know anything, I swear. I'm just a wheel mechanic at a carriage shop around the corner. I can take you there. I can prove it." Maelstrom pointed back up the canal, whose water level was rising. "Well, and I deejay here some nights too. But that's it. Don't have much."

"First, I doubt your little carriage shop is open at this hour," Ralrek said and gave him a shove against the building wall, making Maelstrom groan and me growl.

"Don't do that," I said, too meekly.

"And second," Ralrek continued as if he didn't hear me, "it's not about where you work, it's about what you're involved in. Or should I say *who* you're involved in it with?"

Maelstrom panted. "Who? What? I'm sorry. I really don't know what you're talking about. I'll—I'll tell you anything you want. Just promise me you won't hurt me."

"We won't, but you better tell us what we need to hear," Ralrek said with a snarl.

"Okay, okay. I will. Who do you want to ask me about?"

I leaned my face closer. "Gemini."

And that's when Maelstrom screamed.

6

UNDERWORLD, SECOND CIRCLE

"OH MY SATAN!" Ralrek snapped, pressing his palm over Maelstrom's mouth, cutting the other demon's scream to a muffled whimper. "I'll suffocate you if you don't shut up."

This time, I helped Ralrek shake our target. I felt bad about pressing him into the wall, but his scream was going to draw attention, and at least I didn't slam him like Ralrek had. Around the corner from the nightclub, no one could see what we were up to, but screams would bring eyeballs. We had seconds before we gained witnesses.

"What's wrong with you?" I said, spittle flying from my mouth and landing on Maelstrom's cheek. "We told you we would not hurt you. All we want is information."

Maelstrom's lips trembled. "Yeah ... b—but the information you want is the one thing I don't want to talk about."

"Gemini?" Ralrek asked.

Maelstrom nodded his head like a vertebra had lost its stability.

I placed a hand on Ralrek's arm. He looked at me askance. "Let him go."

"What? He'll run away."

"No, he won't. Isn't that right?" I asked the shaking demon, who nodded.

"I promise, I won't. Don't hurt me."

The street was still clear. "Neither one of us is interested in that. We only want information. Give us that, and we'll leave you alone."

Maelstrom nodded in that childlike fashion again. His Adam's apple bobbed as he swallowed. It would take too much effort to convince him we didn't mean any harm, and we didn't have that kind of time. He wasn't going to trust us, no matter what we said. But we had to proceed carefully, or we would lose this opportunity. That meant I had to do the talking before Ralrek stepped all over the conversation and ruined everything with his bullishness.

Now free from Ralrek's grip, Maelstrom adjusted his shirt.

"What happened to Gemini? Where is he?" I asked, searching his eyes for any sign of dishonesty.

But the demon simply blinked behind that really long and hooked nose, as if I was speaking another language. "How— how do you know about him?"

Ralrek stepped forward and Maelstrom flinched. I put my hand on Ralrek's arm again. He took a single step back. I really did not have the energy to be a referee.

"We work for demons who want to figure out what happened to him. He is very important to them. But they need solid leads. Anything you can tell us would be helpful."

Maelstrom licked his lips, looking up and down the alley. "The demons who talk about Gemini end up going missing too. I don't want that. I have a girlfriend to take care of. So I'm going to need some coin. You understand?"

Oh, I understood. It was the same mentality we faced in the Eighth Circle when we were trying to get information about the Horn of Taurus. No one ever seemed interested in assisting unless it meant coin in their pocket. All the Council's business was expensive, it seemed. What I didn't understand was how someone as homely as Maelstrom had a girlfriend. Like, what did he have to say to land one when I couldn't even form the simplest sentences to interest a succubus?

I reached into my pocket, pulling out a small bag of coin. I had them tucked away in different hiding spots all over me. You can't be too careful.

Maelstrom took it, gave it a heft, and grinned.

Inwardly, I did too, having my first offer please the incubus. This might end up being cheaper than I thought.

"All I've heard is that he was in the Overworld, in a country called Germany."

"Was?"

His mouth widened in a grimace. "Yeah. Don't know much. No one does. He was headed there to do some research on mortal art. Got an approved pass and everything. Something to do with his deejay job. I tried to take it over for him. But Gemini was too good; no one can really replace him. He was supposed to come back and really explode the music scene in the Circle."

"What was he doing there? Just research? What kind?" Germany could have been anything and anywhere, close or far. My only Overworld reference was Seattle. But at least we had something now, a sign pointing in a definite direction.

Maelstrom shrugged. "Gemini and I were friends, mostly because of the deejaying thing, but we weren't that close. He didn't tell me his business. And that's a good thing."

"Why?" Ralrek asked.

Maelstrom jingled the coin bag again. I sighed, understanding the universal negotiation sign.

Only after I handed over another bag did he find his voice. Thank Lucifer I wasn't paying for this mission. "Gemini was more than just some deejay."

"How so?"

"I mean, he was talented. Everyone loved his style, but music wasn't the only thing he had going for him."

I tried to keep my voice even, friendly, but having to drag information out of Maelstrom was trying my patience. "We've paid handsomely. Now would be a perfect time for you to meet us halfway. Give us something we can use because my friend here," I said with a dip of my head in Ralrek's direction, "has an anger control problem and when he gets really upset, there isn't much I can do to keep him from unwinding."

Ralrek growled, making Maelstrom flinch.

"Okay, okay," he said with a shaking voice. "He was wrapped up in a lot, I guess. That dude lived handsomely. Too handsomely for a deejay, if you get me. No clubs in the Circle pay well enough to live like that. Big house. Rented covered carriages wherever he went, and when he was out, he usually paid for the entire party, even if there were fifteen of us."

"Did you ever ask him where his coin came from?" Ralrek asked.

Maelstrom's eyes narrowed. "I would never. That's rude."

"My friend here has difficulty understanding proper decorum," I said, giving Maelstrom a guarded smile, trying to keep the momentum going. "So he was making good coin from something."

He shook his head. "I just enjoyed the ride."

From the first look at Maelstrom in the Council's brief, it was easy to see where he was coming from. He had the intangible hint of somebody who would sell their grandmother if it got him ahead. The hooked nose and stringy hair were just to add insult. Lucifer has a weird sense of humor.

"So is it possible he was attacked in something like a robbery? Maybe flashing his money a little too much for someone's liking and they wanted to free him of it?" It made sense in my head, but I realized I was talking myself through it out loud. I hadn't thought through my theory yet.

Maelstrom took a deep breath. "That's not what rumor

says. Gemini had enemies."

Ralrek growled. "What kind of enemies?"

"Saved if I know," Maelstrom responded. "But that's the feeling everyone had. Whatever Gemini was messed up with, it was bad enough for him to go into hiding, some say."

"So he is hiding?"

"Not sure. Could be dead too. Word is, he was doing some sneaky shit. Pissing off a few powerful business prospectors."

"So, he's both alive and dead at the same time? Great." This was frustrating. I was convinced Maelstrom didn't have any actual information, that he was stringing us along to get as much coin as possible. At the end of the conversation, we wouldn't be any better off than we were now. It was time to call his bluff.

"Give us a name. Who was interested in Gemini no longer being part of the world?" I said, watching his reaction. When I saw nothing worthwhile, I tapped Ralrek on the arm. "Let's get going then. We have our other sources to check out."

Ralrek read my eyes, answering slowly. "Okay."

"Thank you for your time," I said and stepped away. Ralrek followed.

When we were a few feet away, Ralrek whispered, "Are you sure this is a good idea?"

"I'm sure he's trying to sucker us out of more coin."

"Apopis can give us more if we need it."

I shrugged. "I'm not in the mood to interact with Apopis any more than I need to."

Ralrek grunted. "He's tough for a reason, Zeke. Don't be disrespectful."

I lifted my shoulder, smirking. "In my book, respect is earned, not handed out like candy to implings. Plus, my gut tells me Maelstrom doesn't know as much as he's leading on."

"Why would he do that?"

I pinched my pointer finger and thumb together. "Coin. Let's see if this entices him to be a looser with his knowledge."

"And if you're wrong?"

"Then Maelstrom will probably become a wealthy demon. But I don't think I am."

We crossed the street, and I was beginning to wonder if I hadn't made a mistake. I didn't think Maelstrom would even let us walk away, never mind walk this far. With each step, I regretted my decision more. This would cost me more coin if I had to turn back. Plus, it would give Ralrek yet another reason to ridicule me. My existence had given him enough of those since he and Bilba became friends and he came to know about my ... birth defect. So I was more than relieved when quick footsteps raced up from behind.

Ralrek and I turned to see Maelstrom running toward us, waving his arms. I hid my smile under the knowledge that I had him. Even the pissing rain could not dampen this victory —and escape from embarrassment.

"What do you want? We're busy," I said with the driest, most disinterested tone I could muster.

Stopping just short and rubbing his hands, Maelstrom checked our surroundings and leaned in. "Listen, I'm sort of in a tight bind. Got myself into some trouble betting on the aqrabuamelu races."

"What's your point?" Ralrek asked.

The question caught him off-guard, and he stumbled through his response. "Well ... I mean—I thought if I gave you more information, you might—you could help me out? Spare a little more coin?"

"More? We've single-handedly made you a wealthy demon today." I feigned outrage, knowing it would drive his desperation.

"I'm not asking for much, sirs, I promise," Maelstrom responded with a greedy grin. "But it might be worth it to share the name of someone who would know more about Gemini than me."

"Who?" Ralrek asked.

Instead of answering, Maelstrom reached out his hand.

I pulled another small coin bag out of a new pocket. He tucked it away before I'd even retracted my hand. "There's a homeless succubus who is always begging down at the point where the canals meet. Called the hub. Call her Cassie, they do. She's not from around here. Sort of like you two, she showed up one day and started asking questions about Gemini. He was already gone by then. I figure you either know her and you all work together. If you don't, maybe she's involved with whoever took or killed Gemini. That'll help you, won't it?"

Interesting, but I wasn't going to share that. "How will we find her?"

An uncomfortable smile curled one side of his mouth. "You'll know her. She's the most beautiful homeless succubus you'll ever see. Even filthy, she'll take your breath away. Promise." Just as I was about to ask for more detail, Maelstrom patted his pocket and took off.

"Well, there goes our coin and our chance at finding the source."

"Let's head to the canals and see what we can find."

It seems there is no actual terminal point to how drenched you can become if you are out in pouring rain long enough. I had that epiphany as we made our way along the canal, searching for the hub where we would find this succubus. I stopped a passerby and asked for directions and he kindly pointed us down the street, saying we had a few miles' walk ahead. Ralrek joined me in groaning.

After the said few miles the stranger promised us, I was wetter, colder, and hungrier. The only advantage of being so miserable was the motivation it provided to find this homeless succubus as quickly as possible.

"Keep your eye out for her," Ralrek said.

"I'm glad you said that."

"Why?"

"Because, I don't think I could have thought of it on my own without your insightful guidance."

We walked in surprising silence. I expected Ralrek to bite back because, fact was, Ralrek always bit. This time he didn't. He remained quiet.

Half a block later, he spoke up. His voice was timid. "Zeke."

"Ezekial," I corrected.

Eyes cast to the sidewalk, Ralrek's cheeks pulsed as he clenched his jaw. "Ezekial," he said, starting again, "I'm sor—"

Before Ralrek could make the mistake of finishing that sentence and proving himself to have some decency, I pointed. At the intersection of two canals, near a pillar at the corner of a footbridge, a female demon was holding a tin cup out to passersby. The few on the street passed without stopping. She was too far away to hear her comments to those ignoring her.

"Think that could be her?" I asked.

Ralrek nodded.

I dug into my pocket and retrieved a couple coppers. "Hi," I said as I approached the beggar who watched me guardedly.

She looked up, drops of rain cascading from the ragged hood, and extended her tin cup. "Have a coin to spare, Mister?"

Her voice was soft, like creek water trickling over rocks. She was young, much younger than I expected a beggar to be, probably close to my age. And beyond that, she was stunning. Maelstrom was two for two so far. Maybe he did earn his coin today. The beggar's hair was covered in the green hood of her cloak, but the strands that had fallen out looked like vibrant cocoa with hints of blonde mixed into the darker shades. Her smooth face was perfectly symmetrical, nearly horizontal eyebrows, raised just at the corners, highlighted dark eyelashes that surrounded crystal blue eyes. What can I say? I'm a sucker for blue eyes. Okay, I'm a sucker for any beautiful eyes; to that point, I'll concede. This beggar's were bluer than even Seraph's. Her narrow lips drew my attention and in that moment, I forgot my entire purpose for approaching her.

Until she spoke again.

"Have a coin to spare?" She repeated, shaking her cup, which clinked with a solitary coin.

I slid my hand back in my pocket, dropping the coppers I'd pulled free and found a silver. I held it up between us, showing her what I was about to give, and dropped it in.

Her eyes followed my hand until I released the silver, and when she looked back at me with those oval eyes, they were watery, and not from the incessant rain.

"May the Hellfire shine on you."

I smiled, feeling goofy. "You're very welcome. I hope it helps a little."

She shook the can again, the hollow rattling eliciting feelings of guilt that I could have given more. Heavens, I'd just given a slimeball like Maelstrom twenty times what I'd gifted to her. If I knew what the mission required of our coin, I'd give her our entire budget.

Yes, I was thinking clearly, why do you ask?

"Every bit does. I thank you for your kindness," she said softly, her head hung.

"We were wondering if you could return the favor," Ralrek interjected.

I winced.

She lifted her head slightly, only high enough to glance at him, a fire suddenly burning in those crystal eyes. "What favor?"

"Apologies for my tactless friend," I said, trying to rescue the opportunity. "He didn't mean anything, trust me. No, we actually need help with something and we believe you are the demon who can."

"Me?" The beautiful beggar—Lucifer, she was gorgeous, even beneath the dirt-stained cheeks—questioned with a humble laugh. "I doubt I can be of much help to influential and powerful demons such as yourselves. I'm just a simple beggar."

The urge to rescue her flooded over me. I really needed to spend more quality time alone. If a beggar could stir my loins, I wasn't spending enough time looking at succubi magazines.

"We heard differently," Ralrek said.

This process would be much simpler if he would just be a silent partner. There are only so many shards of glass I could step on before I gave up walking around without shoes. I just had to figure out what metaphorical shoes would work with Ralrek.

The beggar cocked her head. A strand of cocoa and blond hair fell forward in a wet clump.

I drew a breath and explained. "We're looking for someone who knows something about a friend. We heard unfortunate news about him and we're trying to figure out what happened."

The beggar's oval eyes turned down at the corners. Her voice dropped an octave. "I'm sorry to hear about your friend."

"Thank you."

"But I don't think I can help. I know so little about anything. I spend my days out here, begging for enough coin to eat, and on the good days, to put a roof over my head. Sorry."

I decided now was the time to take a risk. "Our friend is missing, maybe killed, we believe. And not here."

"Oh, that's terrible. I'm so sorry. But I'm just a simple succubus. My entire world is by the canals and drainage tunnels where the water doesn't rise too high. That's where I sleep at night if I don't get enough coin during the day. I don't know anything about the rest of the Circle."

"Entertain us," Ralrek said flatly. "Tell us what you know about an incubus named Gemini Oso."

Her eyes flickered in recognition, but she covered the slip. Just not soon enough to stop me from seeing it in her eyes. "Gemini? Who?"

I wasn't falling for it. "You know him."

Her thin lips quivered as her shoulders slumped. "He's your friend?"

This beggar was at least aware of Gemini, I was as sure of that as I was that the Council could kiss my ass for sending us to this dreary Circle. Whoever Gemini was in his secret life, deejay or not, he had interesting circles, running from a player like Maelstrom, all the way to a street beggar, on to Lucifer's Council itself.

"Yes, he's the friend we were asking about. Do you know him? Please, we're trying to help." I tried to control my voice, the excitement almost overriding my calmness.

Seconds passed into decades as we waited for the beggar's answer. In that time, her eyes hardened, losing the gratefulness that had softened them moments ago.

"Yes," she said carefully. "I do."

"Great," I clapped my hands, making her jump. "Sorry. Just a little pumped. You might be able to tell us what happened to him. Did he upset anyone enough for them to do harm to him?"

"To kill him," Ralrek said with a subtlety of a carriage train rumbling through a library.

The beggar shook her head and tucked the tin can inside her cloak. "That's the problem. I can't help you."

"What? Why not?" I asked. "You said you know him."

"I do. But I can't be of much help because," she said, drawing the word out as if she were measuring our reactions. "Gemini is in the Overworld. Not here. I can promise you, he is very much not dead. But I think he's in serious trouble."

7

UNDERWORLD, SECOND CIRCLE

"WHAT DO you mean he's in trouble?" I said.

The succubus dropped her head, the cocoa and blond curls drooping. Droplets of cold Second Circle rain dripped to the ground.

"I beg your forgiveness, sirs," she said to the cobblestone. "But Gemini is not dead. That's all I can say beyond the fact that I know he's ... he's hiding."

Ralrek tugged on my arm. "This is nuts. She has no idea what she's talking about."

The beggar snuck peeks at us whenever she thought one of us was not looking. Ralrek was coming from a place of rational deduction, but I saw something in her eyes. She believed what she was saying. To her, Gemini was indeed alive but in trouble.

"Let's give her a chance."

He dropped his arm and gave a quick shake of his head. "This is a waste of our time," he said too loudly.

"Forgive me. But I can only tell you what I know," the succubus said.

"Or what you want us to know?" Ralrek contested.

She found my eyes. "I swear he's alive. I can ... I can feel it.

I wouldn't waste your time, especially not after you were so kind to me. But I can't be absolutely confident."

"Oh, Lucifer," Ralrek snapped.

"Ignore him," I said. "Why can't you be confident?"

"Gemini is a friend. Was—was a friend," she said, holding her two hands in front of her like she was about to have a silent conversation—us demons find the term 'pray' to be offensive, so we just re-categorize it—with Lucifer. "But I can't be sure of anything because he's no longer here."

"So if he was, you'd be straight with us? Why not just tell us where he is and how in the heaven he got there?" Ralrek's edge returned. He shifted his weight from foot to foot more rapidly now.

"I don't mean to upset you, sirs," the beggar woman said. "But I can't tell you for sure if he's okay. Without …" she gave a frustrated sigh, "being able to see him, I can't be sure. I don't expect you to believe it, but it's the truth. I can sense that he's alive."

"You sense?" I said. Maybe Ralrek wasn't wrong.

The beggar nodded mildly. "It may sound silly, but Gemini and I used to be in a relationship, and I would know if harm had come to him."

Ralrek walked in a tight circle to my side. "Come on, Zeke. This is ridiculous. She doesn't know anything."

"Ezekial," I corrected. "And how can we be sure? We haven't given her an opportunity to explain. So unless you want to keep exploring this miserable island, I say we give her a chance."

Still circling, he pointed at the beggar. "Then she needs to start making sense. Either she knows something, or she doesn't. Either she knows where he is, or she doesn't. She's just making this stuff up and hoping for more coin."

The beggar's voice shook. "I'm not seeking any more from you. You've been so kind. I wouldn't do that."

Ralrek didn't even look at her when he waved her away.

"Everyone does. The Circles of Hell are full of greedy, selfish demons."

"Sirs, believe me," her voice rose, emphatic and cutting further across the walkway through the pouring rain. "I want to know what happened with Gemini more than anyone in the Underworld. I told you; we were close, and I miss him dearly. I want answers too. Even more than you. But I feel it in my heart. Gemini is alive."

"In your heart," Ralrek scoffed.

The beggar woman had it hard enough. To have lost someone you cared about and not know where they were or whether they were alive or dead would compound misery. Who would want that for anyone? If Ralrek could not have a little compassion, I would have twice as much.

I softened my voice. "I'm sorry to hear that," I said. "It's possible we can help each other. You tell us about Gemini and his last whereabouts, and we make sure he is safe and finds his way back to you. How does that sound?"

The beggar swallowed back impending tears. "That would be amazing, sir. I would give anything to see him again. But I fear what you are offering is impossible."

"Impossible?"

"I'm afraid so," she said, with a glance toward Ralrek before she continued. "Unless you've come up with a way to travel outside the Underworld."

Ralrek grabbed my arm, but even before he could warn me away from the topic, I asked, "You're absolutely sure he's in the Overworld?"

"Yes. He was ... we were ... intimate," the beggar said.

Well, of course they were.

This beggar—whose name I had yet to get—had a fascinating back story. To be at this lot in life yet have been involved with someone like Gemini, an operative for Lucifer's Council. What would precipitate such a plummet in circumstances?

"That doesn't explain how you believe he's no longer in the Underworld," Ralrek said, the biting comment making the beggar jerk her eyes down.

Submissive. So much to her story. With each little tidbit, she was even more fascinating. "I believe you."

It was a simple statement but seemed to have a profound effect on her, returning that sparkle to her crystal eyes.

"You do?"

I nodded. "And we'd like to help."

Ralrek snapped his head in my direction in mid-stride, pausing his circling, which had slowed. "We would?"

"Yes," I told Ralrek via the beggar woman, "we would. Do you have a name?"

Her eyes blinked rapidly and her lips twitched before she smiled nervously. "Oh, I'm so sorry. I'm so rude. I'm Cassie. And you are?"

"Not believing this," Ralrek said.

I ignored him. "I'm Ezequiel. My friends," I said, stressing the word, shooting Ralrek the nastiest sideways glance I could, "call me Zeke. You can if you'd like."

"Oh, Lucifer," Ralrek said with a big exhale. "Here we go again."

Cassie smiled, this time with confidence. Call me a hopeless romantic, but when you see the potential good your efforts do for someone else, it's kind of cool. My new goal, now that I saw he had potential to feel something besides overconfidence, was to rub off on Ralrek by the end of the mission so he would see that constantly being an asshole was the less effective tactic in life.

"It's very nice to meet you, Z-Zeke," Cassie said, struggling over my name as if it were a foreign word.

"And it's nice to meet you," I said, forcing the corners of my mouth to remain level. There is only so much of looking like a goofball in front of Ralrek I would allow. "And we can help. Honestly."

I couldn't tell if she believed me or not, so I had to be careful. Too much and the Council might shut this down. Too little and we'd be standing in the rain for days to come and still might not get anywhere.

"I believe you think you can, but it's just impossible," Cassie sighed. "Gemini hasn't been in the Underworld for weeks."

"How did he travel to the Overworld?" Ralrek asked.

Cassie's voice dropped. "He only told me he was going. He said he needed to, but he wouldn't tell me why or how. He left and I haven't heard from him since."

I groaned. Keeping her in the dark? What a jerk move.

Cassie must have understood my reaction as defeat. "I told you it was impossible. I appreciate your kindness and your coin, but I've taken enough of your day. I'm sorry for troubling you."

"You weren't any trouble," I said.

"He's not convincing me of that," Cassie said, tipping her head toward Ralrek.

Ralrek was still circling.

"Don't worry about him, he's always like that. The life of the party."

Cassie laughed. It was a sweet laugh, the type I'd imagined angels making, if you believed their biblical propaganda.

"But I have to be honest, if we are going to help you find Gemini, and you're going to help us, we need to see some friends of ours," I said, feeling dirty even halfheartedly referring to the Council as friends. It sullied the word, sullied my thoughts of an actual friend. For a moment, I wondered if he was finding what he needed in the Eighth Circle.

"That's okay, any help I can get, I'll take. I miss him dearly," she said tentatively. "Who are your friends?"

Behind me, Ralrek growled.

"I think it's best if I just show you."

CASSIE HESITATED AT THE GATEWAY.

"It's okay, really. You can step through," I said. Gateways can be intimidating the first few times you see one, not a typical occurrence for regular residents of Hell. Stepping into the ambiguous void is an entirely different level of perplexing.

Ralrek had already stepped through and was presumably waiting on the other side—though I would not put it past him to be sucking up to the Council and blaming me for everything if this was the wrong thing to do.

Cassie continued to look at it as if it would sprout teeth and bite her. "Are you sure it's safe?"

I chuckled, not at her, but at how ironic it was that I was now so worldly compared to other demons. A year ago, the only thing significant about me was the fact that I was the Segregate, the only demon in Hell who needed special handling. Now, here I was acting like the expert on inter-Circle transportation.

"I've done it a few dozen times in the past month," I said, trying to convey confidence through my recent work for the Council that had kept me busy and allowed me to rent my first apartment. "It's unnerving the first few times, but also completely safe."

"But," she dragged the word out, "you're serious? The Council? Lucifer's actual Council is on the other side of this?"

"Yep." I sensed her hesitancy would not lessen any time soon. "Would you feel better if I went through first?"

"You think I'm a coward, don't you?"

I shook my head. "Not at all. The first time I did it, I was scared as heaven too. But if I go first, do you promise to follow me through? No turning back? It's the only way we can find Gemini."

"I promise." Her voice was low, restricted, but still confident.

"Okay, let's do this."

Without looking back, I marched through the gateway, blinded by the intense white light. After the utter void of color faded, I turned to see if Cassie was joining us. A delay gave me doubt.

"Is this friend of yours slinking behind or not coming at all?" Apopis hissed.

I was about to ask the thin tattoo–faced Founder to give her a chance when Cassie's slender, ragged boot tiptoed on the tiled floor, as if she wasn't sure it would be solid or not.

Ralrek snickered.

"Come on, dear. It's okay," Azazel said.

Cassie stepped out, and the gateway zipped closed behind her. She spun at the collapse. Her expression of apprehension made me want to run over to her and hug her. Hers was the face of someone who believed they just made the worst mistake in their life. Instead, I used my go-to. Humor.

"It's alright. They don't bite … usually."

She slid closer, shooting glances at the jade table at the end of the room where Hell's legislators sat. The musty smell of the Second Circle emanated from her cloaked and sodden boots.

"Can you never find males to assist in your missions," Seraph asked, a harsh gaiety in her tone.

The ancient succubus was there during my last major mission, where Marijon helped me see that even demons who claimed to be friends could be traitors. Seraph knew enough about my propensity for the female species and how that sometimes blinded me.

"Actually, your source recommended her." I felt empowered to reply, only because it was backed by fact. Hey, it's not often I can get one up on the Council while, hopefully, distracting them from my testosterone-driven thoughts.

"Glad to see things worked out then," Michael replied. Yes, that Michael, the one from Yahweh's clan and leader of Lucifer's Third Council, redirected the conversation. Seraph was not the only Council member who had once served in Heaven. She and Michael had been sent to Hell in a trade for two high-ranking demons. A peace pact between Lucifer and Yahweh ages ago when hostilities were at a boiling point. Now, no longer an angel, he was still tolerable, for a member of Lucifer's Third Council. Razor sharp wit too. He'd trimmed his beard even shorter than the last time I saw him, making him look thinner. "Let's get down to business. We're behind schedule."

I didn't ask what schedule we were on because I was sure that the three of us weren't part of the Council's plans.

"This is Cassie," I said, starting off the conversation. "She's a friend of Gemini's, and she gave us some bad news about him."

"What bad news, boy?" Beelzebub barked.

"He's no longer in the Underworld," Ralrek said, stealing the spotlight. "We can confirm that."

Azazel whined. Apopis hissed, and Seraph just raised an eyebrow.

"Bless it!" Beelzebub cursed, casting an accusatory glance around the room. "Where in the Overworld is he and how did he create a rift?"

Michael shrugged. "We'll have to worry about the 'how' later, when we have a little more time to consider the." He paused, flashing a look our way. "Implications. For now, let's deal with what we're facing." He squared on us. "Where did Gemini go?"

Cassie came forward. Azazel leaned in, his long white goatee tipped with orange dye bending on the jade table. An intense interest washing over his face. Seraph jerked back like something bit her under the table. Beelzebub growled, forcing Cassie to retreat a step.

"He's all bark," I whispered, moving to her side.

Seraph studied us. Too closely. Was that jealousy? If so, I was a fan. Tens of thousands of years in age difference didn't matter; I was allowed to crush on her, and if I was reading her correctly, I was encouraged. I still had an uncommunicated night of drinks and great conversation planned for her.

Creed warmed against my hip, pulling my thoughts away from Seraph, who was now scowling, focused on Cassie.

"I'll look past that, Mr. Sunstone," Seraph said without warmth or kindness, "because we're more interested in hearing what she knows about Gemini's whereabouts."

Cassie cleared her throat. "He's in a city in the Overworld called Kaiserslautern. At least, that's where he was headed when I spoke to him last. It's in a country called Germany."

"Yes, dear," Azazel said, scratching underneath his long-white goatee, the orange tip bobbing up and down as he did. "What we aren't sure of is why he went there."

"Or by what means," hissed Apopis, his eyes narrowed.

"Not the time," Michael said, reminding his peer. "Please start at the earliest point. Only applicable to Gemini's where-abouts, but don't leave a detail out."

"I don't know that much," she said, "because we were already broken up by then. But he wanted to inform someone he was leaving, and he really didn't have anyone else he trusted."

Apopis splayed his elbows, intertwining his fingers. "Why? What did he fear? Surely he was involved in some-thing he shouldn't have been."

"None of this makes any sense," Beelzebub rumbled, thrusting a hand as thick as a chimera's paw out at Cassie. "Take a look at her. In what circles would she be running where a companion has access to a rift? She is no one."

Azazel leaned back, stroking his goatee. I hoped he would speak, always the one with the most common sense on the Council, even more than Michael. With Michael there was more of a balance. He could be ruthless and overly skeptical at times. With Azazel, that seemed to be his permanent disposition.

"There's a characteristic common in the downfall of all great leaders, be they individuals or a collection, like us," Azazel said, still stroking his goatee. "That is the belief that they are above reproach, that they know and see everything, which of course, is preposterous. We want to believe we hold such a status, that we are not only well-informed, but that we are the sole source of authority, besides Lucifer himself. How do we know all things that happen in the Circles? There's nine of them, for Lucifer's sake. When considered in those terms, wouldn't it make sense that things will slip by us?"

Seraph was nodding. Michael listened throughout Azazel's rationalizing. Now he looked like he saw the sense in what the goateed Council member had to say.

"If a demon from any of the nine Circles is going to the Overworld for any purpose, regardless of what it is, we should be aware," Beelzebub said, planting a fist on the thick table. The goblets and pitcher at the far end, where a sole attendant stood, rattled.

Azazel nodded. "I don't disagree, my friend. But that doesn't mean that we *will*. Just as the Hellfire contains tredecillions of flames, so do the Circles of the Underworld. Individual lives of demons forming a complex network of interactions. As well as we govern, and I truly believe we do, we can't possibly know everything that happens. Lucifer doesn't. So, the way I see it, we have a choice. We can sit here and debate the reasons and rationales for Gemini going to the Overworld, or we can let these three young ones return to their duties. Once we find him, we can fill in the answers at that point."

"I agree," Seraph said, her gaze burning through Cassie. "Let's end this discussion and deal with what we have. If

Gemini is in Germany, then we need to retrieve him. Then we find out how he opened a rift."

"Better still, we send Ezekial and Ralrek," Azazel said in counterargument, to which he received an immediate agreement from Seraph.

"Anyone in disagreement? Beelzebub? Apopis?" Michael said.

They voted, and it was decided. Ralrek and I would go back to the Overworld for the second time in our lives, this time to a place called Germany.

Michael's hand slid back toward his chest, to something unseen. Then, he lifted a gavel and brought it down on the table three times. "It is decided. Tomorrow, you will leave for the Overworld. Return home and make preparations, Ezekial and Ralrek. Apopis will serve as your contact on this mission, though he will remain here."

Ralrek looked determined. "Thank you, sirs and ma'am. We'll find him."

I moved forward, not ready to commit yet. "What about Cassie?"

Having already dismissed us, the four incubi members had pushed away from the table to head off to whatever Council members do when they're not terrorizing minor demons such as myself. All were distracted except for Seraph, who still sat, eyeing Cassie. Heaven knows no fury like an ancient demon scorned, I guess.

Apopis turned back and looked down at something, speaking to it as he answered. "What about her?"

"Does she have your permission to come with Ralrek and me? She has nothing to go back to in the Second. It's a miserable place, by the way. If you could pass word to Lucifer to send them a few cloudless days, that would be great. But she needs more than what that Circle can provide. Can she join us?"

My question got their attention. In reality, I probably

should have been scolded for my flippant opinion about our Lord's involvement with the trivial business of Second Circle weather, but it appeared I'd moved past that point in my relationship with the Council.

"What Ability does she possess?" Seraph asked.

That was a great question. I turned to Cassie, shooting a silent question in her direction.

She looked frightened, intimidated. "My Ability is very weak, I must admit. Not worthy of your time. But I would be honored to go to the Overworld to search for Gemini."

"It is still necessary to know," Seraph said, her voice cool as a Seattle evening—look, it's my only Overworld reference.

Cassie stuttered. "Yes, I—I understand. But I would not be an attribute in that respect. If we find Gemini, I will be though. I will be able to convince him to come back if he gives these two any trouble."

"What Ability do you have?" Seraph said so sternly that even the departing Council members stopped and watched the exchange.

"Discernment," Cassie answered to the floor.

The chamber fell silent. Everyone knew why.

Taurus Hammerwulf had Discernment magic. A strong caster, his Abilities were enhanced because he possessed the Horn, a powerful artifact Bilba geeked out about and the Council wanted back in their control. During our fight to escape, Taurus had cast Discernment spells that slowed my reactions and cost those with me. Nasty things, that type of magic allows the caster to get inside another's head and play mind tricks. Thankfully, I don't have much to play with in the mental realm, so I was able to hold off Taurus long enough to defeat him while Bilba and Ralrek were only beaten to a pulp instead of mush. That magic was no joke and everyone knew it.

Cassie looked at me before stumbling through the rest of

her answer. "But, I—I swear. It's weak. I—I've never been interested in using it and it's never done anything for me."

That much had to be true. If her Ability was even half decent, I doubted she would be homeless.

Seraph's examination turned on me. "Are you comfortable with this, Mr. Sunstone?"

I searched Cassie's eyes. She feared being rejected for this chance to find Gemini. Her Ability was weak, and she was only motivated to find him, not enslave me, as Taurus had been. Bringing her along on the mission was the right thing to do.

"I am."

"Mr. Burning?" Seraph asked without delay.

"Yes, that's fine," Ralrek answered in a guarded tone.

"Does this mean y—you'll allow me to go?" Cassie asked. She was fidgeting with something underneath her cloak, and I willed her to hang in there for a few more minutes and this torture would be over. A few more questions and jibes from the Founders and we would be on our way to reuniting her with Gemini.

"Is that your desire," Michael asked from the back of the room where he had not moved from since pausing to watch this exchange.

"Yes." The answer came from her in a croak.

Apopis hissed. To who, I could not be sure. "We don't entertain the desires of every demon in the Underworld. We have to have a reason."

"If your Ability is weak, what else would you offer that we would send you?" Beelzebub said.

Cassie's lips trembled. She looked to be barely holding herself together. Lucifer's Council of Bullies is what this collection of demons should be called.

"I have little to offer, but I would do anything to return him," she finally answered. "I care about him more than anything in the Underworld, and it could be the difference in whether he returns or not. I'm sure these two," she gestured to Ralrek and me, "are wonderful demons, they've proven their character already. But if we find him, I'm the one he'll trust, not them. If you just send the two of them." She stopped and turned to us, clasping her hands and mouthing 'forgive me,' before resuming. "He will put up a fight. I know him. He can be ... stubborn."

Azazel smiled. "That's a valid argument and would result in a quicker return. I'm in favor."

Apopis swirled his head in a smooth movement toward his counterpart. "The last time I checked, this mission was mine to lead. I didn't realize we were putting this up for a vote."

"I say she can go home and return to her life," Beelzebub said.

Over the past three quarters of a year I had worked closely with the Council. That exposure had changed me. Having Creed at my hip also helped my confidence. They did not like the halberd for some reason, but each time I was in this chamber, it heated against my hip as if to remind it was there. Feeling emboldened, I spoke up.

"She doesn't have anything to go back to!"

From deep inside the bowels of his massive frame, Beelzebub growled. "You're going to have your hands full with this one, Apopis."

"I see."

"It's remarkable that you care for her future so deeply, especially since you've just met her," Seraph remarked. "But it's not your business to save everyone, Mr. Sunstone. In fact, most demons can't be saved if Lucifer's will does not call for it."

Cassie's defense came out in a whisper. "I've tried."

Deep in my chest, my heart tore. "Please, I'm sure all five of you have been to the Second. It's a dark, dreary place. It pisses rain sideways, and she's homeless. Imagine, just try to imagine for a second, what it would be like to live like that. The misery, to be constantly cold and wet. To be hungry, each and every day. To have to shelter in canal storm drains because you have nowhere else to go. None of you would want that for yourselves or anyone you care about, yet you condemn her to that when you have other options?"

My words hung in the air. Shuffling to my side, wisps of material rubbing against itself, crackling of the hearth fire, the only sounds as the five eternal demons considered.

Suddenly Azazel laughed. "Eloquent, Ezekial. Still, my vote remains unchanged. I approve of Cassie joining you in the Overworld. Apopis?"

"As with you, my vote remains unchanged," Apopis said, my spirit dropping. "She should return to her life in the Second. She has no business with us."

"Though I think Mr. Sunstone's intentions are wonderful, his energies could be invested elsewhere with greater effect," Seraph said.

I wanted to shout at her, to give her pause to think. Surely, her time in Hell hadn't beaten the kindness from her. I knew that from spending time with her in the Eighth.

As it turned out, I didn't have to beg or plead. She continued even before my thoughts got away from me. "But it is our duty to give every demon an opportunity to rise from their conditions should it be Lucifer's will. I won't be one to condemn her to that fate, when we have so little to lose by sending her with them. Plus, we know Mr. Sunstone can use all the help he can get." She smiled seductively at me after her comment.

"He wouldn't need all of this help if he had Abilities," Beelzebub said, taking a cheap shot.

"Which is why he was chosen for these missions in the first place," Azazel reminded him. "It separates him from all of our operatives, especially now that he has the halberd."

Beelzebub ignored the interruption. "Maybe if he trained a

little harder, he also wouldn't need to be rescued. Did anyone think it is possible that by sending this weak demon with him, we could do more harm than good? She could hinder the operation, introduce an unnecessary risk. Why would we approve of that? My vote remains unchanged. No."

All heads turned to Michael. His expression was restricted, firm but kind. "So, it seems the decision is mine to make. I understand your reasons for wanting to go, Cassie. And unlike some of my counterparts, I can understand your sentiment, Ezekial. The Council must balance all things when making decisions like this. So it is the decision of the Third Council that Cassie will attend the Overworld with you with the purpose of retrieving the demon known as Gemini."

With his statement, the decision set, Michael walked to the Council's table, picked up and slammed the gavel one more time.

Cassie turned to me, a radiant smile spreading across that beautiful dirt-splotched face. "Thank you so much!" she said, wrapping her arms around me, enveloping me in a subtle dankness, the musty scent of clothes perpetually sodden.

I think I floated.

"You can thank me after you've seen the Overworld. It's not all demons make it out to be. You might hate me forever."

She pulled away, still smiling. "Oh, I doubt that. Thank you for doing this. Thank you for standing up for me. I won't forget this."

Ralrek was already walking away. "Come on."

I turned to thank the Council, but they were departing the chamber, including Apopis. I'd worked with them enough to know I would see him before we left, so it was no great loss.

I released my hold on Cassie, feeling guilty that I'd held the hug as long as I did. Staring into those sharp crystal eyes, rimmed by thick eyelashes, I shared her excitement. "I hope you're ready for an adventure?"

8

OVERWORLD, KAISERSLAUTERN

"I SHOULD HAVE KEPT that blessed rain jacket," I complained, wrapping my arms around myself. "At least that would have helped with the wind."

Ralrek looked more miserable than usual. "I don't remember Seattle being this cold."

"It wasn't."

Gray clouds hung low in the sky, barely escaping the grasp of the green, rolling hills surrounding Kaiserslautern. Even down here, at street level, warmth from the hidden sun seemed incapable of penetrating the thick gray.

"I thought the Overworld would be different from home," Cassie said, looking around with eyes wide, her teeth chattering. I almost wrapped an arm around her.

I understood her perspective, having only spent a few hours in her Circle. Kaiserslautern, Germany looked a lot like where she just came from. Guilt was a companion, reminding me of my part in her being here. Hopefully, the weather and her fortunes would improve.

"What do you say we find our place and then hit a store?" Ralrek said, shaking off the cold.

We agreed and walked toward the apartment from the

side street where Apopis had opened the rift. We had a small advantage in that the descending darkness and overcast skies kept most of the mortals inside. I couldn't understand any other reason why Apopis would drop us in a street instead of an alleyway. But he had, and we moved directly toward the address of the sanctuary, thanks to our prior experience with mortal phone technology in Seattle, before an unfortunate event with any wayward human slowed us.

This was my second visit to the Overworld, and I should have felt more comfortable than I did. Disoriented by what I saw around me, as if I was seeing things for the first time, I was on edge. Everything about this city felt different from Seattle. It had been less than a year since my mission to find Aries. I thought I knew what to expect from the Overworld, but I was learning I wasn't half as smart as I thought. Kaiserslautern looked and smelled nothing like Seattle. The houses were smaller and stacked one after another. In Seattle, the air smelled of vehicle exhaust; here it smell of something that made my mouth water. And it was quieter in Kaiserslautern than Seattle; granted all the Overworld is already quieter than Hell.

The streets were smaller here too, more narrow. As we passed the blocks, some side streets barely passed for alleys back home. That did not seem to bother the humans, who still parked in them. The streets and alleys and few parking lots were crowded, as if this place had existed long before Seattle. Each house, somehow, looked older than what I saw during the first trip. I should have paid better attention during our Overworld geography classes.

Cassie hid her fascination poorly. Her crystal eyes, wide, took in everything all at once. She grimaced more than a few times.

"Not impressed?" I laughed.

"Um, it's dirtier than I imagined," she said, as if she were afraid of offending me.

"I don't think this is normal," Ralrek said, looking slightly disturbed himself. "The last time we came to the Overworld it was nothing like this."

"That's true," I said. "But who knows, maybe it's a lot like the Underworld, you know, that places are unique depending on where you are. The mortals are like us in that respect."

"That makes sense." Cassie drew a deep, satisfied breath. "You're so lucky to have experienced so much. I would love to be as worldly as you two."

"No, you wouldn't," I said.

Ralrek gave a sharp shake of his head. "Don't listen to him. He's the designated cynic of the group. Working for the Council is awesome. You're very lucky they chose you. Appreciate this experience while you have it, because it will probably be the only time you get this chance."

Just when I thought Ralrek was becoming a little more sensitive, he proved old habits were hard to break. What was I thinking? Can't teach a young demon new tricks, I guess? I cut off an oncoming round of mental criticism because an unshaven mortal dressed in a blue uniform with black grease stains approached from the opposite direction.

"Good day," he said, catching me off guard, even though our immortal nature allowed me to understand his native tongue as if he were speaking in our language. Mortals in Seattle didn't talk to us unless we struck up the conversation. They definitely didn't talk to us just passing on the street.

"Hi," I said awkwardly, receiving a strange look as he continued on his path.

"Try not to draw any unnecessary attention, Zeke," Ralrek said.

"Ezekial," I said. "And I was trying to be kind. Give it a shot sometime. The mortals might look on us more favorably than the angels if you were more approachable."

Cassie made a sound, somewhere between a bark and a yelp. I hoped that wasn't her true laugh.

She recovered well. "Are you two always so ... antagonistic toward each other?"

"Only when he's clueless," Ralrek said.

"And only when he's an ass," I said, but with a smile, realizing Cassie might not appreciate the nuances of our relationship. The last thing I wanted to do was scare her off back to the Underworld before we found Gemini. I liked having her around—as long as she didn't turn out to be another Marijon.

"Well, remind me to never get on the wrong side of either of you."

"It's not possible," I said, a little too quickly.

"Gross." That single word was Ralrek's only further contribution.

Block after block, we passed homes that stood side-by-side, crowding the street. This city was so condensed that many of the vehicles had to park with one set of wheels on the sidewalks. No chimera would make it down some of these streets. I was already feeling claustrophobic, and we'd only been in Kaiserslautern for about ten minutes. The green rolling hills I pictured from the mission brief taunted me. Maybe my luck would change, and Gemini was actually hanging around somewhere outside the city. It would be a nice change, to get into the forests. We did not have room for them in Hell and I would love to see what they were all about. Plus, all the trees would block out the gray expanse above my head. My brief time in Seattle had not made me feel any calmer about not floating off the surface into the eternal blackness of space. I just do not understand how that does not freak you mortals out.

Ralrek broke my reflection. "I think we're almost there."

My mouth watered when we rounded the corner. "Oh my Lucifer, what's that glorious smell?"

Ralrek lifted his head, his nose wiggling.

"It's coming from there," Cassie said, pointing across the street.

A single story building with the words *Imbiss Grill* printed on the signed hanging above the entryway proudly stood scrunched between two taller buildings.

"What do you say we drop off our bags at the apartment and then head back here?" Ralrek smiled.

We all agreed it was a good idea. Inside the apartment, we did not waste time checking out the layout or squabbling over which bedroom belonged to who. It seemed like a nice enough place. Plus, everyone seemed motivated to find Gemini as quickly as possible, so the thought we could be here for a while never crossed my mind. After we set our bags down and Cassie took a moment to wash her face—she was just as beautiful without the dirt smudges—we headed for some human food.

As it turns out, the *Imbiss Grill* has some of the best french fries imaginable, the world's best if you believed the menu. They also had the magical treat called chicken. Having had wings in Seattle, there was only one consideration at the moment. Was I going to order a half or full chicken. I went with the full—as if that was a surprise. I seriously planned on petitioning Lucifer to stock the Underworld with this delicacy as soon as I returned. Hey, my connections should be good for something, right?

The meal was fantastic compared to the bland food demons have to chow down on. Food in the Overworld was such a joyous experience, richer, more robust, filled with flavor. We fell silent while greedily filling our faces.

"This might become my main source of nutrients while we're here," I said between large bites. "Screw carbs."

"I've got no problem with that," Ralrek said, smiling behind the thin slab of jagerschnitzel. He'd poked the poor thing with this fork, not bothering to cut smaller portions, before attempting to shove the largest bite he could politely manage into his mouth. He was failing on all accounts.

"Me either," Cassie said, her smooth, impeccable cheeks

smeared with chicken grease. "What?" she asked when she saw that I was laughing.

I wiped my eyes. "You. You should see yourself."

The smile evaporated when Cassie's eyes dropped and she snatched a napkin from the table, covering her face and wiping away most of the grease marks.

"Told you he was a jerk," Ralrek said around a mouthful.

"I didn't mean anything," I said in apology, handing her a second napkin. "You just had grease all over your face. I thought it was—" I cut myself off before I told her how cute she looked.

Cassie conducted a second round of wiping, checking with me to see if she'd cleaned it up. I pointed at the spots she missed on my own face and she mirrored me. Demurely, she bunched the napkins and set them underneath the lip of her plate. "I'm sorry about that. I get a little sensitive about my appearance because demons can be pretty cruel, especially to the homeless."

Her comment brought memories of Aries flooding back. He'd wanted to stay in the Overworld to help the mortal homeless. Hearing Cassie's pained comment only made me feel worse about Aries's death. Immortal homelessness is a problem, if you ask older demons, but I never saw enough to know that. Cassie was only the second I had run across, the other being a beggar in the Eighth. In my Circle, I had yet to see a single homeless demon. Aries had taught me it was a much greater problem with the mortals. I owed Aries so much, and Cassie's comment reminding me of him reminded me of my self-assigned mission to own day repay his memory for failing him. Somehow, some way. Maybe helping home-less would do that?

The more I learned about the Overworld, the more I saw the commonalities we had with mortals, and even spanning the Circles of Hell. Our nature, mortal or immortal, was a shared experience.

"I'm sorry for that," I said.

Cassie picked up a fork now, and I felt even more foolish. I truly hoped I hadn't humiliated her. "It's not for you to apologize for, Eze—Z—Zeke. It's my issue. But thank you for being kind."

I wondered what had happened throughout her life to put her in a place where she now was. What would have to occur to beat a demon down to the point where they couldn't greedily enjoy a meal without shame or guilt?

"Still, I feel terrible," I said.

"Don't. Please." She pulled a slender piece of chicken off the bone with a fork in an awkward, jagged manner, as if she rarely used the utensil. No more commentary from me about her eating habits.

"So, any idea where we can start looking for your friend?" Ralrek said, interjecting business into this awkward conversation, saving me from my downward spiral. I appreciated his unintentional gesture.

We were unprotected by one of the Founder's listening wards, so we had to be careful about what was said. Cassie had been briefed, but she was still new to this, and may not understand the danger of what we were doing. I tried to get out in front of the conversation, to lead her to that conclusion, without embarrassing her.

"Well, he's a deejay, right?"

She nodded.

"Then why don't we look at nightclubs in the city? By the time we're done eating, we can get cleaned up and they should be open."

"Sounds good to me," Ralrek said. "Just give me a chance to grab some food to take back."

"You're still hungry?"

"Don't judge me."

The three of us shared a laugh and then waited for Ralrek to put in another order with the perpetually–pleased woman who didn't move from the counter except to shout orders to the cook. Cassie and I made idle conversation while we waited until it became incredibly uncomfortable. We talked about the chipped resin table top, the way the mortals near us were arguing about something called football, and quaint silence of the neighborhood. We talked about anything to fill the time until Ralrek was done.

"Want to wait with him?" she finally asked, offering a decent validation that I was less than stimulating company—I really needed to learn how to talk to succubi.

We learned a little about Kaiserslautern from the round woman who, we discovered, was the *Imbiss Grill's* owner. She pointed us to a few nightclubs in the immediate area, admitting that her knowledge of such places was limited but that her son talked about them all the time, before going on a short rant about how late he stayed out and his drinking. At points in her commentary, I did not see the problem in his behaviors, though I preferred to drink alone. Still, she provided a wealth of places we could start, and once Ralrek got his food, we headed back to the apartment and prepared for the long night out.

I'm not the biggest fan of nightclubs, so I was not exactly looking forward to this new mission. For all I knew, everyone could be wrong about Gemini's whereabouts. It was possible he wasn't involved in the music scene at all. Just because that was what he loved in the Underworld didn't mean he'd engage in it here, especially if something sinister had gone down between him and this hitman gang of angels. Necessity might require him to do something else. There were one million possibilities for an incubus who seemed so hard to pin down. As day turned to early evening, then to late evening, then approached the early morning, it felt like we explored a million of those million possibilities.

"How many clubs do you think we've hit?" I asked the equally tired Ralrek and Cassie.

"Too many," Ralrek said, looking defeated.

"Thirty-three," Cassie answered, walking—no, bouncing—slightly ahead.

She was still full of energy. My feet were killing me, yet she looked as if she'd just woken and had an excellent meal. Part of me wondered how strong her love was for Gemini. Impressive, to be sure, if her energy levels were any sign. Gemini was a lucky incubus.

"What if we play a game to get to know each other while we walk?" Cassie offered. "That way you two will stay awake."

I laughed. "Is it that obvious?"

"Oh, yes," Cassie smiled. "I take it you don't have very many nightclubs in your Circle?"

"Pubs and restaurants mostly," I admitted sheepishly, thinking about how easy it was to talk to Cassie about anything and everything. With Marijon, we had to hide the fact we were from the Fifth; with Cassie that was addressed in a simple statement. "I never go to our clubs, the few we have."

"Loser," Ralrek said with an exhausted smirk.

"You do? When?"

"Zeke," he interrupted, "it's not like we hang out. There are a ton of clubs back home. They're a lot of fun. If you went out once in a while, you might know that. Anyway, I go out a few times a week. I love dancing."

"Why haven't we seen you on the floor yet then?" Cassie said.

Ralrek cocked an eyebrow. "With the mortals? No way."

"Why not?"

He shrugged. "I don't want to show them up." He was being serious.

I groaned.

Cassie took his hand, lifting it, and spun underneath. Ralrek looked around to see if anyone was watching. I sure was. Cassie moved with the fluidity of a tall-stem flower blowing in a warm wind. Her cocoa hair, streaked with blond, floated outward as she danced. Time stopped. She, the way she moved, was … perfect.

"What are you doing?" he said, half–agitated.

"It's called dancing, silly," she laughed, still circling underneath his arm, spinning this way and that. "I thought you said you danced? The next club we go into, you're taking me onto the floor."

"No way."

"Don't want to be shown up?" she teased.

Ralrek's mouth looked like invisible hands were tugging each corner as he tried to fight a tight smile. "Speaking of, I am getting hungry. I think we should call it a night soon."

With that comment, Cassie released her hold on him, spinning away, a saddened expression passing over her face. I wouldn't have denied her that dance. Ralrek was a dumb bastard.

"It's late, and we can keep looking tomorrow," I said, agreeing with Ralrek. I was exhausted, half from the amount of walking, but mostly by going to so many clubs, filled with sweaty, intoxicated mortals.

"I understand," Cassie said with a pout. "I was just worried that the Council would change their minds and make us return if we didn't find him tonight."

I winced at the mention of the Council outside of our sanctuary. Fortunately, there wasn't a single mortal around at this hour. As late—early—as it was, my brain was not working well enough to come up with a decent explanation if Cassie took the conversation too far and her words fell on an interested ear.

"They won't," Ralrek said, keeping his voice barely above a whisper.

"The opposite will be true. They'll keep us here until we find him, even against our wishes. Be careful what you ask for."

She took a second to examine us. "Do they do that? Do they often hold you against your will?"

Ralrek and I looked at each other, measuring the other's unspoken response. We knew we differed on a lot of things, including our perception of the Council and its demands.

"Go ahead, tell her what you think," I said.

His determined expression told me he appreciated the offer and would take advantage of it.

"They are concerned with the overall picture, ensuring you-know-who's priorities are addressed," Ralrek said in a tone uncommon for him. It was controlled, fair. "For some, and I'm not taking a jab at you, Zeke, it can be a difficult pill to swallow because it doesn't always seem equal. And it's not. Any time I believe I'm hard done, which is rare, I try to remember that."

"What about you?" Cassie said, her head pulling away from Ralrek before her eyes slid to me, as if she was trying to catch him sending silent signals.

"I get what he's saying," I said, wondering how much of a shock to Ralrek's system that might be. "But I also feel there's a certain inappropriateness to how they go about it. No one will tackle that because no one has the power to do so except … you-know-who. They pretty much have impunity, and I think that's dangerous. This isn't me pouting about being made to do things I don't want to do. Well, not totally."

Cassie laughed at that, a sweet, sweet sound.

"I'll be the first to admit, I don't like having to do these things and I don't easily trust other demon's motivations," I said, continuing as long as the opportunity was there. "I don't think anyone should be made to act against their will, regardless of what it is, if that makes sense?"

She nodded, head aimed at the sidewalk. We walked in silence until we rounded the corner. A low, rhythmic thumping greeted us. Ahead, another nightclub, the four billionth of the evening, awaited. Our pace quickened.

We were still alone on the street, no crowd waiting outside the club since it was already so late. Even without a single mortal nearby, I didn't like talking about Hell's business out in the open, but she radiated vulnerability, and I did not want the window of opportunity to close if I could say something that would bring her peace.

"I can tell you, they will probably uphold their end of any agreement," I said. The words failed to convey the message I truly wanted to send. It was difficult to have a conversation like this when I had to self-editorialize every single sentence. My trust of the Council was never strong and only weakened over the months I had been working for and punished by them. "I mean, look, they let you come with us. So that's something. Now, they may have their own reasons and it wouldn't be beyond them to leave you here either. As long as you do your part in this, they'll bring you back. Heavens, they may even pay you enough that you'll be able to get off the streets."

Cassie's eyes grew wide. "They … they would leave me here?"

"No," Ralrek said harshly.

"If it suited their agenda," I said, countering Ralrek. In my mind's eye I could still see Aries, hung from his wall, held in place by the triple attack of Beelzebub, Bilba, and Ralrek. The pleading in his eyes was as raw now, almost a year later, as if I was watching it happen all over again. Beelzebub suffered no consequences. The Council paid Bilba and Ralrek handsomely. The one who did not assist in the murdering of Aries —me—wasn't compensated, but was publicly humiliated and put on house arrest for not following unethical orders. Ralrek could lie to himself all he wanted. But I would not allow him to lie to her.

"I didn't think that would ever happen," Cassie said, stumbling over her thoughts. We'd given her so much to think about, probably too much. The approaching nightclub would serve as a good distraction. We could look for Gemini and allow her to process everything while we searched. Pushing harder wouldn't return more positive results. If we succeeded, all of this would be moot, anyway.

We stood in the red light cast from the neon sign above. The thumping bass of the club music cut through the quiet German evening. The bouncer, sitting inside the inset door-way, asked for our identification. We handed over the fraudu-lent ones the Council had made. Satisfied like all the other bouncers before, he jerked his head toward the club door, giving us permission with a grimace. Sitting on a stool in the cold early morning, I imagined him questioning a lot of his life choices.

The club was dark, like every club we'd been in so far, and reeked of alcohol and sweat. Even at this late hour, bodies crowded the small space. Dark violet neon strips of lights ran along the edges of booths as the only means of navigation. Ralrek led us through the throng toward stairs on the right that led to a second level. From there, we could see the entire club.

When we got to the top, Cassie talked to a group of three mortal men who stood at the half-wall, looking down at the floor below. Thumping bass from the club's speakers drown out whatever she was saying, but the men were smiling, espe-cially the one whose arm she touched. Then the three moved away, freeing up the spot for us. She turned to us, a twinkle in her eyes.

"Nice work," I shouted over the music.

"Thank you," she said, looking down at the dance floor. "It's amazing how similar mortals are to us. A sweet word, a flirtatious touch, and male's brains melt. After all this time, I can't believe their kind hasn't figured out how easily we manipulate them."

I laughed along with her. Ralrek didn't.

"Do you see him?" I asked, changing the subject and

knowing she would pick him out much more easily than Ralrek or I. Gemini's image was burned into my brain from studying the mission brief, but the club was so packed, the dancing bodies moving so quickly, the strobing lights shooting down at the dance floor so distracting, it was a challenge picking out one male from another. The images in the brief showed Gemini as a young, black incubus, with full lips, close cropped hair and off-set eyes. In a sea of white humans, he should have been easy to pick out. He wasn't.

I grew agitated by the combination of noise and flashing light. Throughout our humanology courses, we were taught that mortals, especially young adults, were an angry lot. The overload of stimulus in the clubs over the past few hours went a long way in justifying that theory.

But the humans here, and in the other clubs, seemed happy, lost in the music or in the ritualistic flirting practices. Maybe our teachers and books don't know as much as they claimed?

Cassie shouted. "A few of them look like they could be him, but it's impossible to tell in this light."

"What if I go down to the floor and you direct me from here?" Ralrek offered. "I search, you give me a thumbs up or down when I get near one who might be him?"

It sounded like a good plan, I admitted—to myself. Not to Ralrek. No way.

"Okay," Cassie said, pointing to a corner of the bar below surrounded by dozens of humans. "That guy, on the end. I'm not sure, but it could be him."

Ralrek gave a stiff nod and descended the stairs, weaved his way through the bodies toward Cassie's target. He was careful to not interrupt the dancing rituals of the ones filling the space in the middle.

As she watched Ralrek, I watched her. It's not as creepy as it sounds, I swear. I only stole glances while she stared. She'd cleaned up nicely after we ate, revealing a stunning succubus who matched the wonderful personality of the beggar at the canal bridge. But that wasn't why I was studying her now. I wanted to understand what was behind the way her eyes flared with excitement as Ralrek neared the man who might be Gemini. This was someone yearning to find, to reconnect with another. Her eyes held a longing, an aching to reconnect, for closure. What would that be like, to have someone care that much about me? Whether or not he understood, Gemini was one lucky demon.

I leaned closer. Her scent reminded me of the soft breeze in Eve's Sanctuary. "Can you sense him?"

Without pulling her eyes away from the floor, she nodded. "He's here."

Ralrek made it to the male Cassie pointed out, glancing up. The lighting made it difficult to recognize him. Beside me, she leaned over the railing, squinting before scrunching her face and nodding. Ralrek tapped the male on the shoulder. He turned and frowned at my partner. It wasn't Gemini.

They said something to each other and Ralrek walked away. Cassie pointed out another possible target and Ralrek followed her directions across the floor. Thankfully, there weren't too many dark-skinned men in the club, making our search go much more quickly than it may have otherwise. This second guy was human, not a missing demon who we still had not proved had not been killed by assassin angels. Was it possible Cassie's Discernment Abilities were not the only weak ones she had?

Just as I was about to ask if it would be a better use of our time to head back to the apartment and catch some rest for another search tomorrow, Cassie directed Ralrek toward another target. Tucked in the club's corner, sitting alone at a table over which hung another neon violet light formed in the shape of an armless torso—on a related note, I don't under- stand your human sense of decoration—was a figure fitting Gemini's description.

Ralrek and he talked. My tall incubus partner pointed up at us—well, Cassie—and the figure turned around. His eyes widened.

She snapped erect. Her hands gripped the railing, turning her knuckles white. "It's him, Ez—Ezekial. It's Gemini."

Gemini was on his feet, weaving through the human throng with Ralrek struggling to keep up.

It wasn't until he was halfway up the stairs that I questioned what would happen if Gemini was less than happy about seeing Cassie in the Overworld.

A needless worry.

Once on the second floor, he ran to her. She ran toward him, jumping. He caught her and they embraced. A tender moment, shared by two awkward incubi and a few hundred of our closet mortal friends.

"You're alive! I knew you would be alive!"

9

OVERWORLD, KAISERSLAUTERN

GEMINI PULLED BACK, his off-set eyes radiating with a look of passion. Even in the darkness, his dark skin gleamed. His full lips spread in a smile that slipped when he and Cassie separated and his eyes met mine. Something flickered there.

"Of course I'm alive, babe." Gemini laughed, lifting and squeezing her again. "Why wouldn't I be? And more importantly, what are you doing here?"

I cautiously approached as Ralrek joined us. "How about we move this conversation over there," I said, pointing at an unoccupied table in the far corner of the club, away from this observation deck of the dance floor below. Tucked away as it was, it would give us enough privacy to get the preliminary niceties out of the way.

Gemini looked me up and down. Cassie anticipated his question.

"This is Ez-Zeke and his friend R-Ralrek," she said by way of introductions. "They're the entire reason I'm here and how I was able to find you."

She hugged him once more, and he hugged her back. Ralrek and I stood by awkwardly, looking like two demons who weren't invited to a party but still showed up. "Come on, let's sit down and I can tell you everything."

"You're not working?" I asked him.

"What?" he snapped, his eyes drawing down, reminding me of Apopis.

Oh, so much attitude. This was going to be fun.

"Deejaying?"

His face scrunched. "I'm off tonight, man."

"Cool," I nodded and gave Ralrek that look incubi share when they have just both met someone with a little too much testosterone.

Gemini's abrasiveness wasn't what concerned me. We had to keep our conversation focused and get him back to the apartment where, I hoped, a quick chat would lead to us calling on Apopis to open the rift to home. I was absolutely exhausted after hitting so many clubs and being up late enough to see the next sunrise and wanted nothing more than some Blue Sky vodka and sleep—maybe both in my own bed.

"I'm thirsty," Ralrek said, remaining standing while we took our seats. "What does everyone want to drink?"

We gave him our orders, and he left me with the reunited couple.

"Nice to meet you, Gemini," I said, offering my hand. He looked at it, left me hanging, and only after a playful elbow from Cassie, shook it in a bone-crunching grip.

Somehow, his gaze hardened more when he looked at me. "Likewise," he said tightly, before returning his attention and broad smile to Cassie. "I still can't believe you're here."

She laid her hand on top of his, rubbing it lightly. "And I can't believe we found you. I was starting to lose hope that we actually would find you."

"Is everything back home okay?"

Cassie nodded, excitedly. "As good as expected. You know how things are."

Gemini's gaze and voice dropped. "I do. I'm sorry, babe.

You know I'd be there if I could." The radiating glow returned to his cheeks. "But it's going to get better. I promise. As soon as I'm finished with what I need to do here, I'm coming home and everything will be all right. You'll see."

Cassie mirrored his radiance now. "I know you will. You always do. I was just hoping that one of these days you wouldn't have to rescue me."

Gemini offered his hand. "It's not about rescuing. And plus, this is what you do when you're in love."

She blinked back tears. "We can try again?"

Gemini rolled his thick lips over themselves. "We will try again."

She sat straighter, inhaling deeply. Cassie held his hand in both of hers and she never took her eyes from his. They were fading away into their own world even as I wondered where in the heaven Ralrek was. This discomfort was his to share, the selfish bastard.

As the two reunited lovers got lost in each other, I entered their realm with caution. "Gemini, I'm sure you understand we wouldn't be here," I said, swinging my finger between me and Cassie like an upside down pendulum, "if it weren't important. We can't discuss details openly, so after we have a drink, we'd like to head back to the apartment and finish the conversation."

Gemini sat back, but not breaking the hand holding with Cassie. He lifted his chin, guard raised. This might be a bigger challenge than I thought. Some backup in the form of a tall, handsome devil of a demon would be nice. If I trusted Cassie and Gemini more, I would go get the blessed drinks myself.

"Yeah, we can talk about that in a minute. Right now, I'm just trying to catch up with my girl."

Even ten minutes later, his comment still came across as a challenge. I tried to gauge her interpretation of his level of confrontation. Any time testosterone was involved, things had the possibility of going bad. I didn't want that for our mission or Cassie. She was so happy. This was going to be hard no matter how well it progressed, so any antagonism would only knock us off-course.

"Of course," I said, looking at a human couple in the opposite corner of the second floor who were busy ... coupling. Being the Segregate was easier than sitting around these loving couples, having their intimate exchanges remind me that I had thousands of years of striking out with the attractive half of my own kind. "But it's been a long night." Hey, if he wanted to be an ass, I could too.

Thankfully, she took the clue, squeezing Gemini's hands. "Why ... why are you here?"

"I told you. I have things I needed to take care of, babe," Gemini said in a voice edged with manipulative pleading. "That's why. Just taking care of things."

"But why didn't you tell me back ... back home? If you did, I wouldn't have been so sick with worry." Now it was getting really uncomfortable. "I had no idea where you were or even if you were safe. Then the rumors started. Do you know how hard it's been for me, every single day, wondering if the things I heard were true?"

"I get it," Gemini said easily, making me wonder if he really did. "And one of these days, I'll explain everything, I swear it. But right now, I can't, no matter how much I want to."

"I understand," Cassie said, then drew a deep breath. "It's so good to see you! I can't believe you're here, right in front of me!"

"Crazy, right?" Gemini said and leaned toward her.

I didn't need the script to predict what was about to happen. And I wanted to be nowhere around it when it did. I stood, probably too abruptly based on the reactions from the couple, both of who looked like I'd just caught them doing something they weren't supposed to be doing. They pulled away from each, but only slightly, with hands still locked.

Cassie smirked and Gemini's face gave nothing away. They would be fine on their own for a little while.

Being around this reunification was bad enough, but I getting worried about Ralrek. I hadn't detected anyone conjuring, but this was still the Overworld, a place—the only place—where we could be mortally wounded, and he'd had more than enough time to get our drinks. Something could be wrong, and I was up here watching two love-ravens bat eyes at each other.

"I'm going to see what the deal is with our drinks. I sure as heaven could use one. I'll leave you two to catch up. Remember Cassie, we can't—"

Staring at me stoically, Gemini interrupted. "I've got this, bro. Been here for a while and know the game. I'll make sure we're good."

Cassie said nothing, even when I looked at her, searching for reassurance. So I nodded to the pair—how ridiculous is it to acknowledge your own dismissal?—and made my way downstairs, relieved to get away from the scene the two of them were making, mimicking the coupling humans a few feet away. Sometimes, I just didn't understand love.

The dance floor held slightly fewer bodies now, as the new day dawned, but still enough to ensure the rank mortal funk hadn't dissipated. I hadn't thought to look for Ralrek from the height advantage of the second floor because I was too busy evacuating the love scene. Now I was paying for it. And the toll was wading through this gyrating, sweaty human throng.

"Excuse me," a drunken mortal slurred as he weaved into my path, swaying in the opposite direction as soon as he recognized the almost–collision. I held my hands up, trying to avoid him completely once I saw the front of his shirt speckled with something that looked distinctly like vomit.

Successfully avoiding that calamity, I continued my search along the crowded bar, distracted with trying to blot out thoughts of what was happening up on the second level.

None of the options were appealing. Apopis would be pissed about leaving the pair alone if he knew. But Gemini wasn't going to hear me, and Cassie was too love-struck to think clearly. Reintroducing Ralrek to the conversation was critical to getting Gemini out of the club and back to our apartment, where we could have a real chat. Plus, I only saw one way out of the club, so the pair could not sneak away. I hoped.

The going was slow. Didn't these humans have somewhere else to be, something to get up in the morning for? So few of them looked ready to go anywhere but the dance floor, bar, or toilet.

As I inched along the bar, my focus narrowed. Space was at a premium here as bodies squeezed together, shoulder to shoulder, back almost to back, and sometimes, pelvis to pelvis. I share those minor details because of what happened next, something I couldn't believe at first. Something I initially denied. An incident so unreal to pull my thoughts away from Cassie and Gemini.

The thing about working so closely with Ralrek over the past eight months, and knowing him for thousands of years before that, was that we'd become intimately familiar. Have you ever had someone like that in your life, who you spotted from across the room, even in a crowd? Someone you could pick out within a half second, almost as if you sensed their presence before you saw them? A face that didn't blend into the anonymity of bodies? That's how I recognized him from the back of his stupidly bounteous head of black hair.

And that's exactly why I was shocked to see him acting intimately with someone. Especially in public. Especially affectionately. Especially with a human.

At least now I knew what was taking him so long with the drinks.

The mortal Ralrek was kissing embraced him, hands low on Ralrek's hips. Whatever was in the air that made so many couples want to ... couple was undetectable ... or I was immune. For him to display such divulgence, especially in the middle of a mission, was astonishing.

I edged to him and tapped him on the shoulder. At first, all I saw was Ralrek's face. When he spun, he scowled. His eyes widened, his jaw dropped, and he shot a petrified glance over his shoulder at the mortal he'd been kissing.

Even as I adjusted my stance to look around Ralrek, he swatted away the hands that were still holding onto his waist. It was my turn to widen my eyes.

Behind Ralrek, the human finally relinquished their hold and peered at me. We locked eyes, exchanging looks of confusion. For different reasons, I bet.

I sensed no Abilities in Ralrek's fling. This was no incubus. Ralrek had done the unthinkable.

"Zeke, it's not what it looks like," Ralrek said in a rush.

"What's going on?" I was so stunned that I didn't even bother correcting him about using my nickname.

"Who's this?" the human asked, blowing his blond hair out of his eyes.

"Nevermind," Ralrek said over his shoulder without turning around. "Can I talk to you?" he asked me.

"Sure."

He turned back to the mortal. "I'll be right back." With that, he grabbed me by the shoulders and marched me toward the entrance.

We stepped into the night, much colder than when we'd entered the club. I wrapped my arms around myself, trying to stay warm and hoping it didn't look defensive.

"What's going on?" I asked again.

"I can explain," he said in that rushed speech. "It's not what it looks like. Really. He was asking a question and … and we got to talking. And I didn't say anything, I swear I didn't, but he was interested, and I sort of lost track of time, and—"

"It's okay, Ralrek."

"And I wasn't thinking, I just wanted to get the drinks and get back upstairs to help with you know ... the situation. Before I knew it, he was talking about my hair, and you know how much I like my hair, and—"

"Ralrek," I said, this time much more slowly, "really, it's no big deal."

But Ralrek didn't hear me, his momentum unhindered. "And I don't know what happened. Maybe it was the alcohol, I'm not sure. It's no secret that I'm a lightweight when it comes to drinking."

I decided to let him run with this. He didn't need me calling out on the lack of drinks in his possession at the time I busted him, or the fact that there wasn't an ounce of odor of booze on him or his breath. None of that was important.

"And he must have misunderstood me or took my friend-liness to mean something. That's when he kissed me. I mean, I was shocked. Too shocked to react. And ... and it just happened right before you walked up on us. You believe me, don't you?"

Ralrek's story didn't make sense, as stories fashioned in the spur of the moment typically didn't. But in the bigger scheme, his story didn't matter, not to me. "Ralrek, it's cool."

How many times would I have to repeat that before he believed I didn't care as much about ridiculous rules as he did?

He pulled back slightly, his mouth moving and his eyes dancing back and forth between mine. Then he glanced at the bouncer who we had forgotten about. The large human's drooping eyes told me he wasn't interested in the conversation. I guessed that was his general disposition on life.

"Please, understand. It was a mistake. It won't happen again."

I'd never seen Ralrek suffer a lack of confidence. The demon standing before me was rattled, so unlike the one I'd known for thousands of years.

"Of course," I said and gave him a smile that hid my sudden sadness for him. "These things happen."

He balled a hand and lightly punched my chest. "Thanks."

It was the only response I got. His statement made, he turned and went back inside the nightclub without waiting. I remained on the sidewalk, stunned by what just transpired and by Ralrek's awkward guilt. Ralrek never showed the capacity to care about mortals or even give them the time of day. His homosexuality was as irrelevant as it was natural—well, to us, you humans still have too many hangups—but crossing the line between mortal and immortal wasn't. That was as bad as demons and angels sleeping together—you just don't. Not that I minded. Hey, I'm all for testing the boundaries of rules, like defying the orders of a Founder to kill an innocent. But Ralrek?

To him, this was much more, obviously. I wanted to let him know I was fine with everything as long as he didn't put our mission at risk, but I also wanted to give him time. My heart wanted to shout that I would not create a problem out of this event; my head told me to throttle back.

My heart usually got me in trouble, so I stepped out of the night and back into the club. My entire gang was at our table. Cassie and Gemini were lost in laughing about something I had missed. At least we now had drinks. Ralrek avoided looking at me.

"Welcome back, stranger," Cassie laughed. She flicked the drink in front of the empty chair I was about to sit in. "I got you that."

I looked at the funnel-shaped glass, filled with a pink liquid, a lime slice pinched to the rim.

"The bartender said it was a Cosmopolitan," she answered my unasked question. "He said it's a favorite around here. I hope you like it."

I forced myself to return her smile. "I'm sure it's awesome," I said as I took my seat. "So, are we all caught up?"

The couple shared an intimate look, the type that communicates a million messages only two individuals with a deep connection understand.

"Yeah, we're good," Gemini said coolly.

I nodded, waiting for Ralrek to contribute. He didn't. Instead, he shifted in the chair and shot glances to where the stairs opened to this floor. Was he still thinking about the mortal at the bar? Did he want to go back to him?

I wanted to encourage him to do just that, but I also wanted to get Gemini to the apartment so we could finish this conversation and prepare for the Underworld, either tonight or first thing in the morning. Though I wanted to get home to my payday, I didn't want to risk upsetting Cassie or have Gemini panic and disappear on us. Kaiserslautern had been his home for longer than our few hours, giving him a nice head-start if we spooked him. The prospect of searching for him for wasn't enticing. Plus, who knew what business he had with the Council. They said he was one of theirs, like me and Ralrek, but taking Hell's rulers at their word was no longer on my To Do list.

Where was Bilba when I needed him? He would find a way to direct this conversation, even if he bumbled into it. But without him, and Ralrek completely unengaged, the conversation dragged on as Cassie filled us in on everything Gemini had accomplished in his life. Gemini, not to be outdone, expounded on how epic Cassie was. It was all so adorable, but useless.

It wasn't until after the one hundredth story—I swear—of Gemini's personal conquests that we finally finished our drinks and agreed to head home for the evening, but only after promising the couple we wouldn't call a rift until morning.

As we made our way along the quiet street, the couple taking their time with slow steps; I figured we could save ourselves time tomorrow and get some work done. "Are you good with this, Gemini?"

He laughed cockily. "It was only a matter of time before someone was sent to check on me. I didn't expect this to last forever. Just give us," he looked at Cassie, "the night. Okay?"

"Okay," Ralrek said flatly.

I nodded even though I did not want to.

The rest of the walk was uneventful, Cassie and Gemini breaking off to continue their flirtatious game of catch-up. Ralrek wasn't talking. So I spent the rest of the walk in silent reflection, wondering if I could renegotiate my salary with the Council.

Little hope for that.

I settled in for the night, stretching out on the bed and willing sleep to come over me. The club music was still thumping deep inside, like it had tethered itself to me. Unable to sleep, I pulled out *The Histories of The Balance,* sightlessly fingered for the strip of scrap paper I used as a bookmarker, and picked up where I'd left off. Within moments, my eyes grew heavy as I scanned the section to remind myself where exactly I had stopped.

Deciding I had already read this section about the history of executions and how they were outlawed by demons and angels during the formation of our first Councils after a torrid history of seemingly executing everyone who upset the leaders of the time, I flipped the page and noticed something obvious. Hand written in the margins, a message. I turned the book sideways, interested to see what an ancient book rebel had to say, feeling a certain connection.

I read the passage three times.

From the origin, comes all things. The heavens to the dust, its creation, the Balance maintained.

I WAS CLUELESS AS TO THE MEANING OF THE HANDWRITTEN NOTE but couldn't fight the compulsion to make it Zeke-centric. Was this about Creed? If so, why didn't it give me more?

Tantalizing and teasing, someone had noted this for posterity for a reason. But what? Why? Who?

It's creation?

Creed could be one of a million creations the text was referring to. The possibility that I was way off here was not lost on me.

But still.

Chasing the thought possum up that tree would not happen tonight. My heavy eyelids became clamps, attached to the bottom rims. Closed shop for the night. Sleep came, fast and unrelenting. Thoughts of the meaning of the passage was lost in the wonderment of the subconscious.

10

OVERWORLD/UNDERWORLD

"So what happens now?" Gemini asked.

"Anyone want eggs?" Ralrek asked from the kitchen.

Both Cassie and Gemini said they did. I did too, starvation having visited first thing this morning after making it to the apartment barely before sunrise.

Ralrek set about his work. The early smells emanating from the kitchen hinted at the creation of a masterpiece. Literally anything would qualify at this point.

Once everyone was awake, we agreed on waiting to call on the Council until we ate. Everyone respected it and I woke to the pleasant surprise of having an Apopis-free sanctuary and a chance to stuff my face with someone else's labor. The perfect way to start a payday.

Cassie and her beau sat hip-to-hip at the corner bench of the Bavarian table, holding hands. Her eyes flicked to the potted plant on the coffee table, the beacon we would use to signal the Council. "Z-Zeke, what do you think will happen? Please tell me Gemini won't get in trouble. He doesn't know."

She glanced at him nervously when he snorted at the comment.

"He told me he's not sure." A nervous flick of the eyes at her cherished one. "Because of what he was doing. He wasn't supposed to be here."

"We don't need to get into that," Gemini said to Cassie, leaving me out of the conversation completely.

Genuine concern crossed her face, pinching her thin lips. The answer was not mine to give, and I hated the thought of pandering, platitudes, or false promises. The extent of my role in Gemini's life ended once he was back in the Underworld. What happened with the Council once he was there was anyone's guess. If Gemini was in the Overworld without the Council's permission, I didn't want to tell her what I thought might happen. My mind flashed back to Aries, the other demon who had gone to the Overworld without clearing it with the bosses first. Cassie did not need to know the punitive nature of the Council in those instances.

That Apopis had not come in the early morning to bring Gemini back also gave me reservations about expressing my thoughts. Maybe this would only be an inquisition instead of a murder at the hands of a Founder. But I sucked at lying, the only reprieve being that she didn't know me well enough to know that yet. So I had to say something.

"Never can tell with them. I don't imagine they'll be too happy about what you've done, Gemini, but they'll listen to why you did it. Honestly, that's the best you can hope for with them, I've found."

Gemini scowled. But this was the bed he made. What did he expect?

The aroma of cooking eggs accompanied by the sizzle of bacon drifted out from the kitchen. My stomach clenched in its deprivation and for the first time in forever, I wished Ralrek would hurry and join us. He still hadn't said a word to me and couldn't even look at me. If he was not careful, I would start internalizing his rejection. Almost as much as getting back home to sulk in privacy, clearing the air with him made me yearn for a chance to talk through what transpired between him and a mortal—and a chance to explore his new rule-breaking nature to see if it was, indeed, a new way forward for him.

Who knew? I could end up liking him if it was.

For as long as I've known him, Ralrek had been an asshole, cocky and aggressive to anyone who he felt like being cocky and aggressive toward. But that had been changing over the recent weeks, especially with Bilba tied up in the Eighth Circle with his mother. The forced familiarity of working with him helped both of us understand each other, I think, to see each other in a different light.

Last night gave me the opportunity to see a different Ralrek, one he'd hidden from me for thousands of years and maybe even from others his entire life. Even though I told him I had no problem with what happened, even the fact that it was a mortal he'd chosen to lock faces with, he was still acting as if I'd rejected him. I could speculate for the rest of eternity where that came from, but it wouldn't do our relationship or teamwork any good. We needed to talk this out, but that required privacy. And that wouldn't come until we handed over Gemini.

Me, eager to have alone time with Ralrek. Will miracles never cease?

"He doesn't deserve to get in trouble," Cassie argued, her chest heaving as she took a breath. "He had his reasons. They're good ones too."

"Yeah? What were they?"

Gemini flipped a hand at me. "I don't have to explain myself to you."

I snorted. "No, you don't. You're right. But for your sake, I hope you work on that attitude before you face the Council. They won't react well, trust me. Not that I have a clue about what you've done for them, or what you were supposed to be doing. But in my experience, they're not fans of lesser demons thinking we have a higher place in Hell than we're supposed to." In the big scheme of things, Gemini's attitude did not worry me, and I was only slightly more concerned about his fate. He was a jerk. There were no two ways about it. Totally into Cassie, he saw me and Ralrek as threats. Though she was a beautiful demon who made my skin tingle when I was around her, I was hardly a threat. By all appearances, Cassie lived in a Gemini-centric world.

Still, I didn't have to lower myself to his level, and I did feel for him. Whatever his reasons for coming to the Over-world, justifiable or not, they had driven him to make a huge decision that had profound consequences. Consequences he would pay dearly for, and none of us in this room, or the sulking cook in the kitchen, had the power to influence that.

Cassie's eyes widened, and she bit her lip. In a better state of mind, I would have found that a sexy gesture. As it was, I was too busy spiraling down the negativity hole to make that association.

"What if we didn't bring him back to the Council?" she asked.

"What are you talking about?" I shot a glance at the plant pot as if the beacon would automatically trigger the Council. They could hear us; whether they were listening was anyone's guess.

She scooted forward, her voice dropping. "What if you opened one of those gateway things back to the Second Circle? That way, we can get him home, where they want him without bothering anyone. They'll have to forgive him if we did that."

Ralrek carried plates of food into the room. "They're rifts, not gateways. Besides, that's not going to happen. They'll want information about how he got here, and why he's here in the first place."

I stood to help with the plates. He swerved, somewhat

subtly but not so much that someone paying attention wouldn't notice something awkward had just happened.

I covered my embarrassment by pretending I had stood because of an oncoming cough. Retaking my seat, I said, "Ralrek is right. They'll want to know everything. They won't care about your motivation unless it's of interest to them, but how you did get here is important. You've got to tell them. Plopping down in the Second, even if we could help you do that, won't buy you time." My eyes went to Cassie. "Or forgiveness."

Cassie gulped back a whine, sounding like a mixture between a cough and a stifled yell. "They won't need to know."

She wasn't listening. Time for bluntness. "I can't open rifts. Only the Council can."

"And apparently, Gemini," Ralrek added, his face cast at the plates he was setting around the table.

"And Gemini. How did you do it, anyway? I'm dying to know. That could come in handy one day." No lie, if Gemini could open rifts, maybe Bilba could work on gateways. Gemini was an operative, but so were we, and he didn't seem all that powerful since no one, Council or Cassie, mentioned his Abilities. Man, Bilba creating gateways would come in handy.

Gemini's nose flared, but before he said a word, Cassie was on her feet, arms dropped to her side and hands clenched. "You're telling me they're the only ones who can operate rifts? I don't believe that."

"Well, they're not the only ones. Other major demons are on the payroll to maintain them. But the Council are the only ones who can open them, I'm pretty sure. I'm sorry, but there's no other way. If there was, we would try it."

"Don't make false promises, Ezekial," Ralrek said, squirting mayonnaise on his eggs. I grimaced.

Willingly using my full name now, were we? How many times had I corrected him at his antagonistic misuse of it? Yep, we really needed to talk.

"I wasn't."

"Yes, you were," he said. "There's no other way. In fact, as soon as we're done eating, we need to call on them if they don't show up first. It's time."

"No!" Cassie slammed her palm on the table and scooted out from the corner of the bench, storming out of the room.

We watched her go. I felt like crap. I wasn't sure if Ralrek had the capacity for that.

Gemini appeared annoyed. Standing, he glared. "Way to go, assholes. Have you ever heard of softening the blow? If you're the type of operatives the Council is hiring now, the Underworld needs all the help it can get."

He marched from the room, leaving us stuffing our faces with delicious eggs, mine, mayonnaise-free. The room fell quiet except for the clinking of our utensils on the ceramic plates.

"You're right," I said, staring at in my food.

"I know."

We couldn't get back to Hell fast enough. This was just one more thing making the entire mission unbearable. One more thing in the life of Zeke that was miserable.

"I'm going to call Apopis as soon as I'm done eating if he doesn't show up before then," Ralrek said to his plate.

I nodded.

Cassie's muffled cries drifted out from the back of the apartment, ruining my meal.

"She'll get over it."

"Yeah," I said, Wondering if she would.

That's when the air sizzled. I turned calmly, my mouth stuffed with peppered eggs. Funny, if I cared to find it so, how experienced I was at dealing with the incredible magic possessed by the Council members. The rift peeled apart the air in the middle of the living room, first as a thin vertical line, and then widening into an oval. Once opened, Apopis stepped in the Overworld.

Ralrek stood. "Good morning, sir."

Apopis's slits for eyes slid to my eggs. "A satisfying meal?" Nothing in his tone implied that he cared if it was or not.

"Honestly? Yes, it was." I said, emphasizing the last word. The subtle jab was aimed at both of them.

"Where is he?"

Ralrek pointed to the hallway.

"Bring him out."

He left the table without question. I turned back and attempted to continue eating, though I had definitely lost my appetite. Apopis moved around the table and sat at the couch in the adjoining room. "Where did you find him?"

I slowly set the fork on the plate, eggs unfinished, and got up to join him, realizing I wouldn't get any peace until I'd satisfied all of Apopis's questions. So I quickly filled him in on the events of the previous night, leaving out details about Ralrek's actions. By the time I finished, Ralrek had returned with Gemini. Cassie trailed behind, holding Gemini's hand.

Gemini gave a wide berth around the furniture, standing behind the chair. His eyes met Apopis, without fear or intimidation.

For the longest time, the Founder said nothing, his narrow eyes examining the runaway demon.

It was then that I noticed the rift hadn't been closed.

"Nice to see that you're alive," Apopis said, his voice level. "You'll be returning now."

"I don't want to. My work here is not finished."

Apopis slithered to his full height. "It doesn't matter to me or to the Council what you want. The only thing that matters is that you do what's expected of you. So, make your decision.

Walk through the rift on your own or I drag you back. Either way, you're returning."

Cassie stepped forward, placing herself between Apopis and Gemini. "Please! Isn't there something else he can do if you must punish him? Anything at all? If he says he came here for something important, I believe him. He's been a good servant."

Apopis's tongue flicked at the corner of his mouth. "Don't be ridiculous. And don't impede."

"But he didn't mean any harm," Cassie said, now on the verge of pleading. "He was just—"

"I'll go," Gemini interrupted in a tone so calm that it drew all the attention in the room. "I'll go," he repeated, "but promise that nothing happens to her for advocating for me."

"The Council will treat all of you fairly," Apopis said.

Gemini's grip on the furniture loosened. Cassie's head dropped, and she curled herself into his protective arms.

"Collect your things. I'm giving you twenty minutes. The rift will remain open, so don't think of doing anything stupid." Apopis stood and rounded the coffee table. Cassie skittered back. Gemini moved out of the Founder's way, but never broke his stare. Impressive.

"We'll make sure they're ready," Ralrek said.

"See that you do," the Founder said as he disappeared into the rippling image in the center of the rift. A bright white light flashed at its activation, and he was gone, leaving us with the wayward operative.

The room fell silent, only the sizzle of the rift interrupting the collective quiet.

"Get ready," Ralrek ordered as he moved to the dining area to clear the table.

Gemini turned and headed down the hall, leaving Cassie and me staring at each other.

"Please do something, Z-Zeke. Please help us."

My head dropped. "If I could, I would. Gemini has to

return to the Council. There's no way around that. And please, don't think about doing something irresponsible. If he tries to avoid them again, I fear his fate will be far worse. Their punishment can be ... harsh. Especially if he doesn't explain everything to their satisfaction. The last runaway was a first of his name and they still." I stopped myself, cutting off telling her what really happened to Aries and the general lack of empathy the Council members displayed ever after disagreeing with Beelzebub's actions. That would only worry her more. "Gemini isn't. I don't know how kind they'll be to him. Beg him to be forthcoming, if he'll listen to you. You said he would. Now is the time for that to happen."

Tears formed and ran down her cheek, past her trembling lips. She said nothing, gave me no gesture she understood, agree or disagreed. Nothing. Cassie quietly turned and walked away.

I tried to take solace in the fact that we had reunited her with her lost love. Our work had given her the chance to find a peace that came with knowing he was alive. She would come to see that and understand why we had to follow this mission all the way through. Disappointment might blind her to the situation Gemini had put himself and everyone else in, but in time she would see it for what it was. His fault.

Since I'd given up my bedroom for the couple, my bag was in the living room, already packed. Yanking it off the floor, I didn't realize I left it unzipped until I heard a thump. *The Histories of the Balance* had fallen out. "Bless it."

I stooped, picking up the book, and that's when I noticed something odd. A tiny knob of paper, so small I thought it was a simply malformed bump on a single page, peeked out of the pages toward the back. I set my bag down and used my fingernail to drag the angled nub of paper out of the book. It slid loose. I flipped to the page, being careful, and seeing the bump of loose paper was actually a ripped note slid into the book. I unfolded it.

"Read this," it said in unremarkable handwriting.

Read what? The small tear of paper held no other message. I looked back at the page where the torn piece had been slid and that's when I spotted the handwriting in the margins of the book. The same style I noted last night in an earlier section.

The Balance maintained, its creation of One, gifted to the great prince to bind.

ANOTHER MESSAGE ABOUT CREED, I WAS CONVINCED OF THAT. What were they? Who were they from and why were they hand written in the margins of such an old book tucked away in a corner case of an obscure book store in an insignificant corner of the Fifth? Did Dialphio know someone generations ago had already defaced this book? She probably had a treasure on her hands—well, my hands. And why were these handwritten notes so focused on the theme of balance? And why did someone want to draw attention to this?

So many questions. None with answers.

Not until I got home to Dialphio. Time to get Gemini on the move to face his punishment.

After helping Ralrek clean up, I paced while waiting on the rest of the party. Cassie was the only other one done packing, and she passed the time on the couch, quietly staring out the window with tear-rimmed eyes while I stood around like a doofus. I thought to sit next to her and even moved that way, before I was smart enough to stop myself and continue past toward the chair perpendicular to the couch.

"It'll work out," I said.

Her face crumbled, and she buried it in her hands and cried. I slid the window open and took in the fresh Kaiserslautern air and the quiet of the street below while I waited her out, resisting the urge, strong as it was, to definitely go sit with her now.

"Z-Zeke?"

I drew a breath and faced her.

Her red eyes complemented her blotchy and wet cheeks. Her voice trembled. "Will it? How can you be so sure? He's going to get in trouble. We were just reunited and now he's going to be taken away from me and I don't know for how long."

I swallowed the stupid lump in my throat. I was never good with crying succubi—not that I had a lot of experience with them—including my mother. I never understood them or their motivations, so trying to fix something that was wrong was a monumental task. Cassie was virtually a stranger. Anything I would say would fall short, especially since I had my own needs for finishing this tugging at me. This was going to be tough.

"Cassie," I said, scooting to the edge of the chair and speaking softly, "what was Gemini doing here? Can you tell me that much?"

She only broke down further, making me feel worse for opening my dumb mouth. Cries turned to sobbing, which grew louder, and for a second I imagined Gemini racing from the bedroom and shattering my jaw.

But he didn't, and she controlled her crying enough to speak, her face buried again in her hands. "I don't know. He never told me. We never got that chance." Then her chest heaved. "And now we'll probably never will."

I stood and rubbed her shoulder, letting her know I was there for her the only way I could.

Ralrek joined us next, eyeing me as he set his bag near the rift and busying himself double checking its contents.

Then Gemini's footsteps pounded up the hallway. "Cassie!

Are you okay?" He raced to her, shoving me away even as he kneeled at her feet. "What did you do?"

I'm not the smartest demon in Hell, but I'm smart enough to know to back away from an enraged boyfriend even if I'm faultless. Even if said enraged boyfriend was the jerk who left her to fend for herself in the Second Circle while he somehow snuck around the Overworld doing Lucifer knows what.

"Nothing, man. I swear. We were just talking about you and the Council. That's all."

Behind me, Ralrek grunted in a half-laugh, half-bark.

Gemini shot daggers with his eyes. "How about you stay out of our business, okay? She's scared and doesn't need you to make things worse. You've already done enough."

I had it with Gemini and his attitude. There's a point to kindness, and there's an old saying that no good deed goes unpunished. After everything I had been through thanks to the Council's demands and punishments, I was not in the mood for anyone else to kick me in the shins for trying to help. Gemini put himself, and by extension, Cassie in this position. Not me.

"Screw you, man. You know that?" My temperature flashed in an instant. "None of us are responsible for this mess except for you. You're the dumbass who snuck out of Hell somehow. And your little mysterious act isn't helping you. I didn't leave her high and dry, you did. And this whole thing with the Council? That's on you. If you hadn't done any of this, they wouldn't have cared one bit for you and your decisions. So if you want to be mad, be mad at yourself. I'm not putting up with it anymore, and I'm not going to be shit on because you're upset at being held accountable." Before I told him to get his ass through the rift, I had one jibe left, spurred on by depression, a general lack of tolerating his bravado, and a severe lack of good vodka. "Whatever reasons you had for sneaking out of the Underworld, I hope they were worth it."

Gemini stood.

Behind me, Ralrek stopped what he was doing and moved closer.

"No!" Cassie screamed, getting to her feet, wrapping an arm around Gemini's waist. "Stop. For me, please. You two need to knock it off. This doesn't do any good for a single one of us."

Gemini and I stared one another down. Two bulls ready to charge.

Ralrek was at my side, his hand wrapped around my elbow. In a low tone, he whispered, "Let's get ready, Zeke."

This time, it felt good to hear him call me by the name he wasn't allowed to use.

"WHERE IS SHE?" GEMINI RAGED, HIS SHACKLED HANDS AND FEET clinking the chains.

"The succubus isn't any of your concern," Beelzebub roared back.

It took a certain level of courage mixed with stupidity to confront Beelzebub like Gemini was right now.

But he had a valid point. We'd returned him to the Council's chamber, facing down the five most powerful demons in Hell besides Lucifer himself. Ralrek and I sandwiching Gemini, reporting in.

Three guards waited on us and grabbed Cassie and Gemini as soon as we entered the chamber, shackling him, much to her protestations. I couldn't say I was surprised by the display of aggression. That was when Michael ordered her from the chamber. When she protested, another pair of guards were called and literally dragged her away. I hated that sight more than my inability—or courage—to stop it.

The situation was well out of my hands now. A fat coin purse and a return to my apartment to do some reading of *The Histories of the Balance* were my only interests. Giving everyone a moment to cool down was the best medicine at the moment. And it was not like the Council had imprisoned Cassie. They simply took her from the chamber because of the disruption she was causing. They were not going to punish her for it. Were they?

Seraph watched the proceedings closely, her eyes narrowed as if looking for any wrong move from Gemini to justify unleashing a nasty spell on him. I'd never seen her look so Apopis-like. "It would serve you well to focus on your own situation, Gemini. We understand you concern for Cassie, but our time is precious and our focus is on you and your journey to the Overworld. Let's resolve that, and then we can discuss her punishment."

Gemini growled.

Punishment for Cassie? On what grounds? Unless I'd missed something, she was innocent of everything imaginable. Heaven, she had gone with us to the Overworld with the permission of the Council. What would they would punish her for?

"How is it you reached the Overworld?" Azazel asked, stroking his gray and orange goatee.

Gemini, hands bound behind his back, lifted his chin.

They waited. And waited.

And waited.

"This is where you speak," Apopis said, his tongue jamming the corner of his mouth.

"I have nothing to say," Gemini said, and looked every bit like someone who meant it. If he was going down, he was going down swinging.

I leaned my head closer, speaking from the corner of my mouth. "Just give them what they want. It'll be easier for you in the end."

Gemini didn't move a muscle. He said in a whisper, "Things that are important, aren't always easy."

"They'll punish you," I said. "Harshly."

Uncompromising, he lifted his chin higher. "Let them."

I could do nothing for someone who didn't want help.

Beelzebub straightened, crossing his arms under his massive chest. Apopis and Seraph continued to stare at Gemini as if they were trying to read his soul.

When it was obvious Gemini wasn't going to give them what they wanted, Michael spoke. "Is this your decision? Do you wish to defy Lucifer's Council?"

Gemini said nothing.

The corners of Michael's mouth flattened. "Be that as it may, you've committed an egregious crime. The crime against the Council and against Lucifer himself. You single-handedly put the Balance at risk, and as such, you will be punished."

"Come on," I said, hoping speaking up would encourage Gemini to spare himself, "just tell them how you got to the Overworld. Don't tell them anything else, but at least give them that."

"No." His response was firm.

Michael waved the guards standing at the back of the chamber forward. Four of them, clad in black and red armor molded to their muscular frames, strode toward Gemini. Their sleeveless uniforms exposed arms so muscular that I swore I could see each individual sinew flex and move. They carried long spears burning blue with the power of the Hell-fire in their right hands, and black leather straps in their left. An ominous feeling fell over the room as the clinking of their armor grew louder as they approached.

"Will you not change your mind, son?" Azazel asked, his aged voice croaking with kindness.

Gemini refused to respond, sealing his fate.

Michael pursed his lips. "Very well then. Take him away." He signaled and the four guards surrounded Gemini, wrapping his arms and legs with the black leather straps.

They bound him tightly within seconds before spreading out, stretching the straps and lifting Gemini off the floor. His extremities extended, he grimaced as they pulled him into a horizontal crucifixion pose. I was humiliated for him and looked away. Was this what I looked like to those in the Fifth after refusing to help murder Aries when the Council forced me to ride home strapped to the back of a donkey? Had anyone shared in my humiliation like I was for Gemini now?

No one spoke as the guards marched him to his prison cell.

"What happens to him now?" I asked as I faced Hell's five rulers again.

Apopis grinned as if someone had just thrown him a surprise birthday bash. "That will be determined at a later date. None of which is your concern."

I gave up trying to understand them. Who had the energy for this? "Do you need anything more from us?"

Michael shook his head. "No. In fact, the pair of you have done extremely well retrieving Gemini so quickly. You'll be rewarded handsomely for this."

"Great," I said with half-effort.

"It doesn't sound as if you think it's so," Seraph said, in an ambiguous tone I couldn't quite decipher.

No matter what I said, it would be ridiculed and picked apart. So I kept my big trap shut.

"And don't ask about Cassie, Mr. Sunstone," Seraph said.

"None of my business?"

"Exactly," she said, this time without a flirtatious smile.

"See the financier on your way out," Michael said, flicking his hand toward the large double-doors at the back of the chamber. "She'll have your payment. Be proud of what you've done. Lucifer will be pleased. You've come a long way, and your recent job performance has been outstanding."

"Thank you," Ralrek said proudly.

I couldn't answer even if I wanted to. I felt dirty and something was bothering me about the way the Council not only treated Gemini, but how they behaved throughout the entire situation. I just couldn't put my finger on it.

I couldn't leave the chamber soon enough. The comfort of home called, as did the security of sanity provided by Dial-phio and *The Book Abyss*, which would help me feel not so lost.

Who knew? Maybe she could even help decipher the mysterious messages in the book.

11

UNDERWORLD, FIFTH CIRCLE

"WHAT WERE YOU THINKING?"

The prison cell was dark and rank. The air smelled of permanent moisture. The only light came from a pair of torches on opposite walls of the hallway leading to Gemini's cell, the dim space denying shadows to keep him company. I swore I heard things move in the corners and I had no interest in uncovering what the sounds might be. With each breath, I could taste molecules of mold. If I spent too long in here, I would have to retract the gratitude I expressed to Seraph for allowing me passage back to the First Circle to check in on Gemini in the prison.

"I wasn't?" Gemini coughed.

I smiled and squatted, taking in the image of the broken demon. A week had passed since he stood defiantly in the face of the Council. And in that week, his strength sapped by the horrendous conditions he lived in, and the psychological impact of isolation. Chained to the brimstone wall, his prison clothes were almost as ragged as he was. The last time I saw him, his hair was a mass of tight curls. Now, it was unkempt, with patches of loosened curls poking up and out. Even his skin was ashen now.

Gemini tried to smile at his attempt to make a joke, but it was weak, one that drooped immediately. "Any word on Cassie?" he asked through another coughing fit.

I shook my head. "No," I said through a constricted throat. I wanted better answers for him. But the last time either of us saw her was when the guards dragged her from the Council chamber upon returning from the Overworld. Since then, the Founders were keeping me in the dark. Part of me was convinced they executed a punishment she didn't deserve, such was the lack of trust I had for the Founders who ran Hell.

Gemini's head dropped to his chest. "You've got to find her, Ez-Zeke. Please. If not for me, for her. Whatever happened, she doesn't deserve it. Please help her."

I reached out and put my hand on Gemini's bent knee. In another life, one where we hadn't had to bring him back to the Underworld, I probably would have never seen him as someone close enough to refer to me by that name. Today, none of that mattered. Through the rough fabric of his pants, his leg trembled.

One week. It had only been one week.

"Have they been feeding you?" I tried to keep the rising concern out of my voice. It was nearly impossible.

"They come by from time to time and bring their slop. It's inedible." Gemini laughed weakly and caused himself a wet coughing fit.

My hand moved from his leg to his shoulder. "Easy. Save your strength. You have enough time for bad jokes later."

He raised his head to shake it, wincing as he pressed a fist against his chest. His shackles clinked with each movement. "They will never let me out of here."

"They will. They have to."

Gemini's unfocused eyes searched my face, as if even that required too much energy. "They'll do what they want. Come on, Ze-Zeke, you can't believe they won't keep me here forever?"

"Just tell them how you got to the Overworld. That's all you have to do. Heavens, you were their operative, and they had you on an assignment. For whatever reason, you went quiet and ran away. I don't know what they had you messed up with, but whatever your reasons, forget it. Whoever you're protecting, let them fend for themselves. Give them what they want."

His eyes drifted away. He laugh–coughed again. "You don't get it. I will not tell them."

I removed my hand from his shoulder and dropped it across my bent knee. "You're condemning yourself if you do that."

We sat like that for a few minutes; his head resting against his chest and me listening to his rattling breaths and wondering why he wouldn't do anything he could to get back to Cassie. It hurt to think about her, where she was, and what the Council had done with her. Seraph had given up nothing, saying she was doing enough by letting me check in on Gemini. What secret was this incubus protecting to sacrifice the curse from Lucifer that was having Cassie's love? I waited, hoping he would open up, but just as I was wondering if he had drifted off to sleep, he spoke.

"Please find Cassie. Make sure she's okay. Then I'll be at peace."

"I will."

I sat with him for a little longer, but he had lost the will to speak, and collapsed into a sudden and uneasy sleep. The rattling in his chest unnerved me. Seraph was getting a visit from me to discuss his condition. Of anyone on the Council, though I could possibly include Azazel, she would hear my plea.

Eyes closed and snoring, Gemini was asleep. I patted his

arm lightly and left his cell to find the only succubus to serve on Lucifer's Council.

———————

"SHE'S NOT HERE," APOPIS SAID, FLICKING HIS LIP WITH HIS tongue. "What do you want her for?"

"I need to see her."

He turned, tucking something behind his back. "Leave to find her then or state your business."

"When will she be back?"

Apopis shrugged.

"Will you—" my fire burned. My voice rose.

"What's going on here?" a new voice interrupted. It was Michael.

We turned and greeted him, Apopis less formally than me. Michael's warmth slipped from his expression when he faced me. I swallowed the nervous lump in my throat. "I'm looking for Seraph. Where is she?"

The two Founders eyed each other before answering me. "What does this concern?"

"He won't tell me," Apopis said.

"Because it's none of your business," I replied, feeling good at returning the jab that the Council had trotted out far too often.

Michael turned slightly, angling to address Apopis straight on. "Why don't you head off and I'll take care of this?"

The tattoo-faced Council member dipped his head in reverence and left, but not before scowling at me.

Michael now had my full attention, or I had his.

"Please, where she is. I need to speak with her."

Standing straight, he towered over me, his eyes pinched and as hard as his tone. "Seraph will see you in her own time. I'm more concerned with the fact that you're growing very comfortable making demands of the Council, forgetting your place. You've performed well for us, stellar, in fact. But that doesn't entitle you to treat us as your equal. We are not."

"I'm aware of that."

"Are you?"

"The Council makes that very clear at every opportunity," I said, carefully. Michael wasn't the enemy, even Apopis wasn't, though I was still trying to ascertain how much potential he had to fill that role. Michael had vast responsibilities; I understood that. As much as I hated being directed by the Council to missions that maintained Lucifer's peace and the Balance, my responsibilities paled in comparison to Michael's. If for no other reason than that, he earned my respect. "I need to see her because she understands me. Nothing against the rest of you, but I can be real with her."

Michael cocked an eyebrow. "And you can't with Apopis, who is responsible for this mission?"

"We're finished with that."

A smirk appeared on his lips. "And what about the rest of us?"

I shook my head slowly, Creed warming slightly at my hip, stopping myself from chasing thoughts about why I trusted no one. Michael could read them here. The Gift of Transparency, Seraph had called it.

He sniffed, stretching to look around the chamber. The two ever-present guards were dozens of yards away, bordering the double doors. They were the only demons around to hear us, and I imagined they had been exposed to thousands more juicy conversations than this one over the centuries. Our conversation held nothing that would interest them.

"Is this about Gemini and Cassie?"

"It is."

"Ezekial," Michael said my name like my father when I

was going through my rebellious phase, "this is far above your station. Your mission ended when you brought Gemini back. You've performed well and we are pleased. Don't soil that by getting involved in this any further."

I ran a hand through my hair. What was it with major demons that prevented them from hearing what us regular types actually said? "That's the thing, I don't want to get involved in anything. I have a few questions."

"About them?" He leaned closer—over me. "Or just Cassie?"

"Both."

He inhaled through his nose, prolonged and dramatic. "I'll be sure to let Seraph know you're looking for … Cassie the next time I see her. In the meantime, I would encourage you to move on from the situation. It's unfortunate and will be dealt with appropriately. But to just close the loop, your work here is done. We've paid you, correct?"

I nodded. "Handsomely."

Michael smiled wickedly; it was so uncharacteristic. Unlike Apopis, Michael had not pushed me to being a complete skeptic. Not yet. Still, I squirmed internally when he reached over and laid a hand on my shoulder. "You're special, Ezekial. You've got a great future ahead of you. Stay on the path and you'll do remarkable things. Veer from it and …"

The request for him to finish his comment burned on my lips. It remained unspoken. "Where is she, Michael? Where's Cassie?"

He released my shoulder, his eyes hard. "If we had that answer …"

They didn't know? I wanted to call his bluff. "Send me to the Second Circle. I can find her."

But Michael squashed all hope as soon as my statement was voiced. "There's no need. We're not concerned with her. We've got Gemini and soon enough we will uncover how he was able to travel to the Overworld. This is not your worry any longer. Go back to your life, Ezekial. Enjoy working at the bookstore and keep your nose clean. Don't worry about anything else. This is our job."

Michael emphasized the word "our." I knew exactly what that meant. 'Ezekial, mind your own blessed business and go be a good little demon somewhere else.' I was being dismissed. Again. Like I was nothing more than trash caught against the curb. All I needed was to know if she was okay. For my own peace of mind and to give Gemini his as well.

But Michael wasn't budging. Apparently, I would have to find Seraph on my own.

"ARE YOU OKAY? YOU SEEM DISTRACTED." DIALPHIO SAID AS SHE rearranged a new shipment of books.

"Huh?" I stared at her, feeling like it was the first time I'd seen her today, even though I'd been at work for the past few hours. The symptoms of a troubled mind, I guess.

She had pulled her auburn hair back into a ponytail, something I never thought I would see, especially during store hours. Neither were the sweat droplets beading on her head. She pointed behind me. I turned to see the stack of hardcover books I used to build a parapet display. I thought it would be an effective marketing tool for the new release of *Otherworldly Architecture: The Venerable Influence of The Underworld on The Realm of Angels*. The problem was, I stacked the books upside down, only noticing when my boss pointed it out and after I finished.

"Not sure how that happened," I said lightly.

"Are you doing okay?" Dialphio said.

I couldn't lie. Things were crap and pretending they hadn't been was futile. "No, not really."

"What's going on? Don't tell me they didn't pay you for the job?"

I realized that I needed to stop telling her so much about my work with the Council. I was pretty sure I would get in trouble one of these times. But she was so safe and understanding and she wasn't into lecturing me about how wrong I was all the time, like my father. Supportive and unbiased, she was someone I desperately needed in my life, especially since Bilba still wasn't back from the Eighth.

I shook my head. "No, they paid me. It's not that."

"Then what is it? Trouble with the young succubus?" she said, a playful smile spreading across her face. "Have you not been tipping Gigi again?"

I laughed. Who had time for succubi when no one cared to talk to you, anyway? My plate was full of trouble and I didn't need to add any to my diet. "Not that either. And I'm officially well-educated on tipping ... though the math is hard." I finished with a wink.

Dialphio huffed, not serious at all, and set down the book. The green eye shadow she wore every day made her eyes appear more foreboding today for some reason—the real reason probably lay within the confines of my thick skull. "Ezekial, you've never kept anything from me."

"What makes you think I am now?"

She tilted her head, sending a string of red curls floating across her face. She pushed it back over to the side. "Because you're a terrible liar and I can read you like a book. Something is troubling you and you'll be a much better employee if you just share what it is. You know your secrets are safe."

I did; she was right. Besides Bilba, Dialphio was the only one I trusted with any form of secrets. I thought Ralrek and I were approaching the stage where we could be at least minor ones, but ever since coming back from the Overworld, he'd been acting strangely. We spoke in the week leading up to me seeing Gemini in prison, and not at all in the days since I'd been back. Just Bilba and Dialphio, that was all I had besides my parents. But sharing secrets with them also came with the lessons on being a good servant to Lucifer, and the last time I checked, the big man wasn't that concerned about my troubles. In return, I wasn't concerned with making him happy either.

I leaned on the book parapet. "Am I that transparent?"

A smirk spread across Dialphio's face as she nodded.

I pushed myself up. "It's just this Council business. I'm tired of it. I don't want to do it anymore."

"Then stop."

"It's not that easy."

"Yes it is," Dialphio said. "You walk up to them and say 'I quit.' Just like that. Unless they don't allow you to, and if that's the case, one would have to ask why, wouldn't they?"

I shook my head. "I don't think they accept resignations," I said, my thoughts drifting back to Michael's comments. "At least not until they're done with me. I'm not exactly a volunteer."

Dialphio opened her mouth and then pinched it closed. "Something came in the mail for you today." She walked back toward her desk.

"For me?"

She moved things around. The slight whispering noise of books and papers being rearranged into new yet still chaotic piles drifted out to the storefront.

"Yes. It was sitting on the doorstep. Nearly missed it when I unlocked the store. It had your name on it. Ah, here it is!" She walked out from behind our tucked away office carrying a small tube wrapped in what looked like rawhide. A thin cord was tied around it, keeping it rolled up. Dialphio handed it to me.

"You didn't see who dropped it off?"

"No. And I got in early, so whoever did got here before I did, and that was early."

"That's dedication."

"Or someone desperately wanted to get this to you while remaining anonymous," Dialphio said, a sullen tone lingering over her words.

The tube was tightly wrapped and thin, no broader than a young tree's branch. I pulled on the course rope, inching it along so as not to damage the contents inside the rawhide.

I looked at Dialphio. "I have no idea what anyone would send me. Especially here. Why not mail it to my apartment? If it's important, why take a chance of leaving it at the storefront?"

She shrugged. "Because they couldn't risk being associated with the package?"

"But someone could have stolen it."

"Could have," she agreed, "but with the door being inset, it would have been hard to see. I nearly missed it myself. Plus, stores get deliveries all the time and maybe they were using that as cover? I don't know, Ezekial. Why don't you open it and let's find out?"

It was more of a statement than a question, urging me on. I pulled the string loose and set it on the table next to me. Placing the rawhide on the stack of books, I slowly unfurled it; the material creaked open.

"Okay, so it's a scroll," I said, detaching the paper from the rawhide, which curled back on itself.

"What does it say?"

I read the note, handwritten in squiggly lines, and forced myself to pull my eyes away. It was happening again.

This could not be real. How would anyone know about the things I'd been researching and why would they go to the trouble of leaving me this cryptic message? Was this deliberate or coincidence?

A few words, so much meaning.

"Ezekial?" Dialphio said, concern in her voice. "You've turned white. What does it say?"

I read it to her. "If you want to know your fate, you need to know Creed. Read your *Histories*."

When I looked up, she, too, had turned white.

12

UNDERWORLD, FIFTH CIRCLE

ONE OF THE benefits of being deep in thought was how easy it is to ignore a messy apartment. If you weren't interested in picking up a few piles of dirty clothes or cleaning your living room table of plates of dried food, you didn't have to worry about it. If bills went unpaid, no one complained—especially if you did not care to give attention to the follow-up calls to action. Hot weather went ignored. Bad results for your favorite blazeball team did not matter—which was convenient considering how bad my team, the Sixth Zone Centaurs, are.

Deep thought, really good deep thoughts, can become all-encompassing.

The paint pattern in my ceiling grew more interesting the longer I looked at it. Old Towne was going through a revitalization phase where all interior and exterior facets of the buildings were attempting to reclaim our history while being modern. That resulted in some designer deciding the ceiling in my apartment was a faux stone design. The shades of browns, dozens of them, swirled and faded, blotted and smoothed, created the perception of a blurring stone facade. In those patterns, I saw reality, a maelstrom of

twists and turns, of the deliberate and accidental. Of manip-
ulation.

Gemini. Cassie. Creed and the mysterious scroll that
showed up at the bookstore. Nothing was clear. I was afloat,
wading in the waters of confusion and disorientation.

And the worst part was that my copy of *The Histories of the
Balance* was nowhere. The very thing I was reading, the book I
used to educate myself on why the Council acted like it did,
was gone.

I knew where it was when I left for work because I always
left it in the same place. I'm not going to tell you where, but
I'll give you a hint. It is a place of great solitude and thinking.
Okay, I kept it in my bathroom since that's where I do most of
my reading—please don't judge me, it's been a long few days.
Over the past months, the book had become essential in
helping me understand my role in the bigger picture. I was
seeing connections and political patterns I hadn't seen before.

The book was precious; I wouldn't be careless with that
treasure.

Yet, it wasn't where it was supposed to be.

For an hour, I tore up the apartment looking for it, turning
over every cushion, moving every magazine, sliding dusty
fake plants out of corners, and even rearranging the stacks of
dirty dishes in my effort to find it. Only chaotic piles of
pillows, bedsheets, and cushions showed for the work. *The
Histories* was gone.

After nearly destroying my apartment, I decided I needed
to clear my mind or my frustration would blind me against an
effective search. That's how my brain worked. If I didn't cool
down, it would just continue scrambling away.

Bilba needed to get his ass home. If he were here, he
would come over and help me see things I missed. Good
friends had those skills, they knew you so well that they
anticipated your blind spots. But Bilba was too busy chasing
unconditional love he'd never realize to help me. I wanted to

be mad at him, but couldn't fault him either. Without him, I was on my own, and being alone sucks. A lot.

Heading back to *The Book Abyss* might be my best bet. I planned on distracting myself with work and even double checked with Dialphio that I hadn't left it there—though I hadn't ever brought it to work. My copy of *The Histories* was a unique item, and the last thing I wanted to do was tell her I had somehow lost it.

Bless Felia Ravenous for breaking her son's heart and causing him to chase her around the Eighth until she learned to love him.

I threw on my shoes and headed to my front door when I stopped at the distinct ripping of a gateway opening behind me.

My breath caught when an unknown demon stepped through.

I moved back as he stepped into my living room. A smoke gray cloak hid his frame. He was larger than me, but that's not saying much; almost everyone is. Pulled up over his head, a hood obscured most of his face.

"Who are you?" My voice shook as he continued his approach.

Attempting to be discreet, I slowly slid my hand to my waist, looking for Creed. It wasn't on me and I couldn't see around my visitor or the gateway to see if it was by the couch. I prepared to call it.

"I'm not asking again. Who are you?"

The silent intruder stopped a few feet short and reached inside the cloak. I opened the channel in my mind connected to Creed. Before I finished the call, the stranger withdrew his gloved hand, holding a small satchel.

"Take this," he said in a gruff voice. When I paused, he repeated the order. "I said, take this."

I reached out my hand, careful to keep my distance from him. The satchel was light.

"What's in it?"

The intruder spun, his cloak billowing out as he moved toward the gateway. No fight. No theft. The cloaked head didn't turn around when he responded. "Open it and you'll see."

I unwrapped the loose cord binding the satchel closed and peered inside. A bitter scent wafted out. A pile of gray dust, the only contents. Ashes.

I looked back at the departing stranger. "What the heaven is this?"

Now he turned, the light pulling back parts of the shadow from his face to reveal a hostile smirk. "That which you seek no longer needs to be sought." With this statement, the mysterious demon laughed. I swear, his expression deepened as if he were taking great joy in this news. "When you seek answers sometimes you only find more questions. Maybe you should stop seeking before this becomes dangerous for you."

I was speechless. I finished my call to Creed and extended my hand just as it whipped down the hall. It smacked against my palm.

The uninvited demon flinched at Creed's arrival and stepped halfway through the gateway before pausing, his face cast back into shadow. "You can stop looking for *The Histories of the Balance*, because you just found it."

A wicked laugh followed him into the gateway, which zipped closed.

I slammed Creed back into the loop and stared at the satchel full of ash. The remnants of the most important book in demonology. The book now lost forever.

"WHAT DO YOU MEAN THEY BURNED IT?" DIALPHIO SAID, aghast.

"Exactly what I'm saying!" Dialphio jerked back, and I

drew a deep breath. "I'm sorry. I'm just at a loss. Dialphio, I don't know what to do anymore."

She left to lock the front door, returning with hurried steps. "Ezekial, I need you to think as clearly as possible right now because I'm about to ask you something you have to be one hundred percent sure of."

Her statement gave me pause, but I answered truthfully. "Okay."

"Was it the Council?"

"Dialphio, it has to be."

She moved closer, her voice growing softer. "You said you didn't see his face."

"Well, right. But he got into my apartment through a gateway. Only Council members can open them."

She was already shaking her head. "That's not true. There are instances of others opening them, among other powerful spells. Those aren't restricted to just the Council, though that's what they want us to believe."

"Really?"

"Really," she said. "Now I'm not saying that's what happened, but you need to be sure. Especially before you race off on some half-cocked mission to take on the Council. You don't want to do that. You're not ready."

"They burned the book, Dialphio. Burned! Am I supposed to just sit around and accept that?"

"No." Her tone was flat, like she was lost in thought. Her eyes suddenly cleared, finding focus. "No, none of us should tolerate abuses of power. Ever. But to act without regard will only result in this ending poorly for you." She closed the distance and grabbed my hand. "And I don't want anything bad happening to you. You need to be very smart about how you proceed, from now on. In everything."

It wasn't like I wanted a war with the Council, I just wanted answers and to stop being bullied. In less than a year, they had pushed me into things I didn't want to be part of, forced me to witness horrific abuses and the death of a first of his name, put me in a situation where I accidentally killed another demon in self-defense, all while thinking they could demand my silence.

"What am I supposed to do?" My voice had lost its heat, knowing deep down that I wasn't smart enough to quit. Dialphio was right, I needed to be deliberate about how I proceeded or the Council would take care of my attitude problem.

The cleansing breath and clear thoughts didn't do anything for the heartache of knowing that Seraph was part of this, that she could have made a difference and chose not to.

I didn't need the sureties Dialphio did. The Council opened that gateway and sent a messenger to me. No doubt about that. No one else had a reason to bother with some obscure magic-less demon like me who possessed a cool halberd.

But even so, faulting the Council was not an explanation. I was meaningless to them. What do they care about me and anything I wanted? I was as good as useless, a tool they used to reach their goals, nothing more.

Flashes of memories of their faces after the Aries mission spotted my vision. Possessing Creed was not something they were happy about, even from the first moment. And their displeasure with me having the weapon manifested in subtle comments since then. They had a problem with me owning Creed. Why?

And then a thought hit me. "Dialphio," I said carefully. "You didn't tell anyone that I had the book, did you?"

"Absolutely not, Ezekial."

I didn't truly believe she had, but if it wasn't her then only a handful of other demons could have told the Council, and all of them had been on a mission with me in the recent past. That meant one of my friends or someone I helped had betrayed me. Not that I was a betting demon—it's pretty obvious I have terrible luck—but I would bet a fat coin purse the culprit was spelled M-a-r-i-j-o-n.

"I'm sorry, Ezekial, I really am. I know you wanted to get answers and if I could fix it, I would. But right now, I need you to promise me that you're not going to do anything you'll regret. As long as you are careful, you have a chance. Please know that."

I didn't see the opportunities she did, obviously, but when I looked into Dialphio's eyes, they held unquestionable conviction.

"We'll get your answers, Ezekial," she said with an infinite smile. "I swear it. We move forward with caution."

"We? Oh, no, this is on me. Sorry, boss, but I don't want you getting in trouble too."

She scoffed. "Neither do I. Buy time and let me check into some things. There are resources I have that might be helpful."

"Like what?"

She wagged a finger. "I think it would be best if the answer to that question remained with me. And in the meantime," Dialphio started but was interrupted by a knock vibrating the glass door.

Ralrek stood outside. He was not who I needed to see at this moment, my suspicions about his involvement still unconfirmed. We had come so far, so quickly, I hoped against hope he was not the one who had given me up to the Council.

When we didn't move to the door, he waved his hand in rapid succession, like he was trying to pull a delectable smell to his nose. Anxiety boomeranged in his widened gaze.

"You should probably see what he wants," Dialphio said. When I stepped toward the door, she grabbed my elbow, her eyes as hard as brimstone. "Until you know what's going on, don't trust anyone."

Her words sent chills through me as I walked toward the

incubus on the other side of the door who could have been the one who betrayed me. Taking a deep breath, I faced him. Faking was never my strong suit.

Ralrek fidgeted with the short sleeves of his shirt, pulling them down over his defined biceps repeatedly.

"I'm coming. Relax."

His wide eyes watched my hand as I unlocked the door, taking seconds to ready the necessary words to play off my growing suspicions. But he didn't let me speak.

"Zeke, we've got to go. Hurry."

"Go? Go where?"

Ralrek was already turning to leave. "You haven't heard?"

"Heard what?"

"Gemini."

"What about him?"

Ralrek was thirty paces down the sidewalk. "The Council. They're announcing his trial."

With that, he started away at a slow jog. I turned back to Dialphio.

"Go," she said, "but with caution."

I gave her a stiff nod and raced after Ralrek, the demon who may have betrayed me, costing me the one book that had answers I needed, following him to face the very demons who deprived me of it.

13

UNDERWORLD

THE COUNCIL ROOM was hot and stuffy, filled with Hell's most influential demons. I shuffled my feet in the small amount of room I was afforded by the growing crowd, garnering nasty looks from Ralrek as we were compressed into a tighter and tighter space with each added body. Creed was warm against my skin, making the room even more suffocatingly hot. This was the last place I wanted to be, especially until I uncovered who betrayed me and why the five powerful demons who ran Hell saw fit to destroy the precious book I had.

Of the six pillars lining the room, we stood near the third, tucked neatly in the middle of the pack, going unnoticed by anyone of import, though I suspected the Council was aware of my presence. Call me paranoid if you must, but if I had been earlier, maybe I would still possess *The Histories of the Balance*.

I looked up at the mural of the Hellfire that spread the entire breadth of the chamber's ceiling, wishing I had the connections to get Lucifer's attention. I'd love to know who was behind that mystery, what they did not want me to learn, and just why Creed was so special. But the ceiling—and Lucifer—were unresponsive. You mortals do not understand how lucky you are to have the big man and his angelic coun-terpart listen to your prayers. We regular demons, the servants of Hell, are refused that access, and in times like this, it sucks.

If I maneuvered just right, I could see through the rows of heads in front of me to where the five Founders sat behind the long jade table in their formal black and red robes. A wide half circle formed away from their position of authority, surrounding the incubus in the middle. Gemini faced them, alone.

Shackles bound his feet and hands. With his back turned, I couldn't confirm my suspicions about his overall health, but by looking at how his prison outfit hung loosely, I suspected he wasn't doing any better than the last time I saw him. Time, and the Council's prison, had not been kind to the incubus.

"They're abusing him," I whispered, realizing only after I whispered it that the Council could probably pick up on my dissent, but figured that would be a monumental task, even for them, with so many demons filling the chamber.

"Quiet," Ralrek said out of the corner of his mouth. "I want to hear what they're saying."

But they weren't saying anything. Gemini had been asked about claiming his guilt or innocence well over a minute ago and the entire Council and audience still waited on his response.

Gemini kept his head low, aimed at the floor. His shoul-ders rose and fell in a slow cadence. Thin shoulders. Rule breaker, sneaky bastard, rogue operative; whatever he was to the Founders, he did not deserve this. No one did.

"Speak," Apopis said after the lengthy pause. "Make your claim so we can proceed."

The Council made Gemini wait for days, rotting in a dank cell, getting sicker by the moment. But when they needed something, proceedings had to be swift. Really empathetic from the core group of Lucifer's advisors. How my father deified them was beyond comprehension.

Gemini never pulled his gaze away from the floor.

"What's he doing?" Ralrek said through clenched teeth.

"I thought we were being quiet?"

"It is your right, bestowed on you by Lucifer himself, to submit your claim of innocence or guilt," Michael said, like he was reminding the audience of the formalities more than he was informing the prisoner. As always, he looked as regal as ever, but a dark shadow surrounded him now, cast and only seen by me, after refusing to tell me Cassie's fate. Apathy and I didn't get along.

The chamber had been respectfully quiet, an impressive feat considering how many demons had gathered to watch this spectacle. As Gemini delayed, a slow murmur spread through the crowd. It started in the far back corner and rippled forward, through rows of influential demons. By the time it neared where we stood, demons were more interested in what was happening behind us than with the Council and the demon on trial. I turned to see the heads of the demons in front of me bobbing as the murmur neared.

"Hiding something, he is," a short incubus dressed in fine silks said.

"So guilty," a tall succubus, as tall as Ralrek, said as she faced forward again, rolling her eyes in fabricated offense.

"I cannot wait to see what the Founders do to him," a round-faced succubus agreed with her tall neighbor. "I'll bet they throw the book at him."

The noise continued to grow in volume, and the Council had already noticed.

Beelzebub stood. "There will be silence." His voice boomed around the chamber, tamping down the emboldened spirit of the throng. The murmurs dried up quickly as his commanding presence flowed through the ranks, daring anyone to defy him. When he was satisfied, he re-took his seat.

None of the other Council said a word as they waited for Gemini's answer.

But Gemini, his dark-haired head, its black curls loosening into a towering mess that sat upon sagging shoulders, never looked at the demons sitting behind the raised table.

"Brave," an older demon wearing a cascade of gold necklaces said, nodding his head.

"That takes some courage," another piped in.

"Or complete disrespect," a succubus who could have passed as Apopis's sister countered.

The ripples of murmurs grew again in different pockets of demons all across the chamber.

"Traitor!" someone from deeper within the collection of bodies shouted out.

Dozens of laughs and snickers accompanied the outburst. Someone hissed. An incubus too old to be so brash asked the Council for an opportunity to make Gemini talk.

For his part, he didn't seem disturbed by the vitriol. A newly born enemy of the state, Gemini remained unfazed.

"Gemini, you must enter your claim," Seraph said, her tone sharp.

At her command, Gemini tilted his head up. In that moment, a collective gasp escaped the throng. Even my pulse quickened.

When he spoke, Gemini's voice shook, not from anger or adrenaline, but with frailty. "I must do nothing I wish to not do."

The room went quiet again, as everyone listened for what was to follow the brief statement. But Gemini offered nothing more. Even the Council members seemed surprised, Beelzebub swiveled his head quickly between Michael and Apopis. Azazel shrugged, though none on the Council were looking at him for insight.

Seraph was clamping her jaw.

Gemini was getting to them, and I loved it.

Her brow furrowed, and her top lip pulled back, baring her teeth. "You refuse to enter your claim?"

Gemini answered no one.

Azazel mumbled to himself before entering a coughing fit.

I thought I had a strong game when it came to resisting the Council's machinations, but Gemini was taking this to a new level. From my experience, it took a lot to make an enemy of Seraph. Her distaste for Taurus had been clear from the beginning of that mission, but he was the only one I could recall truly being on her nasty side. Even her fellow Council members, who she admitted to oppressing her opinions simply because she was a succubus, had not earned her ire. Gemini might be volunteering himself to join the Founder's shortlist, not that he looked bothered by her outright aggression.

Michael blinked, his eyes remaining closed for a few seconds. "Then you give us no choice. Tomorrow, we will try you for crimes against Lucifer and your fate decided thusly."

The older succubus next to me gasped, clutching the tiny row of pearls draped around her neck.

"Yes," an incubus behind me chortled.

Michael pounded the gavel, ending the hearing. A trio of guards moved in on Gemini to whisk him away, while the rest of their squad formed a line and edged the crowd toward the double doors.

"That's not right," I said, more to myself than Ralrek, as we were pushed toward the exit.

"He had his opportunity," Ralrek responded evenly. "He sort of forced their hand. What do you want the Council to do if he's unwilling? Just let him go free?"

Two older incubi shuffled along in front of us, their elbows intertwined to stabilize their gait. As we passed, I overheard them talking in hurried tones of excitement.

"Such a shame, this young generation," the short one, his face blotted by age spots, was telling his friend.

Their interlocked arms shook.

"Don't know what the Underworld is coming to," the friend replied.

These pensioners probably hadn't witnessed this kind of excitement in centuries.

"I didn't say that. But what did he really do wrong?"

Ralrek pulled up, grabbing my arm and turning me to face him. "Are you being serious? He opened a rift to the Overworld, or someone else did for him, without permission. They have every right to punish him for that, Zeke. I'm not saying that I'm okay with what they must have done to him." Ralrek's face flinched as his voice softened. Then he blinked and was hard-edged as ever. "But they have to find out how he did it. If they don't, we are all at risk. We have to be honest; Gemini put the Balance at risk."

I looked at Ralrek, trying to read him. On the outside, he looked like the same asshole I had known since he became friends with Bilba. But the events in Kaiserslautern showed me he was not that compliant little being. Not anymore. Ralrek had layers, they were just buried.

I think I let my internal confusion slip because he asked me, "What's that look for?"

"Nothing."

"I don't believe that for a second. If you've got something on your mind, say it."

I stopped again as demons continued streaming by. "You really want that?"

Ralrek nodded.

"Fine. You sound like a blessed mouthpiece for them, and I don't get it. After all our time together I hoped I would have rubbed off on you, at least a little. But you haven't listened to anything I've said." I thrust my finger back in the general direction of the Council room as we neared the mass transport gateways manned by a dozen major demons that would disperse the crowd back to their respective Circles. These gateways were designed to move large crowds, so required more major demons to manage. I had to be careful about what I said. But that still did not fully quench the fire in my gut. "They do this and no one asks questions. Everyone is thrilled to not worry about a thing, as long as the Council handles life's drama for us."

Ralrek bit his lip before shrugging, just without the arrogance he used to display. "That's what it was established for, to govern the Underworld. It's not about convenience or laziness."

"Or control."

Gemini had been an operative for the very demons sentencing him. Who knew what they had him doing under their cloak of sworn secrecy. My own parents had no idea what had happened to me since working for Hell's leaders, so I was confident the same could be said for Gemini. Cassie was deeply in love with him and she was as blind to his dealings as anyone. Typical Council. He could have been snatching enemies of the state and making them disappear in the name of the Council. Would that reality change Ralrek's perception? I doubted it. At his core, Ralrek was still the demon who had been part of the trifecta that killed Aries less than a year ago. No amount of turning over new leafs would ever change that. But this new part of him might recognize the larger range of possibilities here and stop wasting time praising conformity. Then he could start thinking more deeply.

Holding on to that hope was all I had right now because there was little else I had to look forward to.

Ralrek's voice lacked the hostility that was customary. "They have a duty. A responsibility. And it's not an easy one either. From the outside looking in, it's easy to pass judgment for their decisions and actions. But I guarantee you, if you were sitting in that seat, you would have a better understanding of everything they have to balance. Things we don't see, things we don't understand. I'm just saying, if you step back, you would understand that."

"Understand? The Council?"

Ralrek rolled his eyes.

There was the old Ralrek.

"Yes, Zeke. It might do you some good, and heavens, if nothing else, it might reduce your stress and depression. But what do I know? I'm not the demon who drank away every bit of coin he got paid for doing some of the most honorable work any demon could hope to do."

Now he was pushing the boundaries of our new, healthier relationship. I almost reverted to wanting him to swallow my fist. No one talked about my vodka that way. Instead, I spun on my heels, walking back in the direction we'd just come from, away from the mass transit gateways and against the flood of happy, sadistic demons.

"Where are you going?" Ralrek shouted, exasperated.

"To see a Founder about a prisoner," I shouted back.

I hadn't made it a few dozen yards before Ralrek was striding along with me. "What are you up to?"

I wouldn't share my plans with anyone conditioned by the Council. He wasn't brainwashed like my father, but he also was not ready to push boundaries. Sometimes, I swore, Ralrek had a better chance of being my father's son than me. My real father in this alternate reality would be some mysterious freedom fighter who didn't swallow every line forced down his throat.

"I'm talking to Seraph."

"Why?"

"You don't want to know. There's something I need to do. Just head home. You don't want to be part of this."

Ralrek jerked back. I took a deep breath, reminding myself that Bilba would be disappointed and that I needed to act as the better demon. "I'm sorry."

"This may come as a surprise to you, but I want to help. I was there too, in case you forget. I know what I saw."

In the back of my mind, Dialphio's voice floated, reminding me that someone had betrayed me, resulting in the most precious book in my Underworld being destroyed. Ralrek could still be that demon.

"And what was that? What did you see?"

He spread his hands as his lips pinched. "That he wasn't hurting anyone. I don't know how he got to the Overworld or why he was there, but what I saw was harmless and really none of my business if he was on Council business and simply took a detour. We never got an answer, so we can't know. Plus, Cassie is pretty cool, and she believes in him. After Aries … we haven't been good friends."

"We haven't been friends," I interjected.

He dipped his head. "Right. So you wouldn't know, because I never gave you a chance to, but I have done a lot of thinking since Aries. A lot. I don't show it because, well, it's none of your business. I'm questioning a lot of things."

"Like humans?"

He grimaced, his words careful. "Like humans." Ralrek paused and ran a hand through his hair. Ran an actual hand through his hair! "Lucifer, that guy was hot."

I chuckled, patting him on the arm. "Calm down."

"My point is that I have been thinking. With Gemini, if Cassie believes in him like that, there has to be some substance to her perspective. Is she biased? Sure. But that shouldn't completely negate what she thinks or what she told us. That's enough for me to give him a chance at least to tell his side, I guess."

"Give me a moment. I'm not sure you're really Ralrek Burning."

"Zeke, I—" he stopped and clenched his jaw. I waited. "I have a lot going through my head right now. Not just this Council business with Gemini. But you … you've helped me see some things differently. This, but other parts of my life as well. If your gut is telling you to not let this go, then I'm with you. Gemini deserves a fair chance. Cassie too." He drifted away for a brief moment as if he were making the statement to someone I could not see. "We all do."

"And we still don't know where Casse is."

Ralrek opened his mouth and then closed it as if he was swallowing air.

"And that's why I'm going to see Seraph. They denied access to her before, but I will not be denied again. You can come with me or not, but I'm not letting this end here."

SERAPH STRETCHED, HER BLACK BLOUSE PULLING TIGHTLY OVER her chest. For a second I forgot why I was here to see her. My memory came back at the sharp point of Ralrek's elbow.

"So can you help us?" I said after clearing my throat and blushing.

We were in an antechamber, just off the side of the main Council chamber. We were alone with Seraph, the other Council members had left before Ralrek and I returned. I was grateful to the only female Founder for her being willing to accept our request for an audience.

The small room was sparsely decorated, a clothes hanger on one side held Seraph's formal robe. A short, leather chaise lounge Seraph had been sitting on to tie her shoes when we walked in, lined a wall. The door took up most of the opposite one.

All in all, she was being really cool about our request, which I fully appreciated.

Seraph thought before responding. I felt compelled to fill in the silence, to tell her why my rationale was so strong, why she must agree to it. But the Founder didn't need my help. She lived a thousand lifetimes to mine. What could a six-thousand-year-old demon help her see that she hadn't already seen a billion times over?

"If I do this, I do this in complete secrecy. No one can find out." She glanced to the door. "There are certain aspects of this situation which aren't sitting right with me."

"Oh," Ralrek said.

My mouth hung open, my prepared counterargument pointless now.

Seraph's shoulders rose and fell in a quick jerk. "Look. I like you two. Bilba as well. I also have to play the political game. Remember? I told you all about that during the Taurus mission. Not that I enjoy the game, but it's a necessity of my position. However, that doesn't mean I don't have space within those rules to operate at discretion. That's what we'll do here. I'll agree to allow you to go to the Second Circle to find Cassie." She held up a finger to cut me off. She lowered her hand and rubbed her thigh. It almost appeared to be a nervous tick—if it was not so blessed sexy. "I'm not finished, Mr. Sunstone. When you find her, you can have your little reconnection moment, but remember, you are on a mission. Get to work and get back. The reason I'm helping you is to get information."

Of course. There was always a price.

"On what?"

Seraph spread her hands out as if it should be obvious. "On how this all happened. You'll tell me, and only me. Understood?"

"Agreed," Ralrek said without delay.

I felt his attention shift to me. Would I play along with her rules and get to see Cassie or reject the conditions and be rejected? Just like Ralrek, to me, the answer was obvious.

"Agreed."

The Founder nodded and then made a downward spiral with her hand. A gateway appeared on the far wall. "Go."

I DON'T KNOW IF GATEWAYS HAVE A MIND OF THEIR OWN OR IF IT was a sick joke Seraph played, but this one opened about as far away from the canal intersection as possible. Predictably, it was pissing rain.

"This is great," Ralrek said sarcastically, his thick black hair matted to his head. It wasn't as funny as the first time, but I'm sure the seriousness of the situation had a lot to do with that. "I'm glad we thought this through and took five seconds to grab rain jackets."

I stuffed my hands inside my soaked shirt and kept my head cast down, only occasionally casting my eyes up to check our surroundings and receiving a face full of rain for the effort. My skin already prickled with the chill.

Five blocks later I was miserable. All around us, residents of the Second Circle went about their lives, shopping and strolling along the wide streets. The braver were walking their devildogs.

"There is something wrong with these demons."

Ralrek snorted. Then, after a short pause, he said, "Do you think she'll be there?"

"I hope so. We don't even know if the Council followed through on their end of the deal and paid her for the mission. I wouldn't put it past them to renege on that one too."

"Such a cynic," he said tightly. Attributable to his attitude or the chill seeping through him, I couldn't tell.

"Yeah well, I prefer to call myself a realist."

As we neared the canal intersection, I spotted Cassie standing next to a pillar of the bridge. She was begging again. The Council had failed her.

Her face brightened when she recognized us. "Oh my Satan, what are you doing here?" she said, as she ran to give us hugs.

She squeezed me.

"We came for you," I said, gesturing at her collection can. "Don't tell me that the Council didn't pay you."

She looked at the can. "Do you want the truth or to hear that everything is well?"

"I'm so sorry. I can grab some coin when we get back and figure out how—"

"Seriously, they didn't pay you?" Ralrek's question was filled with heat.

"What happened after the guards took you away?" I asked, trying to remain focused on the important information. Who knew when Seraph would bring us back. We might only have minutes, especially if we started bad-mouthing the Council.

"We," her voice was constricted but soft, "we shouldn't discuss this. Everything is fine. I'm home now. How is Gemini?"

Everything wasn't fine. Whatever her motivation, she was lying.

Ralrek studied me. "Tell her."

Her eyes shimmered.

Prolonging this, no matter how hard it was to share, would only hurt her more. "He's been imprisoned since we returned, Cassie. And he's getting sick."

"They're going to sentence him tomorrow," Ralrek interjected.

I grimaced.

Her eyes widened. "What?"

I took her free hand, our grip wet, clammy. "He refused to claim his innocence or guilt, so the Council will proceed with their own determination tomorrow. They're going to sentence him and he'll be punished."

"Wh—what will happen?"

Ralrek and I shared another look, neither one of us wanting to speculate.

She filled the silence. "This can't be happening. There's no chance he'll be set free?"

The pain in her voice was as sharp as jagged brimstone.

"No," I answered softly, "I don't imagine so."

Cassie gulped down tears. "I have to see him, please. I have to."

"That's not possible," Ralrek said

"Z-Zeke?" she pleaded.

Ralrek jumped in before I had a chance to do something spontaneous and irresponsible. "We can't. You know that. They'd have our hides if we did."

I loosed a low growl at being forced into this situation by the Council. This was unnecessary suffering. The demons who created it were the same who did not have to deal with the consequences. Oh, to be elite. To be able to act with true impunity. What a fortunate set of circumstances.

"I'm—I'm sorry, Cassie."

I couldn't finish my sentence before she hunched over, empty tin can dropping from her hands to the sidewalk as she clutched her knees. Her shoulders shook as the sobs wracked her body.

Ralrek and I stood by, as useless as any demons could be.

After a moment, she straightened and looked at me with red eyes, clear mucus running from her nose. "I—I understand. I just wanted to have the chance to say goodbye. I'm sorry I asked that of you."

I found myself unable to swallow. I turned to my partner. "Please."

His bottom jaw jutted out as he twisted his head. "Zeke, we'll get in so much trouble. We are already risking it by being here. If the rest of the Council finds out—"

"They won't," I said with as much force as I dared to avoid turning him off. "Seraph will keep this quiet. And if we get back quickly, she won't even complain about having helped us. We bring her to Seraph, get answers, and the coin Cassie earned. Then we hurry her back here. All before anyone suspects."

Ralrek didn't look convinced, even though I thought my argument was tight.

"It's the right thing to do, Ralrek."

He turned to Cassie, whose big, crystal eyes shimmered. He started, bit off a comment, and then said, "I can't believe I'm saying this, but okay."

"Yes!" I slapped him on the back, rocking him forward a step. "You are a good demon after all!"

"Don't make me regret this," he said, a slight smirk on his lips.

She lunged at him, wrapping her arms around his neck. "Thank you so much! Thank you! Thank you!"

She planted a kiss on his cheek and I could no longer hide my smile at his discomfort, even though a prodding thought inquired where my kiss was. After all, I was the one who championed this.

As it turned out, I didn't have to wait long. Cassie released Ralrek and stepped in front of me, those gorgeous eyes reaching deep into the pit of my stomach, which twisted and turned.

"Thank you, Z-Zeke," she said, moving her face to mine much more slowly. Her lips touched my cheek and the Underworld could have frozen over, for all I cared about anything but experiencing this single second. Wet funk never smelled so good.

But obviously Ralrek didn't feel the same. "If we're going to do this, let's go now before I change my mind."

Cassie released me. Her face dropped, telling me she thought Ralrek's threat was genuine.

"Let's go," I said.

We began our long, cold walk back to the gateway.

And her reunion with Gemini.

14

UNDERWORLD

"I'M GOING to kill you two," Seraph snarled before moving away, her formal black robes swirling as she spun, replacing that nasty look with a pretentious smile for the small group of demons waiting behind her. They were dressed in black robes similar to hers, just without the red embroidery. Outside her open door, a crowd was filing into the Council chamber.

Not a good sign.

The Founder did not act upset about the puddles of water forming on the floor from rainwater dripping off the three of us. There were bigger problems. I was still waiting to find out if we were the cause of them—even though it was obvious from Seraph's tone that we were.

"This is going to be bad," Ralrek whispered.

I agreed. Bringing Cassie to the antechamber that served as Seraph's changing area might not have been the best decision. But it was done.

We might have gotten away with it unscathed if we had come back at any other time than the time we did. The problem was, we returned to Seraph's chamber full of major demons of elevated positions in Lucifer's government. We forced, unintentional though it was, Seraph to deal with the issue of Cassie's unanticipated presence. Thankfully, none of the demons were Founders, but they were demons with eyeballs and voices who could report what they witnessed.

"She doesn't mean it," I mumbled, noticing Cassie had slipped behind me. "She's just pissed. That's all."

Ralrek's bottom lip swallowed his top. "I *knew* we shouldn't have brought her back. What were we thinking? I can't believe I let you talk me into this."

Cassie moved closer, smelling musty in her drenched cloak. "Thank you two so much. If there's ... if there's any punishment, I'll pay it. You don't deserve to. This is my fault. I've brought you nothing but trouble."

I faced her, angling to include Ralrek in the conversation so that we formed a circle. "Guys, calm down. Seraph is upset because she's embarrassed, not because of anything we did. We caused a little work for her by making her explain you being here to those sidekicks of hers, but that's all. She wouldn't be serving on the Council if she wasn't intelligent and influential. She'll figure out a way to make sure those demons forget what they saw."

"There's no forgetting that we walked through the gateway with Cassie right after all that went down with Gemini."

"They might not know where I'm from," she said, bringing a sly grin to my face, "and they definitely don't know who I am."

She was right, but she was probably wrong. The demons in Seraph's chambers were connected enough to have all sorts of insight into the Council's missions. For all we knew, they were administrators who read the after-action reports we had to submit after we had brought Gemini back. The group might not know intimate details, but we had to anticipate they were aware of who Cassie was. A slight panic began to wind me up. My hasty decision might have just created a headache.

I played it off. "See? We're good." I gave Ralrek's shoulder a backhanded slap. "Just relax. We've got this." I was thankful he didn't have the Gift of Transparency—the Ability to read my mind. He would have been lost among the jungle of fears and lies.

Michael stepped into the chamber. He saw Cassie and halted abruptly.

"What is she doing here?" He directed his question at Seraph.

I swallowed the fear now threatening to become convection current of Hellfire. None of us spoke.

The sub-Council demons bowed their heads and scurried out. I was still hoping Seraph would save us when she turned; the heat burning in her eyes. "These two took it upon themselves to retrieve Cassie for Gemini's trial after the recent … developments."

Her lie left me speechless.

Michael's eyes narrowed, swiveling between the three of us. The room felt like it was shrinking, cornering us. When next he spoke, he directed the question at Seraph but watched us. "How did they get there? Who opened the gateway for them?"

Seraph's stabbing eyes never left Cassie, as if she already planned to pin this all on her. But she flinched at Michael's question just the same. Outside the small antechamber, a low murmuring came from the main Council chamber.

"I opened it," she said pointing at the gateway, and I felt the relief of the world fall off my shoulders at her admission. At least she was being partially honest. "I had an errand to run in the Second, but they distracted me. This one." She pointed at Ralrek. "Caught me just as I opened it, putting on quite the act, begging me to talk the Council into sparing Gemini. While this one." Now it was my turn. "Used it to get to Gemini's beggar girlfriend and bring her back. They just returned, so I haven't had a chance to handle it yet."

Betrayal. It's a bitter recipe, like the barberry concoction my mother made me take as a impling when I had an upset stomach.

"Seraph," I started, but Michael cut me off.

"Silence." His head snapped in my direction. "We'll deal with you later. Trust me. Right now, we have other business to attend to. Seraph."

Her eyes dropped at his tone. I had no sympathy for her as Michael left. Once he stepped out, Seraph spun on us, flipping her hand through the air. "You two were so stupid for doing this. This will be dealt with," she said, her eyes taking in Cassie as if she was daring the Second Circle citizen to protest. Seemingly satisfied for the moment, and before I could confront her on her lies, Seraph turned to leave. "Follow me. You're going to attend Gemini's trial. I hope your ploy, whatever your justifications, was worth it."

Ralrek followed without question and then stuttered while I processed what the Founder just said. He was quicker of thought than me.

"Wait. His trial? That's happening tomorrow, I thought."

Seraph's face was hard as slate. "It's happening now. While you were gone, new … information came to light. Information of a critical nature, that needs to be addressed now. Our hands have been forced to act swiftly. You'll see. Now, let's go."

She departed.

My jaw was locked open. Ralrek faced us like he was afraid of what was behind him. In the thick silence that followed, we struggled to provide an answer to what had just changed. Bringing Cassie back without permission was a dumb move, I was beyond arguing that now, but whatever waited on the other side of that wall was bigger. Much bigger. Something of significance beyond which the three of us were ready for.

"Gemini … is on trial … now?" Cassie's voice was brittle.

I lifted my arms, my hands clutching empty air in frustration. Lost in confusion and not knowing what to say or do, I had no answers or solutions, and that bothered me. When we walked out of her chamber, we would walk into a different situation. Something had shifted, and we were the only demons without a clue what changed. That made things precarious, my distrust of the Council aside.

Ralrek's eyes betrayed that he was feeling the same. He ran a hand through his matted hair.

"I've got to get to him," Cassie said in a rush.

Ralrek stepped in front of her. "Take a second before you go out there. You won't be doing him any favors if you're upset."

"Upset? I have a right."

I stepped up beside her, lightly putting my hand on her back. She didn't move it. "Yes, you do. But Ralrek is right. Something is going on. We have to be careful; in everything we say and do. I don't trust them, especially when they act like this. Gemini's trial being brought forward like this tells me that, whatever their reason, the Council is maneuvering. From my experience, I'm pretty sure they're trying to make an example of him. We have to be ready, you have to be ready, Cassie. He'll need you to be at your strongest for him. This isn't about you or the Council. This is for Gemini."

Her eyes searched mine. A quiet minute passed before Ralrek spoke. "I'll leave go find us a spot."

"Are you ready to be strong for him? I've got a terrible feeling."

Cassie's eyes fell to the floor. "I have to be, Ez-Zeke. Gemini needs me to be, I know that. I can feel it. He has no friends here, only enemies. I have to be everything for him."

Once again, I was reminded how fortunate he was.

She shifted her weight from foot to foot. "I'll do whatever I can to ensure you're not punished for doing this for me. Thank you."

I tried to think of something to say, but the momentous event about to happen in the other room would nullify any words I strung together. She had so little as it was.

Cassie took a deep breath. "Let's go before they send guards in." She rubbed my arm lightly and left. I watched her go, wondering what the future held for her. Gemini was only a temporary distraction. If the information was so concerning to the Council to move his trial up, then the former operative had gone out of his way to cause trouble. Nothing she said or did would change a thing. The Council's mind was already set. I knew that; I just couldn't tell her. Her role now was to be the strength for Gemini if he needed it, if Hell's rulers even allowed it. They could be cruel in the best of times. Denying Cassie and Gemini a few moments together would not shock me.

For the life of me, I could not imagine what the incubus had done to garner such a swift reaction from the five Founders. It was time to find out.

Stepping out of the antechamber, I took in the scene before me. Decidedly fewer demons than the session a few hours ago were in attendance, though the chamber was filling rapidly. The double doors were wide open. A group of guards ushered demons in, reminding them of the courtesies to be quiet. A long line of armed guards stood in front of the raised jade table, behind which sat Hell's rulers. The guards held pikes seven feet tall, their points burning blue with the power of the Hellfire. The crowd was quiet as they drifted in and found a place to stand, no one saying a word. I doubted we would be any trouble for the guards or the Council, so I was not sure what the show of force was all about, but it was not surprising that the Council would flex its muscles simply because they could.

The small-but-growing crowd made it easier to find Ralrek's advantageous position at the front U-shape encircling the shackled Gemini. Cassie whimpered when she saw him. I almost put my arm around her, lifting it and then awkwardly pulling it to my side before anyone caught me.

We were only a few feet away from the Council's prisoner. His back was bent as if he was struggling to stand upright and I wondered how much abuse he had suffered in the past few hours. The Founders were really upping their cruelty game. Cassie choked back a cry, and even Ralrek winced.

"What have they been doing to him?" she said.

This time I did put my arm around her but found Ralrek's already there. I pulled mine away like I'd been burned.

"He's been very strong," Ralrek said.

"How ... how do you know?" Her eyes could no longer contain her tears.

"I went to see him in his cell," I said. "If there's one thing I can promise you, it's that Gemini is strong. Brave. They're not beating him down."

She nodded, standing up straighter as she sniffled. "He's still going to need me. I've got to be strong. He's been so much for me."

"And you have for him," I said.

Her head swiveled one more time between Ralrek and I. "Thank you for everything. You've been remarkable and I will miss you." Her hand went to her mouth. "But I'll never forget you."

Michael slammed his gavel on the wood block, making all of us demons not paying attention to the proceedings jump.

"We'll begin as soon as the attendees are in place. Let's have silence so we can proceed," Michael commanded.

The crowd, already quiet, reacted. Those shuffling into place did so with tender steps. The two succubi next to me, who had been whispering to each other, stopped and straightened, as if readying themselves for some sort of military inspection. The five Council members watched the rest of the crowd make its way into the Chamber, a steady flow of demons filling the room, all here to witness the power of the

Founders. Soon there wasn't any space to move except for a center aisle created by a cordon of guards, whose shiny black armor and spears stood out.

"Gemini Oso," Michael started, breaking the quiet, "we, the Third Council, requested your claim for the accusations leveled against you. You are accused of unapproved travel between Circles, and most egregiously, to the Overworld. Secondly, you've also been charged with fabricating your own death for the purposes of avoiding Council inquiries. Additionally, you are charged with risking the security of the Underworld. In pretrial, you refused to make your claim of innocence or guilt. You have refused to reveal your source and method for illegal travel. Though other information has come to light which we are not at liberty to discuss at the moment, you will still stand trial for those original charges. Before we proceed, you have one last opportunity to state your claim of innocence or guilt. You may also find favor with the Council by willingly revealing details. Have you reconsidered?"

The air grew thick with anticipation. The allies of Gemini, if that's what we could be called, seemed to be the only demons compelled to watch from personal angst and loathing for the process. The succubus next to me rubbed her hands like a young imp awaiting a treat.

"Can you move to the side a little so I can see better," someone behind me whispered excitedly next to my ear. Their breath smelled of corn chips. "I don't want to miss this. It's going to be so good."

I did not move.

Air stilled, I could not even swallow and chance missing Gemini's next words.

But the demon we'd found and helped bring back, who hung his head, restrained in handcuffs and binds, did not respond. Defiant until the end, I had to admire his courage even as I watched the Founder's faces twitch in growing frustration and annoyance.

Michael waited, giving Gemini every opportunity to respond. But he still refused. I could relate. I wasn't a fan of caving to the Council either, but they held the power and if he didn't act, he would become their latest victim. How did you convince someone to forgo their stubborn pride from dozens of yards away, witnessed by demons from across the Circles, Council guards, and the powerful Founders themselves?

Michael's face scrunched at Gemini's prolonged silence before he closed his eyes for a few seconds, like the vision of the prisoner irritated him further. He rubbed a hand across his short beard as he contemplated. Michael had always been so even, so composed. Today, Gemini had pushed him beyond that with rebellious denial.

More surprising than Michael's sudden harshness was that Seraph nodded along.

Beelzebub remained stoic, sitting erect, his arms crossed, hands tucked under massive biceps. Seraph kept her icy gaze on the prisoner before them, her focus never wavering, as if she saw something in Gemini's eyes she wanted to pull out of him. Apopis was Apopis, his thin lips curled in a grin. I imagined it was because he knew he would get a chance to punish someone. And lastly, Azazel, at the far end of the string of Founders. His gray hair, tinted with orange highlights from an age long ago, stroked his long goatee as if it brought him comfort. I noticed that he, unlike any of his peers, spent more time examining the room than Gemini. Had he already moved on from the situation?

"Say something," I growled in the quietest voice I could manage.

Next to me, Cassie shivered.

"He won't," an older succubus, dressed in exquisite silks of gold and red, said, leaning in conspiratorially as if she thought I was enjoying this drama as much as she was.

"Guilty as the day is long, he is." She gave me a nod as if we both understood we were on the same team. When I stared at her dumbfounded, she blinked, gave me a double-check, and finally looked away. Ruining her day would be the least I could do for Gemini.

Another moment passed before Michael nodded formally. "You still refuse to answer then?" He paused, offering Gemini one last opportunity to respond.

Gemini didn't.

"Come on," Ralrek urged. Was his encouragement aimed at the Council or prisoner?

Cassie grabbed my hand and squeezed. I squeezed back. I looked at Ralrek, encouraged by his possible support of Gemini. She held his hand as well. It was then that it dawned on me that we were the only friends she had in the Under-world, and definitely the only ones she had in this chamber. If I couldn't help Gemini, at least I could be there for her.

"Very well, then." Michael's voice was firm. "Let us proceed then."

Three sub-Council members stepped behind the Founders and disbursed papers to each of the five. Azazel adjusted, uncomfortable from age or the situation, I could not tell. Beelzebub scribbled notes on whatever the sub-Council members laid out in front of him. Each of the five were busy preparing themselves, except for Seraph. Her hands were folded in front of her and she stared at Cassie as if the succubus to my side was the only demon in the room.

"Gemini Oso, you are hereby charged with first and third-degree desertion, and with falsifying your status as a demon of Lucifer," Michael said with a heavy tone.

Cassie sniffed deeply. I grimaced. The sentence wasn't a shock. How could the Council find anything but guilt for Gemini? That was unavoidable.

I clamped my jaw. Gemini did not need to spend years in jail. Why wouldn't he just tell them? He would still be punished, I had no doubt of that, because the Underworld's rulers loved to punish. But now he was facing forever in a miserable existence, abandoning Cassie. Whoever Gemini was protecting was taking priority over her; Cassie's turmoil and heartache, part of the punishment to be paid.

The crowd grew emboldened with the Council's decision.

"Heretic," a demon a few rows behind us spat.

At first, there were a few nervous snickers at the comment. But a non-reaction from the Council encouraged others.

"Traitor," someone else shouted from deeper in the room.

I looked around, catching Cassie and Ralrek doing the same at the spreading vitriol.

"Sleeps with mortals, I bet." The old incubus behind that particularly nasty comment stood on the other side of the U-shape line around Gemini. He shook his fist at the prisoner as he hurled the insult.

"Angelic scum!"

Aggressive accusations thrown at Gemini from the front of the hostile throng dribbled past. More and more demons hurled insults, first quietly and then growing in volume as more voices joined the rising chorus.

The volume and vitriol only got worse the longer the Council allowed the verbal attacks to go on. I looked at Seraph pleadingly. She remained sitting as she had been. Her eyes, narrowed to slits, burrowed into Gemini. It was the same look she gave Cassie. Never a softy, I still thought Seraph was compassionate and patient. But there was something in her constant examination that hinted of a deeper reasoning. What if that affected the sentence they gave Gemini? If she wasn't willing to give him the benefit of the doubt, he had no hope.

This was not looking good for him. I tried to keep my expression neutral for Cassie, but my heart ached for her and the fate of the incubus she loved.

"Burn him!" a succubus screeched.

"Send 'em to the Isle of Dread!" the incubus next to her—her husband?—cupped his hands around his mouth, tilting his head up, and shouted for the entire chamber to hear.

The crowd roared with grotesque laughter, with a few 'huzzahs' sprinkled in for good measure.

Well, that was unnecessary. Gemini probably deserved some punishment, to set a precedent if nothing else, but he didn't deserve to be sent to the isolated island floating in the middle of nothingness, to struggle for survival against the worst of our society.

With each comment, the crowd grew more aggressive against Gemini. Cassie struggled to contain herself. Even though she held onto the pair of us, she still shook.

Michael held up his hand. "You are to be sentenced," he said callously once quiet had regained control of the room.

Bolts of excitement spread across the chamber's occupants at the proclamation. Heads craned above others as demons attempted to get a better view of what was unfolding. Some shuffled to see around those they could not see above. The annoying corn chip-breath demon behind me tapped me on my shoulder and asked me to take a seat on the floor so she could see better.

All the royalty and influence in the Underworld, but none of the class.

"We, the Third Council of Lucifer, find you, Gemini Oso, guilty as charged for the crimes of desertion and fabrication, of being a risk to society," Michael said formally. "By the power of Lucifer, we have decided that you will be executed by hanging."

The crowd erupted in cheers, drowning out Cassie's cries. Even though both of us held her, she collapsed to her knees. No one needed to see this. No one needed to start asking questions. Only the Council knew of her association with Gemini, and that was enough.

My head swam in the tumult and confusion of what just

happened. I scrambled to think of the next step we needed to take. "Help me!"

We lifted her to her feet.

She was weak, her knees rubbery. We had to drape her arms over our shoulders to keep her upright as she sobbed. I looked toward the front of the room and saw Michael slam the gavel into the wood block again, but the wood-on-wood pounding was drowned out by the cheering, ending this formal tragedy.

Gemini remained bound and unmoving, his shoulders still slouched. A pair of guards moved in and unlocked the latch to the chain connected to the ring on the floor. Even free of that, Gemini refused to move. The guards slid their arms under his, and turned him toward the exit. A line of guards formed a cordon down the length of the room, back to the double doors, separating the crowd into two halves. Gemini was paraded down the middle.

I lost sight of him for a few seconds as the crowd between us adjusted to get their own view. Then he was there, only feet away, and my spirit sank. His eyes were vacant. A life lost. And in one private moment, I was happy for Gemini because I could not imagine a reality like he would experience in those cells until his death. I was happy for him, because his imprisonment had already killed him.

"Gemini!" Cassie screamed as the guards dragged him past. An incubus in front of us turned and shot her distasteful look. A succubus huffed, so bold as to stare at the sobbing succubus from the Second Circle. But none of the reactions registered with Cassie. I don't think she would have cared if she had seen them.

A few nasty insults followed Gemini as the guards led him from the room, but they had no effect on him. His was a strength I admired and envied in equal measure.

The large double-doors remained open, signaling the end of the formalities. The horde of demons departed, sharing opinions of the outcome as they edged forward. None paid a second's attention to Cassie.

We lingered. She unhooked her arms from ours, her gaze distant, and her cries snuffed to nothing more than shaky breaths.

"I'm so sorry," I said, leaning closer.

Ralrek moved to stand in front of her, to block off the last stragglers. "Are you okay enough for us to get you out of here? They're noticing." His eyes shot to the side.

A warning. He wanted me to pick up on something out of place. While still holding her, I stealthily shifted my gaze around the room and noticed Seraph watching, Michael beside her, also analyzing us. Occasionally one of them leaned toward the other to say something.

Maybe Seraph was actually pissed that we had brought Cassie to the chambers. So trivial compared to what just happened, the sentencing of death to a fellow demon, a sentence that required the Ability of Lucifer to carry out since even the Council cannot kill other demons in the Underworld —well, unless your name is Ezekial and you have a magical halberd. I didn't want to hang around any longer than necessary.

"Let's go," I said, gently tugging on Cassie whose steps fell awkwardly. "We need to get you out of here."

She nodded, the life sucked out of her.

We walked against the stream of bodies as we escorted her to Seraph's personal chambers, back to the gateway that would take her to the Second Circle, sparing her from mingling with demons as everyone waited at the mass transit gateways. She deserved better.

So did Seraph. I needed to make right with the Founder. She tried to help us and I overstepped the boundaries. Upsetting her did not sit well with me, and I was more than slightly concerned that she might punish us.

"I think we've got a problem," Ralrek whispered.

"What?"

He dipped his head forward, using the motion to point instead of obligating his arms.

I followed his gaze and saw two guards standing in front of Seraph's chambers.

"Shit."

We would have to charm our way in since Bilba wasn't around to stumble through this for us.

"Hold," the guard on the left said as we approached.

I put on my warmest smile. "Come on, friend. Can't you see that she's in trouble?" I said, tilting my head in Cassie's direction. "She needs a place to sit down for a second. That's all. Be a good demon, will you?"

Behind his visor, I imagined his eyes rolling. Everyone associated with the Council didn't seem to have much in the way of a sense of humor, or personality, for that matter, and empathy was beyond any of them.

"Stand back," the guard replied, not moving.

"Friend," I tried to say calmly, but could hear the edge in my voice. "All we're asking for is a couple minutes to let her sit without getting trampled by this crowd."

"That won't be necessary, Mr. Sunstone," Seraph said behind me.

The three of us turned. Seraph stood tall, arms crossed. Worst still, she wasn't alone. On each side, two guards stood with their pikes at the ready.

"I'm sorry. But she needs to rest at home," I said in the most coded message I could, hoping Seraph was in a forgiving mood.

She wasn't.

The guards moved when she flicked her hand in our direction. They strode up to Cassie and snatched her from our grip.

"Hey!" I said and made to grab Cassie's arm, receiving the butt end of a shaft in the side, knocking the wind out of me and sending me to the floor. The two guards who had been blocking Seraph's chambers were on us, one behind me and the other behind Ralrek, who was also now on the floor. I hadn't even heard him get hit.

"What's going on?" I asked through clenched teeth as one guard grabbed my arms while the other bound my hands in gauntleted cuffs.

Seraph stared down at me even as the guards marched Cassie past. At least she hadn't been hurt. The fire of a small Hellfire burned in Seraph's icy blue eyes. "It's obvious, isn't it, Mr. Sunstone? You and Ralrek are under arrest."

15

UNDERWORLD, UNDISCLOSED

"How long do you think they're going to keep us in here?" I asked for what felt like the four thousandth time since we had been thrust into the cell.

Eight feet away on the other wall where he was chained, Ralrek's head remained dipped. "I don't know, Zeke."

His voice had lost its normal heat days ago. Well, it might have been days. Could have been a week. Down here, the cells were so dark, so deep, the Hellfire was cut off, obscuring day from night and night from day. Our only light came from the fire lamps that hung from the walls, too few and far between to provide much light or comfort. The only way to calculate the passage of time was by keeping track of the irregular meals, which was hardly a reliable measure. The guards seemed to feed us whenever they remembered they had us locked up. There were other prisoners, I could hear muffled voices from time to time, and sometimes even some movements, but wherever their cells were, I could not see them from the slim barred opening to our own. For all intents and purposes, Ralrek and I were alone and lost to pass time by trying to figure out how much time had passed.

Silence fell between us again. That was becoming

commonplace. I had a feeling Ralrek's hope was turning to despair. Mine was as well. The only thing that kept my senses sharp were the mental exercises I had been doing after the first few hours in the cell. When no one came from the Council to see us or tell us this arrest and imprisonment was a bad joke, I refused to sulk. Having no idea of what the charges were against us or how long we would be here, I could have easily slipped into depression again. Well, I mean, I was already depressed; this was just an excellent opportunity to slip further into it. It was dark, lonely, stunk worse than the incubus locker room after blazeball practice, and there was a distinct lack of vodka in the cell. Trust me, I had plenty of opportunities to wallow in my depression. But thinking would keep me busy and sharp. It fed the simmering flame burning inside me at what was happening.

So I thought. A lot.

First, about Creed. When they threw us in the cell, it was obvious the crew had been told they could not take it, because three of them eyed it, caution staining their expressions. Except one. There's always one jackass in a group. As I was being chained with manacles, one guard, a younger half-breed—I swear, if we could breed with ogres, he would have been Example A—with a mashed nose and wide face, reached to my waist to pull the halberd free from the loop.

"I wouldn't do that," I had warned him.

Guess what? He did it anyway.

The second his hand wrapped around the halberd's knob, I felt Creed's energy surge along my leg where it hung to the knob and into the guard's hand. A blue glow radiated from the knob, encircling the guard's hand. He stared at it, wide-eyed. The circle of blue pulsed once and expanded with a violent flash, sending the guard into the cell's stone wall. He did not even have time to yell.

The three remaining guards looked at his limp body, then

to Creed—they did not even bother to make eye contact with me.

"I told him not to touch it," I had said to them with a smile.

I probably shouldn't have smiled.

Whereas they chained Ralrek with his hands clasped in front, the guards took pleasure in chaining mine behind me. My shoulders burned for the first few days; now I could barely feel them except when I laid on one side, and even that sensation of spiked pain usually made me try to sleep in a seated position against the wall.

Beyond the halberd, though, I kept running through everything that happened in the chamber at Gemini's sentencing. The unfairness of it. The vitriol. Seraph's wavering levels of support. And Cassie. A lot.

The beggar from the Second Circle was in love with Gemini. I didn't fault her. She found what she was looking for in him. I envied him because of how deeply her feelings ran. She would do anything for him. To have someone like that in my life—a dream Lucifer had denied me. The only love I'd ever experienced came from my parents, and that couldn't compare to what she had for Gemini. They loved me because they had to; Cassie loved Gemini because she wanted to.

The isolation of the cell—Ralrek was a lousy cellmate—gave me plenty of time to think of the possibilities that awaited us, the reasoning of the Council, the shifting politics, and the mystery behind Gemini's story. I'd almost forgotten to throw in the theft and destruction of *The Histories of the Balance*. So many moving parts. But no clear answers.

"You okay?" Ralrek's hoarse voice broke my thoughts.

I blinked away the image of Cassie, ashamed that she kept rising to the fore when there were so many other things to think about than a succubus already in a relationship. "Huh?"

Ralrek winced as he sat straighter. "I asked if you're okay. Any time you're that quiet, I worry what is going on in your head."

"Why?"

Ralrek's smile was sad. "You get this far-away look in your eyes. Like you've gone somewhere else and left your body behind. Figured that's where you were now and I wanted to call you back here. Don't think for a second that I'm going to rot in here alone." He laughed until a cough cut it off. He raised his manacled hands and pressed them against his chest.

"Sorry," I said shortly. Though I would have liked to have been more of a conversationalist, the energy to engage was not there. Still, a chat would help pass the time. "I was just thinking about everything that went down."

His eyes sparkled with playful deviousness. "You were thinking about her."

"Who?" I asked too quickly.

Ralrek leaned his head back against the wall. "I'm not dumb, Zeke. You've got the hots for her. Anyone who knows you can see that. Don't deny it. Unless you want to pass the time by making me get it out of you." He looked around the cell before raising his arms, locked at the wrists, chains rattling, and spread his hands. "A game of denial might even pass a few hours, so it might be fun. What else do we have to do?"

My eyes found my feet. "Busted."

He hooted. Then coughed, rough and wet. "Gotcha." More coughing.

I looked up. He was pressing his hands to his chest again. His eyes found mine when the fit passed. He sounded almost apologetic. "Sorry. The dampness is getting to me."

Me too. For days, I had been tasting the mold in the air with each breath and every swallow. The more I ingested, the more lethargic I felt. If the shackles were ever lengthened or loosened and they allowed me to stand, I feared I wouldn't be able to. But at least I didn't sound like my partner.

"Are you okay?" I returned the question.

Ralrek's head bobbed as his wet cough rumbled away. "Yeah. I am. Just want to sleep though."

"We sleep a lot."

"What else is there to do?"

"Talk."

"Yeah. Talk." He looked toward the ceiling but stayed quiet.

A torch crackled with the Hellfire outside the cell. In a dark corner, back in the blackness that hid the cell's secrets, a droplet *plunked* against the stone floor.

"What was his name?" I asked, wanting to keep Ralrek engaged. If he was lost to hopelessness, I would soon follow. We needed each other, now more than ever.

Head still tilted toward the ceiling, Ralrek lowered it enough to glance at me sideways as if he didn't trust me to throw my waste bucket in his face. "Who?"

I laughed. "Oh, so now it's your turn to play dumb?"

"I don't know who you're talking about."

"Really? You play dumb better than I do. Maybe there's something behind that."

After a brief moment filled with grinning, Ralrek said, "Hans."

"Huh?"

"No, Hans," he said with emphasis. "Or Horst. I can't remember."

"You don't remember his name?" I chuckled.

Ralrek shrugged, his chains jingling. "It's not like we were dating ... or on a mission with him."

Ouch to the poke in the ribs. "You are such a slut."

Ralrek's head snapped up. We stared at each other for a brief second before breaking out into a hearty round of laughter. It felt good to laugh with him. Who knew I could be pushed so far as to enjoy time with Hell's asshole. Did he even hold that title any longer?

"Too bad we didn't get to stay longer. He was a good-looking guy," I teased, making Ralrek smile.

"Yeah, he was. Excellent kisser, too."

"The two of you were going at it pretty hot and heavy, right in the middle of the club. I never thought I'd see the day the compliant Ralrek Burning ever broke the rules."

His smile evaporated. But before he could reply, the heavy door separating the cells from the floor above echoed down the long hall. We fell into an uneasy silence. The door opening meant guards. A few days ago I would have hoped that it would also mean Seraph coming to apologize and tell us this was nothing but a terrible joke. That entertaining but bubble-headed thought did not last long.

One benefit of living in a place like this was that it was a quiet place that prevented anyone from sneaking up on us. Both of us took the time between the door opening and the arrival of the bodies whose feet slapped the stone floor to sit up, adjust, and run through mental preparations in case it was our cell that would receive the visit.

It was. And it was a pleasant surprise.

"Seraph!" I said, slipping as I scrambled to sit up straighter and jabbing my elbow into the stone. Pain rocketed up my arm, and for a second, I felt my shoulder again. Painful but reassuring, to know that it still had some range of motion.

A behemoth of a guard unlocked the cell door and pulled it open, stepping back to allow her in.

"Relax," Seraph ordered before turning to the guard. "Send a runner to the kitchen and have them bring a meal down. And make it a hearty one."

The guard nodded and walked away, leaving the door open. The temptation of temporary freedom was strong. If my hands were not locked behind me, denying me my full range of motion, I would call Creed, break the chains, and make a run for it. The problem with temporary freedom is that it's only temporary. Even if I got away, I would not be free for long, and when they recaptured me, my imprisonment would be much worse.

"What are you doing here?" I said, my throat scratchy. "I'd offer you a seat but I don't imagine this place is up to your standards. If the Eighth Circle wasn't, this surely isn't."

Seraph stood a few feet away. She folded her hands in front of her and her face was unreadable. "I'm not staying long."

I nodded.

Ralrek lifted his head, his eyes sagging from exhaustion, cold, and the lack of any good food. "Have you brought news of our fate?"

Only Seraph's head moved. Besides that, she was stiff. This would not be a pleasant visit.

"The Council is still deciding what we should do about you two. In the meantime, you'll remain in the cells."

News delivered, Ralrek's head dipped to his chest again.

"It's miserable here," I said. "I get it. You're upset that we brought Cassie back from the Second Circle. I understand it was a dumb thing to do, especially with the controversy surrounding Gemini. But I don't think it justifies being held prisoner for days now."

"Mr. Sunstone," she started, and I knew I was in trouble, "you've been here for nearly two weeks. I recommend you get comfortable with your surroundings, as I expect you will be here for some time yet."

Ralrek groaned, chin against his chest.

"This is unfair," I said, against my better judgment.

"Is it? The Council doesn't see it that way." Seraph gave me an opportunity to prove I wasn't smart enough to keep my mouth shut, and when it appeared I actually wouldn't follow through with a snarky comment, she dipped her head. "I'm glad to see you finally showed a modicum of good judgment. Better than you did when you decided to bring Cassie, not only out of her Circle, but into our chambers."

The Council obviously had a big hangup with my action, but I couldn't honestly understand why. Cassie was a minor demon, no threat to them. They allowed hundreds of demons in that room to watch the sentencing of Gemini, so what did one more matter?

"I tried to be of assistance, as much as my position allows. But you abused that."

"We didn't mean to."

"But you did just the same. And you put the Council at risk."

At risk? In what world would Cassie be a threat to anyone? There were dozens of demons in the chambers that day with enough coin to influence darker segments of the Underworld to raise Abel if they were inclined. If anyone was a threat to the Council, it was the old families, many of whom were guests at the sentencing. Not Cassie.

I wasn't sure if Seraph was intentionally trying to rile me up or not. One minute she was an ally, and the next she was arresting us for doing something she facilitated. I wanted to keep my mouth shut, but this was ridiculous. Everything about it was.

"Yes, we disobeyed you and snuck around," I said, "but don't make it sound like we acted grievously. How did we put you at risk?"

Seraph straightened, throwing her shoulders back and lifting her chin. "Would you consider allowing an angel to have access to the Council and the whole of the Underworld a threat to our way of life?"

Thoughts swirled as I attempted to translate what she just said. Instead of taking time to process her rhetorical question, I stuttered through a response.

"An angel? We didn't do anything like that."

In a croak, Ralrek's question came out as the door separating prisoners from free demons was opened again, echoing down the hall. "Gemini or Cassie?" he asked.

A different guard entered the cell, carrying two plates of steaming food. My mouth watered as Seraph's gaze swiveled between.

"Both," she finally answered.

How? How were they angels? If that was true, we were as good as dead.

Heavens, at least we would eat well before the Council executed us.

16

UNDERWORLD, UNDISCLOSED

I<small>T'S</small> funny how fixated the mind can become when it is stunned by revelation.

At least a day—maybe two—had passed since Seraph's visit. In that time, I only had one thing on my mind. I did not think about escaping the cell. I did not think about the politics of the Underworld and how disgusting and self-serving they were. Nor did I think about the distasteful priorities of the Council, the lack of fidelity, or even betrayal. I was not even thinking about how I could use Creed to free myself.

The only thought that consumed me centered on the fact that the Council accused Gemini and Cassie of being angels.

Crazy talk. They had sent me and Ralrek to the Second Circle to find Gemini because he was one of their operatives and had disappeared, rumored dead. We met Cassie because of Gemini. If the Council hadn't sent us to search for one of their own, we would have never come across her. If the pair of them were angels, then angels were already living around and amongst demons, hidden from the all-seeing eye of Lucifer and his vengeful arm of governance.

That had vast implications. For my entire life, demons feared the power of the Council. It formed our laws and guided actions because everyone understood our leaders could find out about any violations, no matter how small or big. The Council acted to maintain the Balance, the eternal peace between Hell and Heaven, taut with tension because even the smallest slip, like a demon escaping to the Overworld, could throw everything into chaos if both sides were not heavily regulated.

If Gemini was an angel working as an operative right under the noses of Lucifer's Council, that meant anyone could be. And it also meant the Underworld's leaders weren't as powerful and insightful as they led us to believe. This would undermine them on every level.

The clanging of the door at the end of the hall rattled me out of my reflection. Someone was entering the prison, and in our time down here, Ralrek and I were the only prisoners to receive visitors. I guess we were important like that.

Slow footsteps scraped nearer. This wasn't a guard. They walked like mastodons, sometimes even waking me from sleep with their idiosyncratic gait. No, these footsteps indicated a smaller demon, probably a succubus.

Had Seraph returned? To apologize? To share how she was so confident in her assessment that Cassie and Gemini were angels? To admit she and the Council were wrong to treat us like this?

I pushed myself up against the wall, wiping the permanent drowsiness from my eyes.

The footsteps slowed before shuffling to a stop outside the cell.

My skin felt filthy, even underneath the grime created by living in dank conditions, as a slimy sensation ran the length of my arms, neck and face. The visitor had conjured a listening ward. The world muted. Ralrek didn't notice, but my sudden jumpiness drew his attention and he, too, looked toward the door.

A shadow cast by the flickering torches fell on the floor. It was a thin form, convincing me Seraph had come to free us, her political ploys finished. But then the visitor slithered in front of the cell, exposing who it was.

"Apopis," I groaned.

The Founder slid a brass key into the lock, popping the cell open and stepping inside. I noticed he left it open and without a guard.

"Hello sir," Ralrek attempted to push himself up against the wall to sit straighter, proper. His hands slid out from underneath him and he went down in a heap. I winced when his elbows slammed into the floor and he grimaced, too exhausted to even cry out. The last few days had been rough on both of us, but he was wearing out more rapidly than me. How much longer could he last before the cell broke him?

Apopis examined us for what felt like an hour. Whatever he was expecting or looking for, he didn't look displeased at what he found.

"Did you bring dinner?" I said.

"Careful how much you eat, Sunstone," Apopis said with a sneer. "Sitting in the cell inactive and eating too much will only make you fat. And we wouldn't want you to be in poor health."

I had my counter argument ready. "Sitting in the cell isn't good for my health. Have you come to release us?"

Ralrek's droopy gaze stayed on Apopis, who locked his hands at his waist. His mouth twitched as if he'd tasted something that didn't agree with him. Then he paced across the cell, his head cast down.

"No, I'm not here to release you," Apopis said, releasing a long hissing sound I think was supposed to be a laugh.

"Then why are we lucky enough to have you visit?"

Apopis's thin lips spread impossibly wide, his mouth a slit as he hissed before turning the tattooed side of his face in my direction. "You know, I don't like much about you Sunstone, but I do appreciate that."

"What? My ability to cut through bullshit?" Lucifer, I really didn't like Apopis.

He flicked the corner of his mouth with his tongue. "I guess you could say that. Though, to us, it's not as you so eloquently put. To us, having a pair of incubi like you two putting the entire Underworld at risk is hardly what one would say was … how did you categorize it? Bullshit, was it? But I guess we see the world differently, Sunstone, don't we?"

"Oh, yeah."

Apopis continued traveling the width of the room, confidence oozing from him. "So then, let's cut to the chase." Squaring on me, he cut Ralrek out of the conversation, which wasn't that big of a deal since my partner's head was still drooped toward his lap.

"Sure."

"How is it that you came to the decision to bring an angel into our midst?"

I held up a finger—too bad it was useless and unseen behind my back. "First, *I* didn't decide anything. Ralrek and I are a team. Next, the Council was looking for Gemini. Not me."

"I'm not talking about Gemini, you snake," Apopis said, his eyes narrowing as he leaned toward me. Then he blinked and glided back to his full height.

I had to stay calm. "I don't believe Cassie is an angel."

Apopis lifted his chin, thin lips widening and exposing his throat. If I could call on Creed and send it flying into that thin expanse of skin, Apopis would never know what hit him. But I wasn't like him or anyone on the Council; I wasn't a killer—well, Taurus aside.

"Come now, Sunstone. You can't be that naïve."

"None of you did or you would have said something the very instant I brought her into the Council chamber. No one made a peep, not with Cassie, and not with Gemini. They were in your chambers more than once. So, if Lucifer's

Founders can't distinguish an angel from a demon, how am I supposed to?"

Apopis's eyes flashed with hostility. "I could scour you in flames."

"I'm sure you could," I said, trying to remain cool. It was not easy. I was fine with Apopis having this small victory because I wanted to see how far I could push him, maybe into irrationality. "But if you scour me, you won't get the answers you came here seeking."

Apopis slithered backward, a nasty smirk spread across his arrogant mug. "Regardless, Gemini and your Cassie are angelic spies. We don't know exactly how long they've operated in our realm, but it's been long enough to pose a considerable threat. All resources are focused on determining the extent of the breach."

"That sounds like a mess. What is the Council looking to do about it?"

"A lot of that will depend on you," Apopis said without turning around. He had drifted to the far wall of the cell, Ralrek's side, tipping to peer at the gray stone blocks as if he was inspecting them for vulnerabilities. Then he spun without warning, and swung his leg viciously, connecting with Ralrek's shoulder.

I jumped.

Ralrek cried out, falling to the floor.

"Why in the heaven did you do that?" I shouted, pulling against my restraints.

Apopis wasn't about to bother with me. With my cellmate toppled over, Apopis was on him, sending a flurry of kicks to Ralrek's back, shoulders, and legs. Sick and vicious, his strikes filled the cell.

"Stop!"

Apopis paused, hunched over top of Ralrek, and snapped his head in my direction. "Why did you bring those two angels here? Why did you allow them access to the Third Council? Tell me!" He reared back and sent another kick into the middle of Ralrek's back.

Ralrek's yells sickened me. He didn't move or turn over to shield himself from the assault. He just lay on his side, waiting for the next kick.

"Creed!" The scream came out vocally through a raw, dry throat. The halberd did not jump to my hand even though I could feel the connection. Warm against my hip, it remained where it was. If I survived this, I would really have to dedicate some serious training time to improving my calling skills.

"Don't!" Apopis stopped the assault long enough to point his finger at me. "Don't even try it or your parents will suffer."

"My parents?" I croaked, withdrawing my second call to the halberd. "What are you talking about?"

Apopis pulled up from Ralrek, but stayed near, standing full and squaring on me. "Yes, your parents. If you even think about sending a silent command to that blessed weapon, your parents will suffer. In fact, if you do not start cooperating, they will suffer. If you don't admit that you willingly and knowingly brought angels into the Underworld, they suffer."

Was the Council so desperate to cover their own mistakes they would willingly hurt two innocent, middle-aged demons who had no involvement in this business?

"You wouldn't dare," I growled.

Apopis laughed. "Try me, Sunstone."

"What do you want?"

He splayed his arms, palms up. "We just want the truth."

"What version?"

"We simply want to know what your motivations were for exposing us to their threat," Apopis said. "And an admission of your crimes would also be required, of course."

"Admission?"

Apopis nodded, his hands locked in front of him again, signaling the end of the attack on Ralrek who still whimpered on the floor. "Publicly."

The full meaning of Apopis's demand came to light. "You want me to be your scapegoat?"

He didn't reply, but a slimy smile spread across his wide mouth and he flicked the corner of his lips once more.

"I'm not going to admit to something I didn't do!"

Apopis shrugged. "Then I'm sure whoever is responsible for the harm to your lovely mother and hard-working father wouldn't admit their crimes either. Such a shame, to never get justice for your family."

Chained in a prison, I had no way to warn my parents. The only demon with the truth was in the cell with me. My parents, even Dialphio, must have no clue about my situation, probably assuming I was off on Council business. And Bilba, the only demon who would telepathically understand me, was off on his own important business. If I didn't do exactly as Apopis demanded, would they really hurt my parents?

I never felt so pathetic, even as the Segregate, Hell's reject. When I spoke, my voice shook. "But no one knows they're angels." If I played along with his game, I might turn the tide of the negotiation.

"You fool!" Apopis spat. "You have no idea what you got yourself involved in. You're clueless to the streams of influences that have to be manipulated and positioned for the Balance. You're a child, Sunstone, a petulant child. Before this becomes unmanageable, you will admit what you did."

"I didn't do anything I wasn't told to do by the Council."

"But you did."

It was as if he was not hearing me, having some imaginary conversation with another version of me in another dimension.

"And if I do?" My voice didn't sound like my own in my

head. Self-loathing seeped through my entire being. "What happens if I comply?"

Apopis wiggled straighter, appearing leaner and taller. "Then Ralrek will recover and your parents will continue living their full lives as best they can. That's all any demon can ask of Lucifer."

I noticed Apopis had one element missing, one that was of high interest to me. "And what becomes of me?"

Impossibly, his smile grew wider. "You'll stand trial for your crimes. Understand, the Council will be grateful for your admission. You'll have saved us the trouble of carrying out an investigation. Charges will be announced, and a trial will follow, but you'll have done a service to Lucifer and our kind. Without it, I can assure you, your punishment will be much harsher. So, see? It is in the interest of everyone that you make a full admission, and soon. Let us all move on from this unfortunate situation."

Admit wrongdoing I didn't do and get punished. Deny the wrongdoing and be punished far worse. Neither was a solution. A future filled with days, years, possibly millennia of wasting away in this cell while Lucifer knew what happened to my parents, was unconscionable. As unfair as this was, my decision was obvious. That didn't mean I was going down without a fight though. I would test Apopis for everything he was worth while I still had the opportunity.

"If I do this," I said, stressing the first word, "what guarantees do I have that you'll fulfill your end of the deal? How do I know you won't punish them because you have the power to do so?"

Apopis's smile never wavered, never became anything less than creepy. "We would not need to. No one needs to pay unnecessarily."

"Except me."

"Life requires sacrifices, and so does Lucifer."

Creed warmed against my side. I wanted to call on it so

badly that my thoughts were nearly derailed. With the halberd, I would never truly be on my own. Time to call the bullshit for what it was. "What was in *The History of the Balance* that you didn't want me to read?"

"The what?"

"You know what I'm talking about. What was in it?"

Apopis turned his head to Ralrek, who had curled himself into a ball. His whimpering had died down, and I hoped he was asleep. Apopis didn't seem to have that concern. He appeared more interested in determining whether or not Ralrek could hear the conversation. Apparently satisfied, he turned back, grinning.

"You did us no favors by getting your hands on that book. How did you acquire it?"

So Apopis knew about *The Histories*. My instincts confirmed, I felt emboldened. "Can I get an answer to my question before you follow up with even more questions?"

He shook his head. "We have routinely warned you about how you speak to your superiors."

"The time to worry about that has passed. Who was it you sent to my apartment with the bag of ashes?"

Apopis answered with a tip of his head as if he was deciding between what bland dinner to pull from his refrigerator. "Someone we have in our employ for such things. I must admit, visiting you in your own quarters wasn't my idea. But I thought it was a nice touch."

"And the book?"

He only shrugged. "How would I know? I've never read heretical writings. But based on what I've heard of it, a world without it is a better place. Shame you didn't get to finish reading it." He turned toward the cell door, but before leaving, he glanced back at me. "You've made a wise decision, Sunstone, making the sacrifice. Fortune may smile on you yet."

And with his last jibe, Apopis walked out of the cell, not even bothering to look in my direction as he locked the door.

In the silence that followed, I did not check on Ralrek, knowing he needed as much rest as he could get. For me, it was a long, lonely day before sleep finally came. As proof to Lucifer's cruelty, it was a sleep that didn't last forever.

17

UNDERWORLD, FIRST CIRCLE

DAY, indistinguishable from the night without the benefit of the Hellfire.

How many had passed, there was no telling. As if they were aware of my tactic of using meal periods as a gauge for passing time, our feedings became even more erratic. Prolonged hunger was followed by hours where it seemed like we were eating another meal as soon as they'd taken one away. Sleep came in intense waves. Time, at least here, was meaningless.

Unsurprisingly, the Council was doing what it could to ensure we remained disoriented and ignorant. They did not limit the damage to psychological aspects of our situation either. As the hours and days passed, Ralrek's health worsened, as did my willingness to fight.

Since forcing me to agree to admit wrongdoing, Apopis had not returned. No one from the Council had, including, most disappointingly, Seraph. The Overworld continued to spin, with the Underworld along for the ride, without concern or care for two of its heroes locked away in a stinking cell. Ignored and forgotten.

To say I was becoming bitter would be an understatement.

Wasting away wasn't doing much for my physical fitness, but it kindled a fire within me. Over the past few days, I had entertained various manners of death for each one of the Council members. Some ideas were especially twisted—I blame starvation and the constant chill. Of course, I would never do it, most likely because I would never be free again, but it helped pass the time.

Conversations between Ralrek and me dwindled as we ran out of things to say and out of the desire to converse. The talks we held meant we were alive, but if being alive meant continuing this existence, I wanted no part of it. I don't think Ralrek did either.

I thought about my parents and how sick my mother must be. The fact remained that they had gone without hearing from me for weeks. In the void of information, demons completed their own version of a story. Right or wrong, accurate or not, it didn't matter. I didn't want to think about what my parents were telling themselves. Mother would think the worst. Father would fool himself into thinking I was helping keep his precious Balance. I laughed to myself as I thought about Dialphio, crossing my fingers she hadn't filled the vacancy at the bookstore. That spitfire was probably worried sick and scouring the Circle to uncover my whereabouts.

At least I now understood the type of demon Seraph was. No longer a paragon of virtue, she had fallen in my eyes. Politics wasn't a priority, nor was the supposed necessity of wrangling for position and favor. This entire farce was a crime against us, and apparently, the moral masters on the Council were incapable of figuring out another way to reach their goals or admitting they had screwed up. Their absence implied their scheming.

Beelzebub, Marijon, Apopis, Michael; the entire lot of them. Broken trust, broken hope. Sitting in the dark prison cell, unstimulated and underfed, was not doing much for my depression. Can you believe the prison guards or the Council were not kind enough to provide vodka, even after I agreed to their terms?

At some shapeless point in the middle of my misery, the prison door clanged open. Multiple pairs of feet marched down the hall, setting me on edge. Company was coming and this time it wasn't a covert visit by a Council member. The heavy footsteps implied guards, and at their pace, their business was urgent.

I waited for the mysterious visitors to make their appearance. Ralrek stirred at the clanging armor and rhythmic cadence. He struggled to adjust his posture, finally sitting up before our company joined us.

"Wake up," a squad leader ordered as he stepped to the cell door, unlocking it. Behind the armor and helms, they all looked the same, the only diversity coming in their skin tones, so I was not sure if this was a cruel or kind guard. Not that it mattered. The door creaked in protest and he stepped in, accompanied by three of his thick-skulled friends.

"Good morning to you too," I said, not having the slightest clue if it was morning or not. "What's on the agenda today? More gruel, or are you giving us something which might pass as meat?"

To my surprise, the guard laughed, dry and raspy. "No food for you," he said as he approached, flinging the ring of cell keys around his gloved finger, trying to separate one from another.

"Are we going somewhere?" There's a lot of truth in the rumor that males hide their fear behind bravado. I'm not saying I was guilty of it in that moment, but I would not deny it if someone had called me out.

The guard hovered over me and flicked his hand. I sat forward as he reached behind, unlocking the chains tethering me and then the shackles around my wrists.

"In front," he ordered.

Moving my arms forward was a monumental effort. My

shoulders groaned after weeks in this rotting cell, and for a second I was sure they could no longer achieve the range of motion that would bring them to the front of my body. Fire and pins—no, these were not pins, but dagger blades—of pain shot through my shoulders, taking my breath away. I screamed out when the guard yanked my arms forward and slapped the shackles back on.

"Best as I know, the pair of you are getting a little break from the prison." I heard him say behind the gasps of breath I was trying to draw. "Don't be thinking your sentence is done though. We're just taking you up to see the event."

Through watering eyes, I could see the guard standing over Ralrek freed him from his binds.

"Event? What event?"

My guard grunted. "The execution."

A flurry of questions surged through my dulled mind in an instant. I had a suspicion of who was on the docket, but I still needed confirmation. "Whose execution?"

He yanked the chain and, in my weakened state, almost sent me flying into the cell bars. My shoulders radiated with heat, sharp pains and jolts that shot down to my fingertips. His partner pulled Ralrek along more slowly, yet, my cellmate still tripped a few times.

"The angel. Who else?" The guard answered, confirming what I already knew and giving the chain a harder than necessary yank out of the cell.

This time I did fall, scraping up my hands on the rough floor. My guard only laughed and told me to get up. Ralrek didn't even stop. His head hung, wobbling as his guard pulled him along the narrow, quiet hall. I grunted and got back to my feet, the jabs of pain in my shoulders numbed by the Council following through with killing Gemini.

The raspy-voiced guard pulled me through the dungeon that had become my home. I glanced in each cell as we passed, noting that most were empty. The few occupied cells were as dark and depressing as ours; their captives looking as miserable and desperate as I felt. Prisoners to the same situation as Ralrek and I? How many of them were also pawns to the Council's games, suffering a fate undeserved so that the powerful could remain in unquestioned power. So very gross if you ask me.

Prickles of pain danced through my shoulders as the blood flowing to them began the important process of loosening them. I shrugged, and it hurt like heaven, but it was good to feel them move forward again. We were led up narrow stone steps and out of the prison, to the main floor. In this wider atrium, our guards spread out, encircling us without slowing as we neared the exit.

The pair of incubi guarding the entryway pulled the tall, windowless door open and the blue light of the Hellfire burst in. Without thinking, I pulled my hands up to shield my eyes against its burning brilliance. The guard pulled them back down with a jerk. Prickles were now nothing more than a tingling in my fingers, which I wiggled, inviting the blood flow. We were halfway down the wide, black marble stairs leading to the street before I pried my eyes open enough to see where we were being led. The fresh smell of sulfur in the air was fantastic.

A carriage sat at the base of the stairs, pulled up to the curb. A crowd lined both sides of the street to our right as if waiting for a parade. The sight reminded me of my return from the Overworld, when Lucifer's little leadership team paraded me around the Fifth on the back of a donkey to humiliate me for not helping in the murder of Aries. Apparently, they were about to do the same for Gemini.

"A carriage ride? You really shouldn't have. I didn't think the Council would treat us so well," I said, and the guards scoffed.

As we neared the vehicle though, my relief that I would not have to walk on wobbly legs was dashed when Apopis snaked his head out of the carriage window. I took a step back.

"I'm so pleased to see the pair of you joining us for this illustrious event," Apopis said with a hiss.

With my hands bound, I stepped up and reached for the carriage door. "Well, it's not like we had much choice. At least I appreciate the ride."

Apopis slapped his hand on the door. "Oh, you'll be walking. Traitors to Lucifer don't deserve privileges. I'm here to make sure you joined us and that you knew why. Plus..." He leaned his head further out the window and looked down the street. "I wouldn't miss this opportunity. To see you humiliated is something I've missed since ..." He paused, eyes looking up into the hellish blue above in mocking thought. "Well, since the last time we had you paraded around as a warning. You seem to be to racking up these opportunities, Sunstone. I wonder if you'll ever learn? Anyway, shall we?"

At his question that wasn't a question, my guard shoved me forward, down the street to where the observers waited. I stumbled, catching myself after a step or two, receiving snickers from the crowd. Ralrek received the same treatment from his guard and the crowd. When he was pushed, his recovery took longer, and within a few feet I caught up to him. The rest of the prison squad followed behind, just in case I had a change of heart about playing the Founder's ridiculous game.

"You okay?" I asked.

Too weak to respond, he nodded. My fire grew. Lucifer, I was so tired of being treated like yesterday's leftovers by the Council. The guard prodded us along, and Apopis was true to his word, keeping his carriage close enough for us to hear his laughter anytime a particularly cruel comment came from bystanders. Having done nothing to any of these demons, I struggled to understand where their joy in our treatment came from. Even the implings took part in insulting and mocking us. I doubted most of them had any idea what we'd done for them over the past nine months. Yet, here they were, by the thousands if my initial guess was close, lining this main avenue for blocks. This was going to be a long walk.

"Move it," my guard shoved me again when we slowed. I had slowed for Ralrek's sake. The tall demon was barely able to put one foot in front of another.

"Don't push us," I snarled over my shoulder. "He's not feeling well."

"I'm okay, Zeke," Ralrek groaned.

He wasn't.

I received a staff to the head for my troubles, knocking me to the ground. More laughter swept over the crowd before two guards pulled me to my feet. A sylph fluttered in front of me, hanging there in the air just out of reach. She spat a tiny wad of green saliva at my feet before flitting back to the safety of the crowd, which guffawed at her gesture.

My guard eyeballed Ralrek. "He looks fine to me. Move."

We were marched along the street lined by so many of Hell's residents. I did not recognize the neighborhood, it could have been any Circle, even the Fifth. But I doubted that. No one in the sea of faces looked familiar, not that the insults stung less coming from strangers.

I lowered my head and focused on putting one foot in front of the other, trying to block out the jibes. Those could only hurt if I allowed them to. My energy needed to go to the physical requirements of this humiliation parade and supporting Ralrek if he needed it. The ignorant things the crowd—some of them had to be no older than eight hundred years—said would make Lucifer blush.

A loud cheer echoed down the road. Our march finally ended when we rounded the corner of an enormous warehouse and the street opened to a vast square, like one I had never seen before. We definitely were not in the Fifth. Each building lining the open square was three stories, all containing a shop on the bottom floor and residence on the upper two if the laundry strung from roof to roof and flower planters perched on the windowsills were any clue.

Demons crammed into the square, a sea of bodies, and they were happy, elated by something happening further ahead, out of my eyesight. Those closest to the wide aisle we were being marched down noticed us. Elbows jabbed sides, shoulders were tapped, ears were whispered into as we passed.

"We love you, Apopis," a young succubi voice rang out from somewhere in the mass of demons. A localized cheer went up at that.

Oh, if that succubus only knew the truth. The last thing I wanted to do was look back and see his smug face, soaking in the adulation.

At the end of the aisle, the crowd spread apart. Encircled by vocal citizens, a six-foot tall platform rose above the crowd. Upon it, the Council stood at the front, watching the crowd, dressed in their formal black robes with red rope embroidery. Behind them was a hangman's pole, hangman, and said hangman's assistant. Every single demon on the platform wore grim expressions.

Standing beside the hangman's pole was Gemini. Time had done him no favors since I last saw him. Though I doubted Ralrek or I appeared to be holding up well to anyone who had not seen us since our imprisonment, Gemini was wasting away. Thinner, frailer. Even from this distance, I could see him shivering. His head hung against his chest, a mass of loose, black curls forming a large ball of tangles atop his head. The skin I could see had lost its vibrancy and taken on an ashy hue.

Two attendants held onto him from either side—such a kind gesture from the Council, just minutes before they killed him.

Gemini lifted his head and scanned the crowd as the

guards marched us to take our place in the front line of the crowd, near the raised platform. When he looked my way, we made eye contact, but if he recognized me, I couldn't tell.

Lucifer, how I hoped Cassie wasn't here.

"Zeke, look," Ralrek whispered so quietly I almost missed it under the excited noises coming from the crowd. I followed his gaze across the opening to where, to my horror, I recognized two demons. My mother and father were here. In the front row, on the other side of the circle of bodies, they watched our arrival. I wondered if the Council was responsible for their favorable spots. Coincidences and all that.

Mother cried as she raised a shaking hand in my direction. My father stood stone-faced, his eyes locked on me.

Apopis's carriage stopped in front of us, cutting off my view of my parents. The crowd cheered as the last Council member to arrive stepped down, raising a hand. It was all so very self-indulgent. He took his time joining his peers on the platform, soaking in the attention. Once alongside the other four Founders, they all waved. The cheers morphed into a roar.

Had someone canceled the execution and turned it into a party instead?

His carriage pulled away, and I found my mother's eyes again. My father's head, however, was turned to applaud the five who stood in a line across the front of the platform, allowing the crowd to adore them. I wondered what Lucifer thought of this display.

Michael raised his hand as he stepped forward, and a hush rippled backward through the congregants. "Brothers and sisters in Lucifer," he shouted, his voice echoing around the square that was now so quiet I could have heard a faerie's wings flap, "we are honored to have you join us for this important occasion. In the history of our great species, it is rare to find ourselves in a situation like this. Unfortunate, but you can be assured that the Council has done and will continue to do everything in its power to protect you from the ravages of the great evil that is Yahweh and his minions."

The crowd hissed. It was like Michael was trying to provoke them into open hostility. Gemini wasn't going to receive any favors today.

Being out of the prison, in the open day underneath the glorious blue of the Hellfire, I scrambled to think of a way to intervene or at least slow down the proceedings. But the muddled mess that was my mind could come up with nothing. My shoulders had finally stopped burning; my fingers no longer tingled; the fire inside me burned at the injustice of all this, and yet my mind refused to cooperate.

"This demon," Michael punched a finger in Gemini's direction, "is no demon at all. Through Lucifer's guidance, we have confirmed his identity as an angel, working in a concerted effort with others, as a spy for Yahweh. He infiltrated the Underworld by leveraging the naivety of other demons in our employ. This is the first breach in fifty thousand years, and we are taking measures to ensure it will be the last."

Someone lit a few more fires inside me at Michael's half-truths. Convenient, that he did not mention that the Council had Gemini working for them or that they had lost track of him. Though, keeping Hell's residents informed was hardly a strength of its rulers. Heat rose in my cheeks. Even though we'd done nothing wrong, having it implied that I was responsible was infuriating. The fact I was powerless to change anything only made matters worse. I ached for the power to disappear into the brimstone, since I lacked the freedom and power to break things in a fitful rage.

"And today, you will witness Lucifer's justice!" Michael shouted, and the crowd erupted.

My heart, afire with anger, sank when I looked across the expanse and saw my father raise long arms above his head, clapping so aggressively his head jerked with each smashing together of his hands. My mother had her arms wrapped around her waist, hugging herself, stealing a glance in my direction.

"Gemini Oso has been found to be a celestial spy for Yahweh," Michael announced as the crowd quieted again. "The most egregious crime. Today, we will discharge Lucifer's justice and this spy will pay for his crimes against the king of kings. He will die by hanging!"

The square erupted with cheers. Some incubi threw their hats in the air. Some tossed their implings—don't worry, they were responsible fathers and caught each one. Others pumped their staffs above their heads. Faeries and sylphs danced in sharp swoops and dives above the heads of the demon crowd. Off in one of the square's corner, bodies swayed together almost as one, like they were dancing to music only they could hear. A string of armored guards quick-stepped inside the circle in case things got out of hand and the crowd decided to rush the platform.

"Disgusting," I whispered to Ralrek. He only grunted, in agreement or not, I couldn't tell.

In a neat row of four, the other Council members stoically watched. Michael seemed to be taking great joy in this spectacle, the first execution in generations. Even though I trusted none of them, I expected better of him. This was a role for Beelzebub or Apopis.

Gemini didn't stand a chance.

My stupid brain and its inability to come up with a plan.

The most disappointing observation of all was that Seraph looked not only unreadable, but unbothered. In the time since we were marched into the square, she had not moved except to wave at the crowd.

Was she so bought into this?

I was never so happy to not have Cassie around.

Michael raised his arms, and every eye fell on him as he slowly lowered them. He half–turned to Gemini. "Do you have any final words?"

A few demons hissed. Most were hushed or received a swat from their neighbor. All around the circle, spots of demons leaned forward to hear better. A succubus directly across from me, no older than ten thousand years, clamped her teeth down on a white handkerchief.

None of them need worry about missing a word from Gemini, because he did not look to have the strength to do it. The attendants on either side, holding his arms, were likely the only reason he was upright.

Gemini's head lazily shook to one side, then the other.

"The prisoner has nothing to say about his crimes. Hardly surprising for someone so guilty. This type will stoop to the lowest levels to ensure success in their mission to destroy what we have. Who we are! Hear Lucifer's charge. As you go about the days to follow, do not forget what you see and hear today. This rare event is a lesson for all of us to keep our guard up and to be wary of those who act suspiciously. After this moment, carry word of Gemini's guilt with you for the rest of your life and teach those who are too young to understand. Stay alert. Remain aware of the danger. Report suspicions to your local authorities. We cannot have our way of life threatened!"

Michael nodded to the hangman. A barrel chested, hooded demon in a black vest, pants, and boots, stepped behind the hangman's pole, to stand beside a long lever. The two attendants who held Gemini's arms walked him toward the pole.

They were really doing this. In front of a square full of demons, the Council was going to hang Gemini.

Parts of the crowd surged forward until the armed guards halted them. On the side of the circle opposite me, demons moving to get a better view, swallowed my parents. That was the one fortunate event during this travesty. At least I would not have to witness my father's exuberance. I knew who he was; a demon who gave his full, unquestioning allegiance to Lucifer's Council. I didn't need the validation.

My head hurt. From the exhaustion. From the humiliation. The hunger. The crowd noise. For Gemini's fate. From the seething anger and helplessness. The base of my skull felt like it was being stepped on by an iron shod boot.

I wanted to shout out that this was beneath us, that we should be better. But looking around the crowd, seeing the wave of faces devouring every second, I realized how wrong I was. An extraordinary event, it only appealed to an existing nature. My kind hungered for this.

With each preparatory movement of the hangman, the intensity of anticipation grew amongst those watching. The air crackled.

"It's really going to happen," I moaned.

"Let it go, Zeke," Ralrek huffed in a low tone, his eyes blinking slowly.

I shook my head. "I can't."

"He's an angel. It doesn't matter. Don't waste your energy on it. We can't help, especially since we're ..." He lifted his hand to show his manacles.

I would have taken a step away from Ralrek if there wasn't a crowd of demons tightly packed behind me. He couldn't quit on Gemini. Not now. We had just spent weeks suffering in a cell. He suffered just as I had, and all because we did what the Council demanded and they needed fall guys. How he could live through that and not empathize with Gemini was unfathomable.

"Why does that matter?"

He shrugged. It was excruciatingly slow.

"Remember, we found him in the Overworld, doing nothing. Hardly a crime worth punishment. He came back willingly. None of this makes sense." I winced against the pressure at the base of my skull.

Ralrek's chest rose in jerking movements. "We can't do anything. Gemini lied, faked his death. He knew the risks, man. You've got to see that?"

My eyes narrowed. Was I the crazy one? Did Gemini's victimless crime deserve the use of Lucifer's Ability to create a dangling corpse? Did seeking fulfillment require the ultimate punishment?

Of course not. The demons sharing this square in some obscure Circle proved themselves as bloodthirsty as the Council. I swept my gaze around the throng trying to close in on the platform, my parents now hidden by the sea of bodies.

The noose fashioned, the hangman's hand on the lever, the crowd cheered. The assistant lowered the noose over Gemini's head, tucked it under his chin with a few jerks of his meaty fist and tightened the knot. Lucifer wasn't present, which was strange because only he could kill a demon while in the Underworld—yes, I did too, but stay with me on this one. I figured he would be here. Especially at an execution. The last one happened well before my recollection. So how did this work? Did He imbue them with a spell, a part of his power, to carry out His justice? Or, worse, did the Council have some twisted fun and leave Gemini dangling until the crowd dispersed and the big man came by to finish the job?

I could barely swallow as the assistant shimmied Gemini backward, into position atop the trapdoor. The hangman's thick fingers gripped the top of the lever like he was kneading dough. My thoughts drifted to Cassie, hoping she escaped somehow to a place where the Council would never find her. I hadn't seen her during our march through the street and could not see her now. Maybe Seraph had intervened on Cassie's behalf after all, and she was safe, or at worst, serving her punishment in a comfortable cell. Was it possible they would make some deal with Heaven? Use her in a trade? As long as she was safe, that was all that mattered. As much as Gemini didn't deserve this, Cassie deserved it less.

Michael glided forward now that the executioner and victim were prepared. This time, Michael didn't need to quiet the crowd. As the reality of this event sank in with each procedural step completed, the crowd had grown quieter.

My headache was turning into a migraine. When we returned to the prison, I would demand proper hydration, as close to vomiting as I suddenly felt.

Michael raised his arm, tall and long, and opened his mouth to give the command. But the crowd did not want words. A roar rose into the air, echoing off the buildings. Even from where I stood, I could see the fire in Apopis's eyes raging to life as he fed off the fervor. Beelzebub grinned, smug and confident. Only Azazel and Seraph remained reserved, but they also didn't look like they disapproved of Michael's message. Azazel was grimacing and Seraph scowled.

Politics, I'll never understand it.

"Just kill 'em already!" an aged voice shouted from a few feet away. The owner of the voice was a wrinkled succubus with more facial orifices than teeth. She shook her fist in the air toward the raised platform. Demons around her laughed and shouted approval.

Her encouraging cry was echoed at other miscellaneous spots around the horde, rippling back toward the buildings that were homes and businesses, and now also the walls of Gemini's death cell.

Michael waited for the noise to die down. His chest swelled. "Gemini Oso, with Lucifer's blessing, it has been bestowed upon me to carry out your judgment. It is time."

He rejoined his four peers, who adjusted their stances to watch the proceeding.

The attendants backed away from Gemini, and my heart broke when he didn't struggle. He simply stood, arms at his side, unmoving until he lifted his head. His watery eyes examined the crowd below, those who had taken time from their day to celebrate his demise. In this moment, he was bigger, better than they were, than all of them combined. Including me.

When my time came to stand on that raised platform, I wondered if my father would stand in the crowd raising his fists in celebration.

With everyone in position, the hangman planted his two meaty hands on the long lever. This was it. The end of Gemini.

Before the hangman pulled and sent Gemini's worn body accelerating toward the brimstone below, sharp, disorienting pain stabbed the corners of my eyes. I winced. It was like miniature implings were plunging microscopic daggers in to my eyes.

A signal of a powerful spell.

I doubled over, yanking Ralrek down with me. He fell.

"You ass," he said as he held his elbow.

The guards assigned to watch over us turned. I tried to lift my bound hands to my eyes to press back against the pain, but the chain stopped my hands a few inches short.

I'd never felt this—thankfully—and knew it wasn't an Ability I was familiar with. This was not a migraine. This was magic. Under the circumstances, I was too preoccupied with my exploding eyeballs to worry about who was casting, from where they were casting, or why they were casting.

The world exploded.

Even with my eyes closed, the spell set everything alight. My eyelids transitioned from pink to a white so intense every bit of definition, of space and dimension, disappeared.

The day filled with screams.

The pressure in my head squeezed, sending me to the ground as another, and then another, and then another spell was cast. Each spell ripped the air apart. My heart stopped beating, I swear. The light was so intense I couldn't dare open my eyes. I moved to my knees, holding on to the brimstone as if it was the only thing that grounded me to reality.

More screams.

I cowered, grasping the ground and sending a thought to Lucifer to help me get through this before my eyeballs melted inside my skull.

Panting, I waited as the brightness faded.

The world came into view again. Bodies were spread across the square in a chaotic display. Many demons were injured, while many more, too many, lay unmoving. No one stood.

I pulled my hands under me and pushed up. Dust showered from my hair. Squinting, I reached for Ralrek. He groaned.

Pushing myself up, I saw what the square had become. A sea of bodies, now undulating with panic. Demons toward the back of the square, furthest away from the platform, were getting to their feet. The stronger ones ran from the square, taking the streets and alleys to escape.

On the platform, the five Council members were in varying states. Azazel was laid out on his back. Michael was on his knees, holding his head. Beelzebub took a single knee, both his massive paws on the bent one as if he was trying to push to a standing position. Seraph held onto a pole, swaying. And Apopis stumbled while getting to his feet.

Magic. Too much magic was being conjured, wracking my body with sensations. Until this moment, I had never felt uncomfortable in my skin. I did now. The sliminess, scratching, hair raising, stickiness, and more overwhelmed my capacity to think. I froze.

"What's going on?" Ralrek asked in a weakened groan.

"Magic. Lots of it," I replied.

"Don't move, you two!" the guard who pulled me from the cell snarled, pointing to the ground as if we were hellhounds who needed to learn our place.

"Are you serious?" I said, biting back. "Unchain us."

He swallowed, wiggling his nose and sniffing. "Not a chance in heaven."

The invisible boot crushing my head pressed down again.

"Down!" I pushed Ralrek just as explosions knocked everyone healthy enough to stand back to the ground.

A bright stream of white light, thick as a felled tree, shot across the open square from a nearby rooftop. It struck the middle of the crowd, tossing bodies in the air in whirling circles. The screams of the demons hit by the stream were cut short, meaning …

No, that wasn't possible.

"We're under attack, you idiot," I shouted to the other guard, having already given mine a chance to save us. This guard scrambled to his feet but looked at me like he could not fathom what species I was. "Unhook us now!"

My raspy-voiced guard slapped him on the arm, lowering his pike in a defensive position. The second guard copied him and they scanned the square.

Everyone who could crawl, walk, or run was doing it now to find defensive positions. The disorientation still not fully abated, most moved in a malaise. Azazel nearly walked off the front of the platform while trying to find something to hide behind. It was then that I noticed a major detail no one else seemed to notice.

The Council was on the platform. The hangman and his assistants were hiding behind the weapons rack. The one individual not in the equation was Gemini.

Then the stairs to the platform burst apart when another stream of light hit it, projecting a shower of shards and splinters. The demons closest to them crashed against the buildings in the back of the square, then flopped to the ground.

Air crackled. Two more beams of light, from different directions, targeted the platform. Sections of it rocketed upward when struck, the splinters even catching fire as they rained down among the demon corpses splayed across the brimstone.

The small part not yet destroyed, the platform upon which Gemini would die, burned with white fire.

I focused on the Council members, who were conjuring their spells now in defense, trying to turn it into attack. Michael hid as he worked on his. Beelzebub threw boulder sized balls of fire toward the roofs of different buildings, trying to get lucky with one of them. Seraph waved her hands in uncharacteristically wild movements, pulling tiles from the rooftops. There, they floated and swirled. Apopis worked a Deception spell. By its stickiness, I knew once he released it, the spell would be frighteningly large.

Two streams of light raced from the rooftop to my right toward where Apopis hid. Both missed, but came close enough to the front of the platform to shower the sky with splinters.

I grabbed the guard closest to me and spun him. His eyes were wide. The incubus's rational brain had departed, reverting him to a mass of meat and bone that would not act unless acted upon.

"Unlock these blessed chains!" I said, shaking him. Creed uselessly hung at my waist. I could do at least some good with it if I had free hands to use it. "We'll die if you don't!"

The thousand-yard stare didn't break. But thankfully his partner was slightly more aware. With a shaking hand, he dropped his spear and snagged the keys from his belt, trying to unlock our shackles.

"Give me that!" I ordered, grabbing the key ring from him without waiting. My eyes watered from the thick pressure in my head, making finding the keyhole on Ralrek's shackles nearly impossible. Freeing him, I turned the key to my hands. Just as I unlocked the bolt, the air sizzled.

"Down!" I shouted again, diving in the direction I felt the sizzle coming from.

Just as I struck the brimstone, another white stream hit the ground a few feet in front of where the two guards had been standing. The attack hit with such force that it tore a three foot deep crater into the brimstone.

As pebbles and chunks of the ground fell back to the surface, I noticed the two guards were gone, lost in the bodies that lay around.

The road and alleyways leading from the square were filling with fleeing demons now. Some shoved others out of the way to escape. Even older succubi were not immune to the flash of demon-on-demon violence. There were too many of us and not enough avenues out, causing demons to panic. One fortune, if anything in this could be considered fortunate, was that whoever was behind the attack ignored the easy target of so many packed so tightly together as they fled, instead concentrating their attacks on where they had the Council pinned down.

The area around the platform was under constant assault. The Council sent spells racing back toward the rooftops.

Magic and bodies everywhere.

The attackers' hiding positions gave them an advantage, forcing the Founders to throw aimless and hopeful spells and counterspells. The Council fought to maintain what they had at this point. It was a losing proposition.

The air rippled. Not from the platform, but from above. The stabbing pain in my eyes crippled me and I fell to the brimstone again.

Through tears, I cried out. "Move! Get off the platform!"

Seraph turned to her counterparts and waved wildly. All five jumped free just as a thick bolt of light, the thickest of the battle so far, punctured the platform. Anything that remained of the platform was obliterated, including the hangman and his assistants, leaving the structure and the demons who were about to kill Gemini as smoldering piles of ash.

I jumped to my feet, racing to find Hell's rulers, half hoping I'd find nothing.

Michael was down and bleeding. Beelzebub, who already had Seraph wrapped in one arm, was bending to lift the Council's leader with the other. Azazel held his head with one hand while supporting himself on a pile of rubble with the other. His goatee had turned pink with someone's blood.

"You've got to get undercover!" I instructed, pointing to the nearest building's outcropping. "Hide under there until we can figure out where this is coming from."

Beelzebub gave Michael a jerk, thrusting the taller incubus up and almost onto the muscular demon's shoulder. With grim determination on his face, he carried the two Council members to hiding. Azazel hobbled along and almost fell, until I jumped to his side and caught him. We made it under cover of the outcropping. That's when I noticed Apopis hadn't caught up.

He had been coming up behind me as I assisted Azazel. Now, he was on the ground sprawled over a corpse.

Out in the open, he was ripe for an attack from above.

The invisible boot stomped on my brain.

This wasn't a headache, it was my Ability. I was sensing someone conjuring. Unknown magic, but magic nonetheless.

Forcing my eyes to stay open against the stabs inside my skull, I sprinted toward Apopis as he pulled himself up and limped in our direction.

The air sizzled. Too late. I was too late. Twenty feet still separated us.

At full speed, I did something I hadn't tried to do since the prison cell. I called to Creed.

The connection was there immediately. A longing. Intense.

Fifteen feet.

Creed rattled in the loop.

Ten feet.

It slapped into my palm.

Connection complete.

My hand was one with the petrified cherry wood. As I neared Apopis, the air tore behind me. I was in the direct path of the next attack, the only thing between it and one of the Founders.

Even as the beam of light raced toward my back, I skidded to a halt in front of Apopis and thrust Creed out. Spinning the halberd, it quickly picked up speed to form a rotating shield, the defensive tactic I always used against Bilba that he hated. Now I was glad I practiced it so often. Hand over hand, it arced through the empty air, spinning faster and faster.

I growled as fear blinded me to the very real possibility that I was about to die. For Apopis. This sucked.

Face-on with the white stream of light magic, its immense brightness blotted out everything. I lowered my head, spinning Creed as quickly as my burning muscles allowed, and waiting for impact.

The stream struck. The force rocketed me into Apopis. He stumbled, taking the brunt of my weight, and I almost went over him. That would have been the end for both of us. But I kept my feet as the spell drove against me. Creed's haft warmed under the assault, heating until the light dissipated.

Exhausted but alive, I nearly dropped the halberd.

"Run!" I shouted through gasps. Apopis started toward the cover where the other Council members now cast, sending spells toward the spot where the latest stream of light had been unleashed. Even Ralrek had joined them and was sending tiny fireballs in the direction of the attacker. If I lived, I was going to give him shit about that.

A thudding of air preceded the boom of the roof shattering from the attack. The Council moved to the next roof and then the next. Everyone who could fight now was.

Another rooftop, obliterated. Then another. The tide was turning.

The attack of light had ended, gone as quickly and mysteriously as it had appeared.

All across the square, demons squatted, kneeled, tended to the injured, and wailed over the dead. And underneath that, everyone held their spells. Just in case.

As the minutes of silence passed, it became obvious that the attack had ended. Whether or not the attackers were killed, no one could be sure, but the worst was over.

Demons trickled out from their hiding spots to look for loved ones and friends. In the span of minutes, the square had become ground zero for Hell's own apocalypse. Bodies lay scattered, prone, broken. Rubble was strewn on top of many of them, remnants of the buildings that formed this square, serving as homes and businesses for the lives attached to them.

"I don't understand," I said, running a hand through my gritty hair as I took in the degree of death around the square. "Demons can't be killed here."

"Celestial magic does not care about the rules of the Underworld," Seraph said sorrowfully as she walked among the dead. I followed.

"You mean ..."

She nodded. "Angels, Mr. Sunstone."

"Th-that's not possible."

She stopped and looked at me, huffed, and then turned her back to me when Michael joined. The pair walked away, followed by Beelzebub, who supported both Azazel and Apopis. Apopis didn't even thank me for saving his life.

"We need to get back to the Council room and open the reporting channel to Lucifer," Michael was saying as they departed.

A cordon of guards streamed into the square, a dozen breaking off the formation and surrounding the Founders, escorting them to a carriage that waited on the other side of a wall of rubble. They left me standing alone and unsupervised.

Part of me doubted I was free, and the other part didn't care because I actually was, at least for the moment.

Standing in the square was not an ideal way to spend whatever moments of freedom I had while I waited for some authority to re-arrest and imprison me. I couldn't help the dead, and the injured were making their way out of the area.

So I went in search of my parents. My gut ached during the hours it took to move from body to body, ensuring they weren't among the dead. Rubble and dust covered the dead, too many broken and bloodied to easily confirm they were not my loved ones. Each body I turned over came with tense apprehension and delayed relief and sorrow.

So much loss. Ralrek tried to help with my search but he had turned as white as parchment and I demanded he sit down until I finished or until someone could get him home. I breathed easily again when I'd searched all I could and didn't find them. My parents had escaped.

I needed to get home and figure out what was next; I was at peace not helping anyone besides Ralrek at the moment. These demons didn't have to worry about retribution from the Council. We still did. Staying in the square wouldn't give me the time I needed to think through a response.

I was halfway across the square, past the deceased and the rubble when a cloaked figure scurried across toward me. I yanked Creed out of the loop, extending it and prepared an exhausted attack.

The cloaked figure pulled up short, raising brown gloved hands in surrender. This was the easiest fight I'd had in a long time. Good thing too, Ralrek hadn't even bothered to conjure. He didn't even try to fake it.

The figured lowered one chubby hand, the other one remaining raised. I watched guardedly as their hand slipped into the cloak and pulled a slip of rolled parchment free.

Their face still hidden behind the hood and that downcast

head, the demon took a tentative step forward, offering the parchment.

My heart thumped in my ears. As soon as I took it, the figure turned and raced away, hurriedly weaving around obstacles and into the crowd at the mouth of an alley. I watched them go, mystified. Only when they disappeared did I collapse Creed and place it back in its loop.

"What was that?" Ralrek asked, rubbing his face, smearing gray ash up his cheeks.

I wanted to say something smart about his lack of response to the stranger, but it had been a long, miserable day, and honestly, I was done.

I unfurled the parchment and read the message, immediately regretting that I hadn't when the stranger was standing here.

One in creation, bound to the false prince, deceitful by design or accident, the triple-rendering, no eternal Masters, the redeemer chooses its own fate.

CREED. THIS WAS ANOTHER LIKE THE MESSAGES FROM *THE Histories of the Balance*.

My head snapped up, I searched for the figure I knew had already disappeared.

"What's it say?" Ralrek asked.

Even though he was a few feet away and seated, I folded the note with haphazard attention, and shoved it in my pocket, offering him a pathetic smile. "Later, bud. Now isn't the time."

But now was the time because the message couldn't be ignored.

A day that started in a prison cell as punishment for a

crime I didn't commit, a battle against angelic invaders, ended with a stranger handing me a message from a book destroyed by the demons who set all these wheels in motion? Just what in the heavens was going on, and what was the story with Creed?

And where was Gemini?

And Cassie.

Was she safe?

Was she with Gemini?

18

UNDERWORLD, FIFTH CIRCLE

MY BED BECAME my home after the attack on the square. I kept no company besides my Blue Sky vodka—my first stop after coming through the gateway back into the Fifth was to pick up a new bottle from the corner liquor store. I should have picked up two, the empty bottle on the coffee table reminded me. I'd stopped mixing the vodka with ghost berry juice because that only delayed the desired effect. Straight vodka made the heaven that Hell had become easier to deal with.

In the days following the attack, the Council was silent, not even sending a patrol to re-arrest me. Even though all the Fifth Circle talked about the tragedy and the lives lost, for the first time in the history of the Underworld, our leaders remained eerily quiet. They appeared on the news and were interviewed in the papers, but those were nothing more than scripted public relations moves if you ask me. They served the purpose of reminding demons all around Hell that the Council was hard at work, but they never actually talked about what work they were accomplishing. To me, the interviews only resulted in me finding out that the attack happened in the First Circle, making that the third Circle I had traveled to on Lucifer's coin. Call it an accomplishment, but I could not have cared less.

I wasn't hiding from them, holing up in my apartment except to make quick runs to the fast food stands dotting the pedestrian zone of Old Towne after the food in the apartment ran out. I was going to get fat. I didn't care.

The Council could find me if they wanted. For whatever reason, they hadn't, and I was grateful. My alcohol infused mind came up with many situations and scenarios why that was the case.

Too bad I did not have Bilba around—heavens, I did not have anyone around—to bounce the theories off to see if they made sense.

Though Ralrek had called on me a half dozen times in the past few days, increasing in occurrence the more I ignored him, that did not count. Not that I was mad. I felt for him, actually. But I couldn't put two coherent thoughts together for myself, never mind him and the inevitable questions he would have. Before I talked to anyone, I needed to figure things out for myself. Thankfully for my brain and analytical skills, I did not have the motivation to head to the liquor store after the vodka ran dry.

How did I figure anything out when I was still unsure if I was an enemy of Lucifer or not?

Friends or enemies? Where did I stand with the Council, and for that matter, where did I stand with the rest of the Fifth Circle? For almost a year, I had an undesirable reputation here. My parents could not have been the only Fivers at the execution. Others would have been there too. They would have seen me shackled, a prisoner of the Council. And if there is one thing I know about demons, it's that they fill in the missing details around an unfamiliar situation and always follow their leader's story, no matter how true or false it was. On that day, untold scores of demons identified me as an enemy.

If there was any saving grace of the events in the square—and how could there be when so many died?—it was that Michael and the Council never named and shamed me and Ralrek. No trial or sentencing. Not even a public condemnation or one-off humiliation event.

We hadn't had reconciliation yet, but that was not on the top of my list of things to do once I found where I left my motivation to do anything.

Disillusioned and burned out on life, I honestly wasn't concerned with much, including the piece of paper sitting on my coffee table.

Returning from that tragedy in the First Circle, I'd come home to a note slipped under my door. I tossed it on the table, thinking it was an overdue bill. Two days later I decided to open it and see who I hadn't paid. Much to my surprise and frustration, it wasn't a bill, but a handwritten note advising me to read the included parchment and to think. No signature, no name, no address. The note writer obviously couldn't even be bothered to sign it as a 'friend of Ezekial' or something equally cryptic yet playful. Whoever left it didn't want to be associated with me. Based on the message in the parchment, I understood why.

The rending maintains through the cycle, beyond the celestial, its creator, through a fate chosen of its own volition. Guarded by the first of his name, the first of the Zodiac.

MY MIND STILL BOUNCED THROUGH SCATTERED THOUGHTS FROM the implications.

Secret notes. Scrawled messages in the margins of old books. Signs pointing me back to Creed. And now this?

If I was reading this correctly, the unnamed author of this

message was trying to clarify that Aries was involved in Creed's destiny. At least, in part. The consistent messages made this clearer, now more than ever.

"Guarded by the first of his name, the first of the Zodiac." A sad smile spread across my face at re-reading it. Aries was the first of his name, and the first of the Zodiac. And Aries had gifted Creed to me, linking me to my destiny, saying that I was 'the one'.

Bat dung-crazy, that old incubus.

Twinges of regret swarmed over me at the thought of how I failed him, crazy or not.

That set me on a days–long review of the previous cryptic messages about Creed. Long after the vodka had run dry and my mind once again cleared, I reviewed those notes, attempting to decipher their meaning before ultimately giving up. It was too much, too soon. I was still struggling with the fact that the Council had imprisoned us for a crime we did not commit and, had a travesty not struck Hell, I would have been forced to admit guilt or watch my parents suffer.

The Council's silence consumed my energy. Consumed me. This went beyond bitter. This was deeper. You didn't sacrifice for an organization and then turn around and have them punish you to cover their own tracks. Ever since I'd been involved with them, it seemed like I was lined up for a series of betrayals, starting with my parents, carrying through to Beelzebub in the Overworld, to Marijon in the Eighth Circle, and lastly, with the Council over Cassie and Gemini.

In that tangled mess, I was now supposed to add mysteries about Creed?

Dialphio had been asking me to return to *The Book Abyss*, saying it would be good for me to get out of the apartment. She even came by twice during the week and promised more frequent and longer visits until I returned to work. I conceded, fully planning to go in tomorrow, if for no other reason than to have a change of scenery. But for today, the plan was to spend time with my closest friend.

Speaking of which …

I needed to head to the liquor store.

"COME HERE, YOU," DIALPHIO SHOUTED AS SOON AS I WALKED through the front door. I don't think I got out the second word of my greeting when the short, auburn–haired demon locked me in an embrace. She pulled back but still held my arms at the triceps, looking me up and down, her smile slipping. The pro that the bookstore owners was, she recovered quickly, I had to give her that. "You've been losing weight, Ezekial."

I had? Dare I tell her I felt like crap?

"I've been better," I answered, a thick guilt hanging on my every word. "How have you been? The bookstore looks great."

It didn't. It looked the same as it always did whenever I missed more than a few days of work—a chaotic, unorganized mess of various titles.

A chaotic mess. My ears were burning.

She was looking around at her offspring, her proud eyes seeing something I didn't. I loved the store and enjoyed Dialphio's company. But one of these days when life didn't suck and she wasn't looking, I would reorganize everything. We have an old saying in Hell about asking for forgetfulness instead of permission that bounced around my distracted mind.

"Well," she said with a wave of her hand, "come on in and get settled. I want to chat."

I walked to the back of the store, behind the half-wall that held stacks of books that hid our desks. The few personal items I kept at work, a picture of me and my parents, a news article from when I scored the winning goal in our sector's blazeball tournament, and an old picture of my childhood devildog, Powder, were in their place. My coffee mug was on the same coaster I always used. Even my drawer was organized with red pens in the left bin and black in the right. My notepad was also where I left it.

Home.

I didn't bother hiding my smile.

I must have stood in front of the desk longer than I thought because Dialphio moved to my side, rubbing my arm. "It's good to have you back, Ezekial," she said with a soft, motherly voice.

I turned and hugged her. "It's so good to be back. I've needed this."

Dialphio's smile rippled like it was trying to fight off an army of sadness all on its own. "I can tell. From what I've heard, it sounds like you had a rough go of things."

Boy, was that true. "You could say that."

Dialphio's eyes jumped to the front of the store as if she checking for something or someone. "If you need to talk through any of this, I'm all ears."

"I really appreciate it. I don't have a lot of demons I can confide in. Especially now."

"What happened?" Dialphio's voice was heavy but encouraging. She wasn't seeking the latest gossip or juicy news. She was the one who reached out to me during my absence, the one who checked in on me, Ralrek not forgotten—though, if I had entertained him we probably would have just sat around and watched movies or played video games instead of working through our issues, as incubi do. My own parents—safe at home—hadn't. Not that I went out of my way to check in on them either. But I would, once I had the energy for the hour-long walk.

But I wasn't sure I wanted to tell her. Informing her might somehow, in this twisted world, result in the Council targeting her.

"The mission went bad, that's all."

She tilted her head, her eyes losing their joy. "A lot has happened to you, but please don't treat me like an impling. You can be honest with me, Ezekial. No matter how much you hide, you won't stop the rumors. And in case you don't remember, I encouraged you to be very careful about who you trusted. Right? If you don't allow me to help, I fear the toll it will take on you."

"How bad are the rumors?"

She chirped, filled with disgust. "Bad enough. You know how demons can get when there's exciting news and they're bored. The Circle is full of them, no matter where you go. I was in the fourteenth zone the other day, picking up a rare item, and they were talking about it over there too. Rumors. About you and Ralrek. About that angel. Some say you are one·too, that you're a Council cover-up, secret agent type thing. Some say you have hidden wings. Silly, really. In a good way, if you can say that, the attack on the First keeps most demons distracted from only talking about the pair of you. But time will numb the sting of that horrible event and, soon, rumors about you will grow legs. Soon the entire Fifth will claim you can freeze demons alive with just a flicker of your eyes. Just watch."

"Did they ever say how many died?" I decided focusing on the attack would stave off another wave of depression I was valiantly trying to hide from my caring boss.

Dialphio nodded. "At least three hundred. From Angelfire, no less. Angelfire in the Underworld! The worst incident ever."

Oh, my Lucifer. Angelfire? That's what that was? I mean, we're taught all about it in school, that it is the strongest of angelic magic, but now that I'd seen its power, I understood why it held such an ominous reputation.

"Do they know who did it?"

She shrugged. "One report quoted the Council saying it

was a squad of angels, of course. I've heard various guesses, from only a few to a dozen or more. I don't think anyone knows for sure since none of us knows what it takes to cast their magic. Such a shame that so many innocents had to die."

This time I nodded, though I struggled to agree with her. No one deserved to die, but I'll be blessed if what I heard and saw that day were the words and actions of innocent demons.

Dialphio took a moment to walk to her desk. She pulled a drawer open and reached in. I figured she was going back to work, which was fine with me. If one thing could rescue me from my self-loathing over the past few months, it might be falling back into a routine with the shop owner and leaving this Council stuff behind.

As long as the Council decided to leave me behind.

I set Creed on the desk and headed straight for the coffee machine. "It's good to see you still have this."

Dialphio yanked her hand out of the desk, sitting against it and blocking my view of the drawer. She saw I was referring to the coffeemaker and cracked a smile. "Of course. There's no way I could operate without it. Especially not a bookstore. It's deathly quiet in here too often."

She returned to whatever she was doing at her desk while I finished making myself the sweetest cup of coffee I could, missing the Overworld sugar. The more I was exposed to that realm, the more our bland food and additives stung. Was it really too much to ask to live for millennia while also enjoying the finer things? Instead, I said, "I just need to get settled and then I'll get on the floor."

"Huh?" She blinked, then shook her head as if clearing cobwebs. "Oh, okay. That's fine."

I watched her for a moment while pretending to organize papers. Something was off. Either something was bothering her or she was regretting not replacing me when I was off on the mission. Whatever it was, Dialphio was lost in thought.

Getting back into the rhythm wasn't as difficult as I'd

imagined, and I cursed myself for not challenging myself to do this earlier instead of wasting days in the apartment drinking away my problems. I couldn't change that now. The only thing I could do was work, to help her and to get back into the flow of life. If the Council ever decided they weren't happy with my freedom, they could take it up with me. Until that day, I would do my best to live the life I had.

I hadn't even noticed her hanging by my desk; I was so lost in thought. When I found her eyes, she had a thousand-yard stare. She was seeing me and not seeing me, like she was looking deeper into my being to find what rotted tangle lay at my core. Hers was not a look of confusion, but of dilemma.

"Dialphio? Is everything okay?"

"Huh? Oh, yes, I'm sorry," she said, looking at the note she held before extending it to me. "This was sent for you. I think you should read it."

I did. The letters were written in big loops, fluid handwriting. I found Dialphio's eyes. "When did it come?"

"Not long ago. Came through my notebook." She pointed at it, even though I knew what she was talking about.

As thick as a loaf of bread, her notebook sat on the center of her desk. A bronze-gilded cover had two swirling lines, each arcing from the edges of the cover and looping toward the center where a teardrop gem was set into a raised bezel of silver. Dialphio's demonic notebook. Rare items only the higher middle classes and the rich could afford, demonic notebooks allowed demons to communicate over great distances and even between Circles. The sender simply needed to address the recipient. How a bookstore owner could afford one was beyond me, but I was glad she had it now.

"You've read it?"

Dialphio nodded. "It didn't have your name on it." She read my unspoken conclusion. "It is my store after all," she said with a forced chirp. "I think you should do it."

"You do?"

"Ezekial," she said carefully, "there are forces at play that are far more powerful than anything you or I understand. But you're important to all of this. That's why they're treating you like they are. There's something about you they fear. That's the box you need to unlock. If you don't, you'll always be reacting to their actions. Do you think what they did was fair?"

My desk suddenly demanded my attention. Since returning home I had successfully—depending on how you look at healthy and unhealthy behaviors—suppressed the anger boiling inside me. That fire had been quenched by one-point-seventy-five liters of vodka and depression. Dialphio brought that anger back to the surface with her comments, and I knew she did not intend to rile me, but it was the result. So was shame. Shame at my inaction. Shame at my avoidance. Shame over my pouting.

"No, but you don't understand the full situation," I said, finally answering her.

"Oh, balderdash," Dialphio said in a heated voice. "All over the Underworld, demons know, or at least have an idea, what happened. Enough to know you didn't do anything wrong. Most of us, anyway." A sly smile spread across her face and she chirped. "Though there are some who are convinced you're Yahweh himself."

I laughed halfheartedly. "I'm evil, but not that evil."

Dialphio pointed at the note. "If she's asking to see you, you need to go. Now, before the Council finds out."

"But I don't know how," I said. "It's not like I can open gateways."

"If you have the will, there's a way. And if Cassie wants to see you, which is what she clearly says in that note, then I think you should do it. Act. Soon. And by soon, I mean, why are you still sitting here. Go see Seraph. She'll help, won't she?"

"I don't know," I mumbled, rubbing my thumb over the swirling letters in Cassie's handwriting. "You need me here."

"I hired you because I needed the help. I don't keep you around because of your work ethic, which is mediocre at best," she said with a huge flavor of humor. "You're a good incubus, Ezekial. But you're also wrapped up in big things. Things more complex than we understand. You have a good heart. I've seen that. Don't worry about me or this silly store. Get to her before it's too late."

"They burned it, Dialphio. They burned *The Histories of the Balance*." The admission fell out of my mouth easily, even though I knew it would disappoint her.

"I know," she said. "It's a significant loss. Generations from now, when that knowledge has been wiped from our species, whoever is around will vilify us for our neglect. But we can't do anything about that. The only thing we can do is react to the situation. Sitting idly by and letting it happen is not the right answer. We can be proactive and direct it toward the course we want. We simply have to choose to act. So, Ezekial, which do you choose?"

I stood, snagging Creed. Dialphio narrowed her gaze. I snickered. She still distrusted my halberd. "If you're okay with it, I'd like to take off and see if I can hitch a ride to find Cassie." I moved to her and gave her a hug. She embraced me back. "You're amazing, Dialphio."

When we moved apart, she said, "As are you, Ezekial. You're a special demon. I just don't think you know how special right now."

"Yeah, not feeling that special to be honest."

I started to walk away, but she stopped me with a chubby hand on my elbow, the arm holding Creed.

Confusion etched her expression. She wasn't looking at me, but at my hand.

"Is everything okay?" I asked, moving my hand, half out

of self-consciousness and the other half because of her scrutiny.

"Can I see that again?" She pointed at Creed. "Can you … oh, I can't believe I'm asking this, but can you open it?"

"Sure," I said. I backed away and activated Creed. The ting of its blades opening rang through the narrow bookstore. I held it out for her inspection. "What's wrong?"

Dialphio examined it. She did this once before, and that turned out to be an early catalyst to me understanding the weapon's nature. The inscription she interpreted. The notes in *The Histories* and ones left by secret courier.

"This inscription," Dialphio said, hovering her finger over the bottom of Creed's haft. "Remember what I told you it says?"

"Yes." My mouth felt dry.

Dialphio didn't respond. Instead, her thumb hovered over the minuscule message etched in an ancient language into the petrified cherry. "I need to check on something. Go see what you can do about Cassie."

It was an awkward dismissal, yet I still walked away full of regret. Because walking away meant I had to accomplish the next thing on my to-do list. I needed to see Seraph.

I made it to the front door before Dialphio warned, "Be careful, Ezekial. Be very careful."

19

UNDERWORLD/OVERWORLD

HERE'S the thing that might break hearts; there is no such thing as fate. Take it from me. We get brainwashed into believing there is; I'm guilty of falling for it too. As a resident of the Underworld and a demon, though minor, I speak with a certain air of authority. After all, I've been working for Lucifer's Council for nearly a year, so I'm pretty close to the source. Not saying I'm all that—I'm not—but the information I have access to is about as solid as solid gets. And I can say with confidence, what humans think they know about Lucifer and Yahweh is misleading.

Buckle in.

The two great powers don't have everything under control, in Hell or Heaven, and they're not omniscient. Those are just ploys of the powerful to keep subordinates subordinated. Everything is about patterns and association. You see something happen and you have to understand its purpose. We all, immortal and mortal, are guilty of that. It's our nature to associate stimulus to something in our subconscious or preferred perspective, refusing to see it for what it really is, an incident of chance.

I was doing that now.

After leaving *The Book Abyss*, I pondered how else I could get to Cassie. Going through Seraph was less than ideal, but it was the only realistic way. My options were severely limited. One of these days I would need to befriend major demons instead of the minor ones I hung out with.

Cassie was in the Second Circle and wanted me to meet her because something was about to happen and we needed to speak—her words, not mine—before she left. She didn't say where she was going or what was about to happen, but I had my inclinations.

My conundrum was solved for me. I didn't need to figure out how to find Cassie because someone was already doing that for me. I opened my apartment door and felt the slimy murkiness of a listening ward. I had company.

Normally, I don't believe in wearing shoes inside a home. It's just not right. Something about cleanliness and deityness. But with someone in my place, I had neither the time nor inclination to worry about shoes. They remained on and I pulled Creed out of the loop. I wasn't interested in being on the disadvantage to whoever was here, wondering if I was going to get a second chance at the hooded visitor who destroyed my book.

Walking into the living room, I can't say I was surprised to see a Founder sitting on my couch.

"Hello, Mr. Sunstone," Seraph said, her icy blue eyes sparkling with trouble.

In that moment, everything I wanted to say boiled inside.

"Hey." I needed to be on the defensive, prepared to react. Never one for politics, I didn't care to fake displaying pleasure at her presence.

"I imagine you're not excited to see me," Seraph said. Good to know she was socially aware enough to pick up on the obvious. "I'll keep this quick. I'm sending you to the Overworld."

I adjusted my grip on Creed. "What? Why?"

Seraph pushed herself up off the couch. "Let's just say I owe someone a favor. And I want you to understand something."

"What?"

"That she really is an angel. Cassie, I mean. Listen to how she says your name. Does she stutter?"

"What?"

Seraph's eyes lost their sparkle, and she looked away. "If we'd only trained you better." A deep sigh, and then. "Angels aren't able to say demon's names, not easily. Only the most highly trained of them can at all."

My mouth dropped open. Every time Cassie had said my name, she stuttered. It was cute, I thought, ignorant to the fact that it was a clue about her future deceit. Gemini had stuttered too; how did I not notice?

"Why don't you stutter then?" I said, full of bitter fire.

She breathed deeply, her chest rising. Thank Lucifer for depression, I barely noticed. "That's because I'm not an angel, Mr. Sunstone. You should have learned that long ago. But, I guess it's never fully out of my nature, is it? That's what clued me in to the fact that they were angels. I never worked with Gemini, so never had close enough contact to pick up on the subtle clues. Having him and her in the chamber, my suspicions were raised almost immediately. Now, can we focus on why I'm here or would you prefer to verbally spar?"

I smiled at provoking her, even though the Founder remained composed. Shrugging and trying to appear equally contained, I said, "And what if I don't want to go?"

One corner of her mouth curled upward. "You will. Trust me."

I scoffed. "Sorry, I'm all out of trust. Check back in with me in a few weeks. I might get a new shipment."

Seraph rolled her bottom lip into her mouth, biting down on it. "I can't say that's not justified. One day, you may come to understand. Today is not that day. Today is the day for you to go to be lifted up, and apologies, but you need to go now. Time is running short."

"Yeah, I have other things I need to do. Sorry."

Seraph slapped her leg. "Do you want to see her Cassie or not?"

I stopped, connecting with those icy blue eyes. "Is she okay?"

Seraph nodded. "She escaped before Gemini's public ... event and is in the Overworld. She's been asking to see you. We have about," Seraph swung her head side to side, looking up, "an hour or two before this window of opportunity closes. So, either you go now, or you never see her again. Which will it be?"

"I'll go."

The Founder turned, waved her hand in a S–motion, and the rift formed in my living room, knocking over a plant on an end table. The room sizzled with energy.

"Hurry."

Not waiting for a follow-up, I stepped through the rift between the worlds. The light blinded me. I kept Creed ready as the vertigo swarmed, and I closed my eyes and hung on for the ride. Who knew what waited for me on the other side if Seraph was being truthful about any of this. A fool, I would no longer be. Dialphio had taught me better than that.

Seconds later, I was standing in the apartment in Kaiserslautern. Simultaneously, I was right and wrong about an ambush.

"Z-Zeke!" Cassie said, springing off the couch and running to me, her arms wide. We collided in a tangle of arms and ... bless it, did it feel good. "They really sent you!"

We hugged until she pulled back, dropping her arms quickly and looking sheepish.

"I'm sorry if I upset you over all of this. I can explain everything," she said.

Seraph said we only had a brief time together. I needed to hit the high points. "Is it true?"

"Is what true?"

I grimaced. "You know what I'm talking about. The Council accused you and Gemini of being angels. And," I breathed, trying to calm the advancing hurt and anger. It came through in my words even though I tried to keep it down. "Why in the heavens did you use me? I thought we … I thought we were friends. I helped you when I didn't have to. Why?"

Unbelievably, she winced. "I didn't use you! I wasn't completely honest with you, I'll admit that. But there were reasons, good reasons. If you felt used, I apologize, but that wasn't my intention. Not you."

"The heaven you didn't!"

Cassie turned away, walking behind the chair. "It's not that simple. I feel terrible about the way it all turned out and I hated manipulating you and Ralrek, but it was a necessity. Please, no matter what you think about me or what happened, you are a friend, Z-Zeke."

"Friends don't use their friends," I said matter-of-factly, feeling every inch of the moral high ground.

She took a big breath and her face twitched as if she was struggling with the biggest secret in the world. "You don't understand a lot of things that are going on. I would never use you. It wasn't like that for me. I truly like you. R—Ralrek too. You're both very good demons, kind souls. And I'm glad I got to know you. The plan wasn't for me to actually like the demons I was working with, trust me."

"Is that why you wanted to say goodbye, so you could feel better about abusing our friendship?"

"Don't be a jerk," she said, pressing down on the chair cushions from behind. Her voice softened. "Please, just … don't be like that. I don't want my last memory of you to be this."

"Who are you? Really, I mean. Who are you?"

Cassie's mouth opened, but nothing followed.

The true tragedy was that she never had time to answer me.

A hot sizzle came from the kitchen. From Cassie's expression, she hadn't expected the noise either. We turned and watched as a new rift formed in the room. As soon as it was wide enough to fit through, a figure jumped out. The demon was cloaked just as was the visitor who'd burned *The Histories of the Balance* for the Council. My hand went to Creed.

As soon as they were through the rift, they were casting. A wave of familiar scratchiness raked my skin.

"Down!" I shouted to Cassie, taking cover behind the television stand. She dropped to the floor behind the chair.

The figure paused for a fraction of a second, surprised at my warning. Even as they released their spell, Creed was in my hand and the blades clinked open, ready to ravage. And so was I.

This was the breaking point. Used and manipulated, hurt and rejected, scapegoated, I was no longer willing to be the toy of Hell's great leaders. The memory of Apopis's imperious sneer when he admitted that the Council played a role in this thug burning my treasured book came to mind as I darted around the television to get a better vantage point.

The cloaked assassin release a three–ball stream of fire at Cassie.

I sprinted forward only to trip over a cord laying on the floor when my eyes flashed with pain. Just like in the First Circle square. The crushing pressure at the base of my skull returned.

Blinded, I crashed into the half wall, my shoulder searing as it separated.

The roar of newborn fire meeting another magical force filled my ears. When I pried my eyes open, I couldn't see clearly. But I could see enough to pick out blue fire balls battering a shield of white.

I swallowed the lump in my throat, knowing what this all meant. Her inability to say my name without stuttering, the reason I was blinded and tripped. Confirmed, the blue-eyed beauty now battling Hell's assassin, was an angel.

I got my answer about Cassie after all, and I didn't know how I felt about it now that I had.

Abandoned by a few, made a second priority by others, being important to an angel was against everything I was supposed to understand and believe.

Yet, I could not deny what I felt. Cassie cared about me, and I cared about her. And she was now being attacked.

Fire scorched through the air as another assassin's spell flew from the kitchen, striking Cassie's white shield. Four feet in diameter, it was impressive, in size and duration. Whereas the assassin could only shoot fireballs every few seconds, Cassie's spell had lasted the entire fight.

Head down, she pushed toward the kitchen, toward the attacker. Her steps were short and slow, methodical and calculating. As she neared me, she glanced over.

I tried to not let my eyes fill with tears, but my body had its own ideas of what it wanted. My shoulder was burning hotter than the fire balls being thrown at the angel. Thankfully, Cassie was classy enough to not ridicule me. Her thin smile sprinkled joy on my fire. It asked for forgiveness, and I was only willing to give it.

"Are you okay?" I said through clenched teeth as I tried to sit up, pressing my back against the wall.

She nodded. "Are you?"

I wanted to tell her I was physically okay—even though my screaming shoulder would have argued differently. A fresh round of rough scratching sensations of fire magic signaled an oncoming attack.

"Be careful!" I said in warning, pushing my hand against my separated shoulder. Lucifer, it hurt.

Cassie squatted, holding her shield. Beads of sweat, which already dotted her forehead, swelled under the exertion of the spell as a thick stream of fire struck it. The assassin was ramping up the intensity, now knowing he was not fighting a minor angel. He swept the stream from side to side, catching the couch and wall, both of which began to burn.

The spell was cut off. Too early. They were not done; the scratching over my exposed skin warned me of that. This assassin had stamina.

Cassie lowered her shield and raced into the kitchen.

"No!" I shouted, sensing the assassin's tremendous spell.

The pressure at the back of my skull lessened. A sign that Cassie was weakening?

Even before I could contemplate the question, her shield slipped as she approached the final confrontation. The assassin had her right where they wanted her, weakened and aggressive, overconfident. If she wasn't careful—

I tried to pull myself to a standing position to peer into the next room. It was so hard to think or see clearly, with my immobile shoulder on fire. Every movement was jarring. I crept up the wall, each inch calculated to minimize the pain.

Before I got to my feet, the assassin released their spell. I didn't see it strike Cassie's shield, but I saw the aftermath.

She screamed as she flew through the doorway and into the living room, crashing against the far wall and cracking it. She slumped to the floor, her chin collapsing against her chest, her shield evaporated. Now she was vulnerable.

I was on my feet, using the top of the half wall separating the livingroom from the kitchen to support myself as I held my injured arm against my body. Creed was a halberd, making it useless now that I was down to a single arm. If Cassie was unconscious, or worse, the assassin could have their way with both of us. It was a fight that wouldn't last long. I had to do something. The angel may have lied and used me for some greater purpose, but just as with Gemini, she didn't deserve the Council's justice. It was in my hands to fix the balance the Council denied them.

"Come on," I growled at the weapon, holding it out in front of me in my right arm, "work a miracle."

I don't believe in miracles, but I needed every bit of help I could get. Cassie was in a crumpled heap against the far wall and I couldn't see if she was breathing. My head had cleared though, no longer filled with a stabbing knives from her angelic Abilities. I inched along the wall, trying to arc my neck out to create a wide angle that would allow me to see into the kitchen.

It worked.

The assassin was not giving away their location until a shuffling came from behind the refrigerator. That's when I noticed the lack of the scratching of a fire spell. Either the assassin was resting or trying to sucker me into the room as they did to Cassie.

"Who are you? What do you want?" I asked. There was no sense in trying to disguise my location, I was sure the assassin was aware and waiting for the moment to strike or flee.

"Just you, Sunstone." The voice. The same incubus who delivered the bag of ashes that used to be *The Histories*.

"Who sent you?"

"That doesn't matter."

He would not give up information easily, but I had to get something out of him to learn who was behind this. Friends and enemies, so difficult to distinguish sometimes.

"Who sent you? Tell me and I won't stop you from jumping through the rift."

The assassin guffawed, actually guffawed. I gripped Creed.

"You can't be serious, Sunstone. Please tell me you're not."

"Tell me and I won't hurt you."

"You're an impling. You couldn't hurt me on your best day."

I didn't want to have to prove him wrong, but he wasn't giving me much of a choice.

"They didn't tell you what I did to Taurus Hammerwulf, did they?" I waited and listened. The silence from the other room told me I had his attention. At least I wasn't recalling that traumatic incident for fun. "Funny thing; that wasn't even my best day."

Sandpaper on my skin signaled the readying of another round of dancing.

Oops, maybe the Council had told him.

And here I was with only one arm. Thankfully, it was my good one. I was ready, whether or not he knew that. When the fire crackled through the room, I had already slid further down the wall, moving back in the direction I'd came from. Now, I ran back to the corner, farther away.

Just in time, too. The assassin's fireball struck a few feet shy of where I'd been hiding, blasting a hole in drywall. Two more fireballs hit further down the wall as he searched me out. He was getting closer, and I was running out of time.

Under normal circumstances I would have spun Creed to create a movement shield—I'll come up with a better name for the move when my life isn't being threatened. I tried, but the length of the weapon and being restricted to a single arm made it impossible. I only had seconds to spare before another fireball would come my way, and I didn't have much fight left.

"Stop resisting, Sunstone. You've been an inconvenience for too long. Give up now. It'll be better that way. Do the right thing."

My right thing was surviving. But how to accomplish that with few options and an unconscious ally.

His energy refilled, the assassin began conjuring. Did he ever get tired?

"You're going to die, Sunstone," the assassin bragged.

"I'm well aware of that!" I shouted back, completely out of answers and hope. "You've served me well, my friend," I told Creed. As silly as that may sound to you mortals, it felt right at the moment.

I closed my eyes, gripping Creed's haft. The assassin released his spell. The last remaining part of the wall separating us exploded, showering the room with splinters of studs and drywall.

I clenched my teeth as he began another.

The Council was killing me after I gave everything to them, including my dignity. As the Segregate, I had little of that in the first place. I watched as they murdered Aries; I suffered a lifetime a shame for my parents; I followed questionable orders for coin, and I killed another demon—accident or not, that did not matter. I never wanted to be Hell's hero, but neither did I want to be its scapegoat.

My hand clamped Creed's haft, threatening to crush the petrified wood.

The scratching of the rough fire magic raked across my body, burrowing into my arms, my fingers, my neck. My face tingled with the thousands of pricks underneath my skin. This spell was going to be bigger than his last strike against Cassie. With good aim, the assassin would obliterate me and deprive me of the chance to say goodbye to those I cared for.

Harder, I squeezed.

Warmth, its radiance shooting through my hand. My arms. My chest shook with adrenaline. Power. Hunger. Rage. Pushing out the scratching.

Creed's blades burst into fiery blue steel, the hue of the Hellfire.

His spell finished, the crackle of newborn fire raged to life, setting every molecule of oxygen ablaze.

My grip was steel. Power surged through me, filled me.

My injured shoulder responded, popping back into the socket, flexing as if the injury hadn't occurred at all.

Uncontrollable power surged through me, cutting off my breath.

The assassin's fire stream bore down on me. I jumped to my feet and feasted on the power surging inside, thrusting Creed out. A blue light exploded from the double ax head and raced toward the fire stream.

The two spells collided inches away, Creed's blue swallowing the assassin's fire in a tsunami of energy, racing back toward his hiding spot as if it was following his stream.

I held Creed, screaming in rage, only half aware of the murderous act I was about to commit.

But I couldn't stop it. I didn't know what I'd done or how I'd done it, but Creed was not going to be denied. We were in the Overworld; if I didn't kill the assassin, he would kill me and Cassie. The blue beam swallowed the fire as it raced into the kitchen, past the obliterated wall. In the last seconds of his life, the assassin tried to dive for his open rift, his eyes wide.

Creed's blue stream struck true. The assassin collapsed, and he wasn't even flung back into the wall as he had done to Cassie. Instead, Creed obliterated our attacker, his body blasted apart into thousands of fragments like a dandelion's white seed plume blown by a wishful impling.

At his destruction, Creed's blue stream evaporated, and the ax heads cooled as blackness fell over my eyes.

I DON'T REMEMBER COLLAPSING, BUT THE NEXT THING I SAW WAS Cassie standing over me, smiling. It was a glorious sight.

"Oh, thank Yahweh you're okay," she beamed.

I tried to sit up.

"Be careful," she said as she helped.

I looked around the apartment. "The fire?" I said in a scratchy voice.

Cassie looked over her shoulder at the scorched couch and wall. "I put it out. Hopefully, it didn't do too much damage, but I don't imagine the Council will get the security deposit back on this one." Her laugh was light, as if nothing significant had happened.

I tried to sit up again. My head swam, but my shoulder no longer arched. A little stiff and tired, I was alive and smiling … until bile rose in my throat.

"Take it slow, Ze-Zeke," she said, there to steady me. "It'll take a while for you to get used to that type of magic. You can't push yourself."

I was holding my head, but took my hand away and opened my eyes to read her face. "Hey, talk to me about this whole not-being-able-to-say-demon's-names-thing. Is it true? And what's this talk of magic?"

She snorted. It was cute. "It's not easy, saying your names. As much as they make us work on it, you would think it would be easier. It's not, that's for sure."

I answered my own question on the second part—well, sort of. I had done something I didn't know was possible. Was Creed so powerful it could neutralize the handicap of being the Segregate? Visions of that blue light swallowing the assassin's fire spell and obliterating him flooded back.

I'd cast a spell. I actually cast a spell.

Cassie must have read the realization on my face. "Yes, that was all your magic. Well, you and that," she said, pointing at Creed, which lay parallel to my leg.

I reached down and picked it up, collapsing the blades. Once Creed was back to its truncheon size, I cradled it in both hands, staring at it, almost as if seeing it for the first time.

Cassie moved closer, placing a warm hand on my shoulder. She no longer smelled like the Second Circle. "It will take time, even decades, but you'll get used to it. Well, with regular practice. Plus," she stopped to snort-laugh again, "that was a pretty powerful spell you used. What made you choose that one?"

I rubbed my face that still tingled. "I don't even know what I did."

"I imagine it's overwhelming."

I squinted at her, noticing that she looked much healthier than I did. "How do you know so much about this?"

She smirked. "Do you really want the answer to that?"

"A few answers from you would be nice, yes. Like how you know about Creed, if Gemini is alive and are you two really a couple, why demons can say your names but you can't say ours and … well, that's an excellent start."

Cassie sat back on her feet, resting her hands on her thighs. "I don't have a lot of time to explain. Why you can say our names? No idea. I'm not that important. Gemini, yes, he's alive and home, thank Yahweh. That was a little too close for comfort. And as for Creed, my knowledge is limited to what we're taught. Honestly, there's probably someone in the Underworld who would be better to ask than me."

"You missed one."

"I did?"

I smirked like a goofball. "You didn't say if you were a couple or not."

"We're not," she smiled, her nose twitching. "That was all part of the act." She shrugged apologetically. "Sorry about that."

I moved on quickly, distracted by wondering if that meant she was single. "I can't ask anyone. I don't trust many back there."

"Maybe you should try?"

"You could help."

"How?"

I shrugged. My head was clearing. "Was this all a ploy by

you and Gemini? What was the point of it? I mean, tons of demons died."

"They almost killed him."

My head dipped, forcing the point. "Yes, because he was an angel who invaded Hell."

"Invaded," she said quietly, sitting back on her haunches and looking away. "Hardly an invasion with two angels."

"You?" The thought seized my mind. Cassie was the architect of the attack on the First? All those killed, at the hands of a single angel? "You did that?"

"The square?" she said with a huff. "Are you kidding? I'm good, but not that good. No, that was an entire squad." The edge vanished from her voice. "And some never made it out."

"I still don't understand why."

"We are spies, Z-Zeke. Well, we were. It's not like Heaven can use us again. Not for that."

"Spies? You send spies to Hell?" The heat was being ignited again. This was an act of war. Above her pay-grade or not, that did not matter.

"You do it too."

"We send demons to Heaven to spy?" I barked in disbelief. "That's ridiculous."

"Ridiculous to you or not, it's true," she said, resting a hand on my knee. "Both sides do it, Z-Zeke. No one is innocent. No one is free from blame." Suddenly, she was on her feet. "I have to go very soon. I was hoping we would have more time."

"Time for what?"

"To explain everything," Cassie said.

"Then stay longer."

A shadow passed over her face. "I can't. I have to go." She backed away. "I wanted to make sure you were okay before I went."

"Wait," I said, urging her to pause. "You ... you owe me

this. How did I cast? I'm the Segregate. I don't ..." my voice lowered, "I don't have any Abilities."

She shook her head, before she clapped her hands in straight arms in front of her. It was a sharp sound, one that made my ears ring.

A white rift sparkled in the air next to her. Instead of sizzling, like rifts were supposed to, this one filled the room with a low tinkling, as if a dozen wind chimes swayed in the breeze.

Cassie stepped toward it, pausing. "Ez-Ezekial, you don't know how special you are. But know this. It's no longer a big deal that you're the only demon without magic; that entire Segregate thing is useless, just something to keep you doubting yourself. Your true nature. You never were a Segregate. You just didn't know it."

My head spun. "What? Nevermind. How, Cassie? How did I cast a spell?" The threat of tears prickled my eyes. I had to get this answer before this wonder angel disappeared from my life forever.

Answers. From an angel. An immortal enemy.

"It's because of Creed."

"Creed?"

She nodded, her face dragging down. "You've been able to cast ever since Aries gave to you what was always yours."

"What kind of magic?"

Cassie shrugged, one foot through the angelic rift. "Any kind."

Any kind of magic?

She was almost gone.

"Wait! How does it allow me to do that?"

Half her body was through, a white glow distorting her features. "Because ... Creed was fashioned by One."

With that, the angel stepped into the rift and it blinked out, leaving me sitting on the floor of an apartment in the Overworld wondering what in the heaven just happened.

20

UNDERWORLD, FIFTH CIRCLE

DIALPHIO DROPPED her gaze from me to the paper in her hands and read the note again.

I wrote it out because to speak the words might draw the attention of the Council. The last thing I wanted right now—or ever again—was any of their focus. Thankfully, they were no longer a concern, having privately but officially dropped all charges against Ralrek and me, giving us our freedom once more. No, I did not expect it to last, not with the way Apopis glared like he was seconds away from snatching me and swallowing me whole. Instead, he sent thugs to harass my parents into staying away from me.

I missed them, especially Mother, but I wanted them to be safe, so I made do with hiring merlins to deliver letters to them. It was expensive, but the coin I earned from the Gemini mission allowed me to send as many as I wanted.

I would not forget what Apopis was doing, though. One day, he would get his.

When she finished, she didn't react like I thought she would. My boss hadn't been exposed to any of the crap that happened to me over the past few weeks, like false charges, threats, and imprisonment—oh yeah, and an assassination attempt—and only knew of the players in this game through my testimony.

"My ability is Constructive so I'll give this back to you since I can't torch it with a Fire spell," she chirped, not sounding humored in the least. She shouldn't be. "I don't imagine that needs to be anywhere but with you until you destroy it."

"You don't seem surprised." I watched her carefully.

"I'm not," she shrugged.

"Why?" The question sounded harsher than I intended but I was tired. So very tired.

To her credit, Dialphio was more level-headed. "I want to show you something I found."

"Okay."

When she disappeared behind the stacks of books forming the wall that separated our desks from the customer area, the door chimed. I was so out of rhythm because of my disjointed work history that I forgot the greeting Dialphio wanted me to use.

Thankfully, the customer was someone who would forgive my poor service.

"Bilba!"

"Hey Zeke." He beamed, in such a hurry to get to me he let the door slam closed.

"Careful with that, please," Dialphio called out from behind the book wall.

"Sorry," Bilba said while throwing his arms around me and lifting me off the ground.

We laughed. And then I realized how awkward it was to be hugged by him, not only because he was strong enough to lift me off the floor, but that he didn't have to do so over his stout belly.

When he set me down, I backed away. "What the heaven happened to you? Where did all of this go?" I poked his now-firmer belly. It was squishy, but about half the volume of the last time I saw him. The weight loss wasn't restricted to just his stomach either. His arms were firmer, and his face looked healthy for the first time since we were imps. His cheekbones had definition and shape.

"What's this noise about?" Dialphio came from around the book wall, tucking something in her pocket. Her eyes widened at the sight. She hugged him. "Bilba, it's so good to see you. Are you home for good?"

She asked the question I needed an answer to but hadn't had the chance to ask.

When he nodded, I felt the weight of a hundred lifetimes lift from my back. Bilba home. Suddenly, everything felt right in the Fifth. As much as I adored Dialphio, even if I wasn't worried about being betrayed by her, she wasn't enough. Bilba was. He was my balance. He was safe. Maybe I could finally break up with vodka.

"Man, I'm so glad to hear that," I said. This time I initiated the hug. "And even better that you'll be around finally."

"Yes, he'll need a drinking buddy," Dialphio said in a teasing voice that also included a mother's disapproving tone for good measure. "It's sad when a young demon with promise drinks alone so often."

Lucifer-damned perceptive, that one.

Bilba threw his arm around my shoulder, facing the most wonderful business owner in all the Underworld. "Don't worry, ma'am, I'll take care of him."

"See that you do," she said with an unyielding look. "Well, I'll leave you two to whatever it is young incubi discuss. Lucifer knows neither of you will simply admit to missing each other and getting that out of the way. It was nice seeing you again, Bilba. Be sure to come back from time to time and pick up a book. Just." Dialphio raised a finger. "If you're going to *borrow* anything, please return it in one piece instead of ashes."

"Ashes?" Bilba asked, dropping his arm, but she was already rounding the corner to her desk.

"I'll let Ezekial explain *that*," she called.

Bilba looked at me like he'd just forgotten my name.

"It's a long story," I answered. "I'll catch you up later, when you've settled in. Maybe we can go out for a drink and food? I haven't done that since before we went to the Second Circle together."

"Really?" His disbelief seemed genuine. "What have you been doing?"

"That's a long story too."

Bilba smiled the all-knowing smile that close friends shared. "I can't wait to talk."

"So," I said, trying to shift things before we inadvertently stepped into Council business, "what's up with your mother. Did you reconcile?"

For the first time, Bilba's face dropped.

"Oh," I said, softening my voice, "it didn't go well?"

"Um, it's just that ... well," Bilba smiled sadly.

"We really need to have a drink," I said, offering the way out incubi usually needed because admitting vulnerabilities wasn't in our nature—or had been programmed out. Either way, we'd address it in a typical round-about manner, just when we had faces full of bland Underworld food.

"We do, buddy," Bilba said in agreement and grabbed my shoulder in a meaty paw. "And let's do it soon. When are you getting off?"

"I'm closing," I said, and added before he asked, "and I can't ask her to let me sneak out. I haven't been much help to her lately, and I don't want to take advantage of the situation."

If he was disappointed, he didn't show it. "No worries. Let's do something tomorrow? I've got to get back to my father, anyway; I left him to fend for himself and we need some bonding time."

"Not happy about you staying in the Second?"

Bilba thought about his answer before replying. "It's not that. He's okay with it, even said he understands why I needed to have that time with her. I think he's still hurt, hasn't gotten over her leaving. But him and I are okay."

"I'm glad to hear that, bud. I really am. If you need anything tonight, just say the word. But it's going to be great catching up with you. I've … missed having you around."

He nodded. "Same. And I will, I promise. But hey," he said with a snort and clapped his hands, "I'm excited to hear what you've been up to. It's been eventful. Dad even talked about you."

We were getting close to a topic near and dear to the Council's spies and eavesdroppers, so I cut him off. Best friend or not, or *because* he was a friend, discussing this in the open wouldn't happen, not until I was sure who to trust.

"Well, look," I said, "I want to hear everything and tell you about my latest adventure, but let's do that when we can enjoy ourselves." I raised my voice even though I didn't need to. "No offense, Dialphio, I love being here."

"None taken," the nosy bookstore owner responded too quickly to hide the fact that she had been listening.

Both me and Bilba cracked a laugh. She chirped from behind the book wall. Life was good again.

"Okay, tomorrow then?" I said.

"Tomorrow," Bilba agreed, and we hugged each other one more time.

I watched him go, not going back to work until the door slammed—he was a slow learner in some respects—and he was gone.

Dialphio joined me. "He's a good incubus, even if he doesn't know how to close doors."

"He is."

"Keep that one close," she said.

"I will."

"I mean it," she said, and she did.

Dialphio would never betray me. She cared about me for *my* sake. Not for family pride—hers was broken worse than mine, and she did not have a Founder to blame it on—or the Balance; not for what she could get out of me or what I could do for her; nor for who I was or wasn't. Dialphio cared because she cared. Sometimes it was as simple as that.

I grabbed her hand and squeezed. "I know. And thank you."

She looked at me with a hint of genuine curiosity in her eyes. "For what?"

"Everything."

Dialphio grabbed my other hand. We faced each other. "There's something about you, Zeke. I doubt you see it. I'm confident you don't. But it's there, inside you, burning to come out. Something that goes beyond your upbringing or the demons you surround yourself with. The Segregate? It means nothing unless you let it. You are your own demon. A curse from Lucifer Himself if you ask me. Embrace it. You're a good demon and deserve to be treated kindly. I will always be here for you, as will a few others. Just," she paused to squeeze my hands, bouncing them up and down, "let us help you."

"What do you mean?"

"You can't do everything yourself and you can choose to believe that until the Hellfire fades," Dialphio said, "but you'll burn out before it does. Be careful who you trust, but trust in those you can."

I laughed, trying to keep the bitterness from my voice. "I've tried, and I got burned. What's that they say about fooling me once, shame on you; fool me twice, and I'm a minotaur's ass?"

Her squeeze intensified. "That's what I'm talking about, right there. Let them be part of your journey. Walking alone won't serve you well. One day, you'll understand, but for now I want you to trust me on this; others want to help. They already have. I'm here. Bilba is too. Ralrek even." We shared a laugh. Her voice lowered, turning serious. "Let us in."

How could I let go with the world spinning out of control?

I squeezed her hands. "I'll think about it, I promise. But I'm sorry. You don't get it. You haven't been there and don't know what it's like to have demons lie to you all the time."

She raised a disapproving eyebrow. "You'd do well to not assume the experience of others, Ezekial. And stop with the hyperbole; it doesn't suit someone of your status. Some demons have been truthful with you. Maybe too truthful, so much that you missed the signs. You have been blinded by your distrust and have missed the message. The truth."

And she was right. Demons cared, and I was not in this on my own. I needed to wake up to the fact that others suffered as well. I needed to wake up to the fact that I needed them.

I was going to keep Bilba close. Ralrek too. I was done taking crap from the Council, done being pulled and shoved and positioned where they needed me. I was done feeling guilty about Taurus and how much I drank. I would never forget Aries, but my guilt over his death would no longer cripple me.

I just needed to clean the slate.

Dialphio released my hands and reached into her pocket, pulling out a parchment. She handed it to me.

"What is this?" I said, unrolling and reading it. It was gibberish; the characters weren't letters more than they were designs of disorganization; no rhyme or reason to their pattern.

"It's a guide, used for deciphering."

"Deciphering what?" I asked, my eyes finding Dialphio's.

"The language of One," she replied with a twinkle in her eyes. "I've had that hidden because it's a treasure someone would need one day. I just didn't think it would be me. I'm glad I still had it when you came into my life."

I swallowed the massive lump in my throat. "Me? Why?"

"Remember when I saw Creed, that inscription?"

"Of course."

"Well, there is more I was holding back until I could be sure."

"You lied?" Did we not just talk about letting demons in?

Dialphio touched my arm, holding it like she was grounding herself to me. After a moment, she loosened her grip and patted me affectionately. "The language of One is old, yes. Older than Fa'Hersei, though."

One. There was that name again. Cassie was the last one to speak about it to me. The Council never brought it up. My parents never mentioned the name. Even Bilba and his photographic memory were silent about the name.

"How old?"

"This language," Dialphio said, her eyes never wavered. Their intensity pulled me in. Tension pressed on my chest. "Is the language of One."

"Who is One?" My throat squeezed.

"Not who," Dialphio corrected. "But what. Please forgive me, Ezekial. I never wanted to hold information back, and would not have if it wasn't absolutely necessary."

"What does this mean, Dialphio. Please? Be straight with me."

Her face scrunched, as if she was second-guessing whether or not she wanted to say anything.

"Please." My voice croaked.

"I needed to be sure. What Cassie told you about Creed was the truth. You own, by right, the weapon of One, the creator of all."

"All? Like … everything."

She nodded.

"Even Lucifer? Yahweh? The earth? Solar system? The universe?"

Dialphio chirped. "And beyond. Do you really not understand what the word 'all' means?"

I swallowed, my eyes locked on hers. "But ... why?"

Dialphio shrugged, turning away to organize a stack of new arrivals. "Maybe Aries was talking about more than just that cursed halberd when he gave it to you? Either way," she said with a teasing smile, "it looks like you have some exciting times ahead."

THE END

WHAT'S NEXT?

The weapon of One? The creator of all? What has Zeke stumbled into? Or is he being pushed?

Keep reading The Zodiac series to find out.

Pick up book 4, Cancer's Curse, today!

REVIEWS HELP

If you enjoyed this book, I would appreciate your review.

Your time is valuable, but reviews not only help other readers find something they might like, but they help me as an author. They are important to me because they allow me to see what readers like you enjoyed about the book and what I could have done better.

Thank you to every one of you who takes the time to leave a review!

DON'T MISS OUT!

Get the latest news, special deals, exclusive stories, first looks at book covers, and more by signing up for Paul Sating's newsletter!

Sign up for Paul's newsletter to follow all the news and special deals for upcoming novels, and to catch up on the latest regarding his podcast at http://www.paulsating.com.

EXCLUSIVE STORIES AND CONTENT

More stories on-the-go! Get exclusive access to Paul Sating's
fiction, including free audio books, in podcast form!

Get more stories each month by becoming a Patron! New
exclusive fiction each month!

Become a Patron & enjoy more content!

ALSO BY PAUL SATING

Fiction

Fantasy

The Zodiac Series

The Fall of Aries (Free for newsletter subscribers)

Bitter Aries

The Horn of Taurus

The Gemini Paradox

Cancer's Curse

The Pride of Leo

Virgo's Vigilantes

Libra's Liberation (2022)

Battleborn Series

Battleborbn Trilogy

Fireborn (Coming 2022)

Rageborn (Coming 2022)

Battleborn (Coming 2022)

BoneBreaker Trilogy

King of Bones (Coming 2022)

War of Bones (Coming 2022)

Breaker of Bones (Coming 2022)

Crown of Thieves

Birth of a Thief (Free for newsletter subscribers)

Horror

The Scales

12 Deaths of Christmas

The Plant (Free for newsletter subscribers)

Suspense

RIP

Chasing the Demon

Nonfiction

Novel Idea to Podcast: How to Sell More Books Through Podcasting

Podcasts

Audio Fiction with Paul Sating

(Free for Patreon supporters!)

Urban Fantasy Author Podcast

(Available on all major podcast apps)

ACKNOWLEDGMENTS

This book would not have been possible if it was not for some amazing people. People who I am eternally grateful to have in my life.

Always, my wife, Maddie. No joke, every author needs support of the type I get from her. What an amazing 'curse' of Lucifer! She is the sacrificial lamb who is forced to read all the first drafts of these books, and let me tell you, it is such a sacrifice. She does that, she gives me her thoughts, she suffers through the rough copy, and even feeds me treats when I write something clever. You all just don't understand how tickled I make myself with some of the stupid lines I come up with. She has the patience of a saint, she really does.

My daughters are always so excited whenever I release a new book. To me, building a legacy is an important thing. We all only ride on this dustball flying through space for a finite time, and the only thing that lives on is what we leave behind in the minds and hearts of those we've touched. With each book, I'm able to leave behind one more thing for them to remember me by, to tell my future grandchildren I might have, about me, and to maybe even be proud of me.

Kevin Baker has stood by me for years and helped push me to not quitting on myself. For too many years after high school, we lost touch, and we only came into each other's lives after life and the military separated us for far too long. He's a gem. I love the man—even with all the strange and inappropriate videos he sends.

Erica Stensrud has consumed my stories for far longer than any mortal should have to. Not only does she fake it really well when claiming she enjoys my stories, but she encourages me to make more! An absolute glutton for punishment, I cannot express how much I appreciate her.

Adam Burke, a warrior in the truest sense of the world; there reason why I've already written one character based on him, and have an entire future trilogy's character who will be modeled on Adam's personality.

Straight shooters are always people I can get along with, and my British brother Louis Jackson is definitely that. This man has stood by my side for a number of years, and I still cannot scare him away. He's one stubborn incubus. And I would not have it any other way.

And no acknowledgments would be complete without the amazing group of authors and writers in the *Horrible Writing Writers Support Group* on Facebook, and the Mastermind that spun off that group. From this collective, I have learned so much, about writing, about publishing and audio books, and about myself.

I am eternally grateful for every single one of these people. They make me the author I am today. They make a the better person.

And, as always, I don't write these books because they're good for my health—they're not; I stress a lot. But that's because I care about what happens on the other side of the pages. The journey I take readers on is *the* priority for me. Zeke's adventures would not consume my life the way they did if no one cared to read them. If you're holding this in your hands right now, I have dispatched a merlin your way and it is carrying my eternal gratitude. Thank you for making sure I never walk alone.

.

ABOUT THE AUTHOR

Paul Sating is an author, podcaster, and self-professed coolest dad on the planet, hailing from the Pacific Northwest of the United States. At the end of his military career, he decided to reconnect with his first love (that wouldn't get him in trouble with his wife) and once again picked up the pen. Years on, he has published eight novels and he hasn't even screwed up his podcasts, which have garnered over a million downloads.

When he's not working on stories, you can find him talking to himself in his backyard working on failed landscaping projects or hiking around the gorgeous Olympic Peninsula. He is married to the patient and wonderful, Madeline, and has two daughters—thus the reason for his follicle challenges.

Find out more about his other books and free podcasts from his website: www.paulsating.com.

CONTACT PAUL

How to Contact Paul Sating

Published by Paul Sating Productions
    P.O. Box 15166
    Tumwater, WA 98511
    paul@paulsating.com

Follow Paul:
    Facebook: www.facebook.com/authorpaulsating
    Bookbub: bookbub.com/paul-sating
    Goodreads:
goodreads.com/author/show/16982359.Paul_Sating
    Instagram: @paulsating
    Pinterest: pinterest.com/paulsating
    Twitter: @paulsating

FROM BOOK 4 OF THE ZODIAC SERIES

"CANCER'S CURSE"

(Click Here To Order Your Copy)

Underworld, Fifth Circle
One Year After Gemini

Bless it, it was hot.

Yes, I know you mortals have this general perception of Hell being all about Hellfire and brimstone, and it is. Well, sort of. But the Underworld—or Hell, as I prefer to call it because it's simply so much easier to say—is much more than trite stereotypes.

We have the Hellfire—it's blue, by the way—and brimstone—which is all our streets seem to be made of—but we also have oceans, lakes, prairies, cities, city parks, old towns, new towns, dancing and bar districts, and even walking trails and coffee shops for all the old demons to do old demon things in and around.

When you boil—get it?—it all down, Hell is a lot like the human world. I should know; I've been there twice and consider myself an expert in my circles, though my circles extend to just two other incubi, my boss, and my parents.

My point is, Hell is similar to the Overworld and, today, here in the Fifth Circle, it was hot.

Like, suffocatingly hot.

Though that might have something to do with me standing in the middle of a pack of demons in the height of the day, smack-dab in the center of the Samhain carnival.

Bless it, today was hot.

The one difference I guess I would have to recognize if I'm being honest, is that Hell doesn't have seasons. As I learned from my time in the Overworld, those are common for mortals. Here, not so much. Not at all, actually.

There are no seasons because—axial tilt aside—the Hell-fire, our version of your sun, misses the mark. We get our light and sense of passing time from it, when the Grand Chamber is opened and closed each day. Callers, magical purple creatures, ensure the Underworld's residents who do not live near clock towers start their days on-time, even before the blue light escapes. Life here is a well-oiled machine. Day-in and day-out, each one is the same as the previous, identical to the next.

Don't feel for us; it's our reality, our truth. The vast majority of demons don't know any better. I like the predictability of life here. To most demons it's one less thing to worry ourselves about, one less distraction from serving Lucifer and His grand plan. At least for typical demons—which I am not.

The only thing I was serving right now was my face. With corn dogs, cotton candy, and deep-fried hamburgers.

"Wipe your face," Ralrek said, flicking a finger at the corner of my mouth. "You're wearing more food than you're eating."

Placing the crock of my elbow against my mouth, I watched his face twist in disgust before yanking my sleeve across and away. "Better?"

He looked away. "You're gross."

Bilba, my best friend, laughed at the observation, covering his much-slimmer stomach with both hands, decorated with his typical black fingernail polish.

"But my mouth is clean."

Bilba laughed harder, the tips of his ears turning pink.

My argument game was solid. Ralrek didn't bother to argue. Such was the newfound healthy status of our relationship.

The only time I now saw the pair was on social occasions like this. I still had my job at The Book Abyss, working for that slave-driver Dialphio, but in the past year, none of us had received any work from Lucifer's Third Council. That lack of work deprived us of those moments of intensity that usually led to us fighting or getting at each other's throats. Things were much more peaceful now, so I had to antagonize him somehow. Can't have life becoming boring now, can we?

"Which one do you want to ride next?" Bilba was in front, leading the way through the crowd of demons hanging around gaming booths, standing in ridiculously lengthy lines for a ride, those waiting to lose coin in one of the rip-off schemes otherwise known as carnival games.

It was the opening night of Samhain, the annual carnival celebrating our liberation from Yahweh's reign of terror. Now, now; don't get offended until you've walked a mile in our shoes. None of us were there at the beginning and we can't be sure what went down between the two behemoths that control the fates of immortal and mortal alike—well, I used to think that until Dialphio educated me on One, but that story is for another time. For now, it was about Lucifer and his escape from Yahweh; the Fall according to angels and any mortals who believed them. It's a very festive time for us.

I love Samhain. Not only is it our biggest holiday, it is also the most lavish and most revered. Literally everything except the Hellfire factories and retail outlets—because demons just cannot imagine a shopping-less day—close for a few days before and after Samhain. So revered is it that we fill hours of our free time with conversations about the stories of how mortals have blasphemed our holiday by culturally appropriating it, dressing their kids up in costumes to "scare off evil."

Mortal ignorance can hurt sometimes.

But we don't let it dampen our festive season, keeping those chats restricted to nights, when demons have finished a day of celebrating, overeating, and spending time with family. It's in those times, at night, when the implings are in bed, and exhausted parents are trying to catch their breath, that the childless and more liberated sit around, sharing drinks and other pleasures of the imbibing type, along with opinions of what mortals have done to our most sacred period. Outside that, Samhain is all about the celebration of demonhood.

And the holiday's high point is the carnival. A time for unadulterated fun. Which was exactly what the three of us were doing now, with Bilba leading the way.

"I swear, every year, you turn into an impling," Ralrek said at Bilba's back, because Bilba slowed for no one when it came to fitting in as many rides as possible on a day ticket.

"We've only been on twenty-two rides!" he replied without looking over his shoulder. "And it's getting late."

Ralrek and I shared a look. "It's early. There's plenty of time," I said. "You're going to trample a little one."

"Then they need to stay out of my way," Bilba laughed. I didn't think he was joking.

I grabbed for his shirt, which was a feat. Bilba moved through the crowd with a ride-inspired grace completely unbecoming of him and his typical abilities. It was adorable. But annoying. His newfound sprite came from dropping some seriously unhealthy weight he carried for thousands of years while he was in the Eighth Circle trying to force his truant mother to love him. Though he wasn't fit by our health department standards, he was getting healthier every day and gaining some agility, which would be great in a fight, not so great when we were packed in clump of bodies at the Samhain celebration.

"Slow down," I said after missing my swipe at his shirt. "Seriously. This is supposed to be fun and, in case you hadn't heard, sweating is not fun."

Bilba finally pulled up, glancing around.

"What are you looking for?"

"A clock tower," he said, his eyes never finding mine. "I need to know what time it is."

"Why?"

"Zeke, we haven't broken even yet." His tone was flat, uninterested in carrying on a conversation that would hinder him reaching his goals.

Bilba had this principle of frugality. It came from being raised in a single-income home since his mother abandoned their family half a lifetime ago. He'd always been cheap, but that personality quirk was exasperated by her absence, even after he started working for the Council and getting fat paydays every time we'd finished a job. Being cheap meant managing his coin carefully and one way he did that was to calculate how much a ticket cost per ride ridden. The standard was variable—I never bothered asking why—depending on his mood, but each year he let us know what an acceptable rate was. This year's rate was three coppers, a higher-than-normal-Bilba-rate, and we were currently averaging nearly double that. All that meant we had serious riding ahead of us before he allowed us to slow.

The things you do for friends.

"We're not implings," I countered. "We can stay out all night until they close for cleanup if we want to."

"Can't take that chance," Bilba said, turning to dash through the crowd.

"When we catch him, I'm going to kill him," Ralrek said,

bringing a hand up to his perfect oil-black hair and smoothing one side that didn't need to be smoothed.

"I would too, but I feel bad for him." I mirrored Ralrek's hair-fixing, tussling my shaggy cut. He didn't notice the subtle jibe.

"Why? He's the dumbass that blew everything he'd earned."

Ralrek and I never had the healthiest of relationships. In fact, it wasn't until we were forced to work together by the Council that we spoke more than a sentence or two whenever we had the distinct displeasure of crossing each other's paths. That changed, slowly, after our first mission to the Overworld to capture an ancient demon called Aries the First. Ralrek teamed with Beelzebub and Bilba to kill him instead, and our relationship suffered as a consequence. During our last mission I discovered his secret, one he'd only recently shared with Bilba, that he was into mortals. By sheer luck, I earned Ralrek's trust enough that I could now chastise him for his insensitivity without setting off a round of verbal sparring. But only after I earned his trust enough to believe that he was not the one who stole and burned The Histories of the Balance, only the most important book in my world, in the middle of our Gemini adventure.

In the year since, we'd grown enough that I considered him a friend.

"Don't give him crap about that, okay? He finally found her and wanted to help because, be honest, you've both earned a lot of coin from the Council. How was he supposed to guess that it would dry up so quickly, especially after he spent it all trying to help his mother's stupid flower shop stay open?"

If any comment was coming, Ralrek bit it off, which was nice. The old Ralrek would have loosed it, regardless of the pain it would have caused. The improved version of this tall, handsome demon at least considered the cost of being an ass before proving himself so. It was refreshing, even if I was still skeptical of its viability.

We caught up with Bilba at the end of the line to the most popular roller coaster called Heaven's Gate, the scariest ride at the carnival. White beams of steel twisted and turned in waves and loops, arcing high into the Hellfire blue sky. Just as we joined him, a cart carrying a dozen screaming demons corkscrewed over our heads, thrusting them into a tunnel of blinding white light.

"I love this one," Bilba said once the cart passed and we could hear again. Another cranked up the long climb, about ready to release another screaming torrent of pleased passengers. I swallowed. He laughed. "What's the problem, Zeke? Not ready for this?"

"Since when did I like roller coasters?" The beams rattled above us as the cart had completed its climb and was loosed, the momentum sending it spiraling down. The memory of the last time I felt that drop was immediate, and I felt myself dropping along with the actual occupants of the cart racing toward the first loop.

"You've done more dangerous things than this," Bilba said, turning to watch the new cart carry its occupants up and around. "This should be nothing."

"Well, it is something, and it's something I don't like," I said, pointing as the cart shot out of the massive loop, jettisoning into the first of a series of corkscrew turns. "There is no control when you're trapped in those blessed things. Honestly, I don't understand how more demons don't die on them every year."

"Physics," Ralrek answered. "But seriously, Zeke. It's just a roller coaster." He moved closer, lowering his voice. "You've faced scarier things before. This is nothing. Plus, you can cast some freaking amazing spells now. Just magic yourself out of any trouble."

Wagging my finger at Ralrek, I looked around, making

sure no one was listening, not that we could be heard over the rumble of the cart racing around the coaster even as another one was cranking its way up the initial climb. The crowd of excited demons in front and behind us appeared to be more fascinated by their impending death at the hands of this mechanism than our conversation. "I have control, well, sort of, over the things I have faced. At least how I responded to them. That, I don't." My finger found the speeding cart zipping over our heads, filled with petrified faces, distracting me from thinking about my new Abilities, thanks to the ancient halberd. "If I could use Creed's power, which I control, on that coaster, I would. If nothing else, it would make me feel a little better about this."

"Well, I'm glad you can't, because you have no control over your new Abilities," Bilba said.

"They're not new," I countered. "It's been a year."

"Ohhhh, an entire year," Ralrek said, Bilba joining him in laughing at my infantile skills.

When you're thousands of years old, a single year is hardly impressive. But when those years were lived as the only demon in Hell's history without magical Abilities, a year of possessing them was significant no matter how it was sliced. I just tried to ignore the fact that sometimes Creed seemed to have a mind of its own, altering spells even as I was in mid-conjure. If the weapon was sentient, I'd swear it was screwing with me.

The coaster line inched forward. Just like mortal males act when they're together, incubi don't like holding long conversations. Any situation that forces us to talk about things that don't involve movies, sports, or succubi aren't enjoyable. It was only a matter of time before someone said something stupid. Thankfully, it wasn't me.

"Do you think we're actually being punished?" Bilba broke the silence between the three of us.

"Punished? For what?" Ralrek said while I tried to ignore the conversation as the roller coaster's disembarking passengers taunted me with their smiles and yelps of joy. Liars, all of them.

Bilba sighed. It was heavy and a little too dramatic for a carnival atmostphere. "For what happened with Gemini." He turned away from looking forward to address the cyclops in the room we'd avoided for the past year.

Neither Ralrek nor I wanted to dive back into that piece of history. It was behind us and had been for a year. The memories of that entire situation, however, were as fresh as if it happened yesterday. With only the slight prompt from Bilba, the brightness of the Angelfire attack that killed hundreds of demons at Gemini's execution ceremony flashed through my mind. The burned air, the death cries. All of it, raw, simply from Bilba mentioning Gemini's name. For me, there was no mystery why this particular cyclops went ignored.

"We didn't do anything wrong," I finally answered Bilba.

"I didn't say you did," Bilba said, sounding hurt. "What I meant was, if you look at the facts, the Council has ignored us since they absolved you and Ralrek of any wrongdoing. A year, and ever since that incident, how many assignments have you gotten, Ralrek?"

He shrugged. "None."

"Zeke?"

"Zilch."

Bilba rolled his hands as if our answers proved his point. "See?"

"No."

"No," I echoed Ralrek. "And I'm in no big hurry to either," I said, dipping my head and giving Bilba that look. You know, the one that tells your friend he should know better than to tread on soft hearts.

He knew the story, knew that Ralrek and I had been

arrested for a crime we did not commit and that we likely would have been executed right after Gemini had angels not attacked to save their own. He knew, because I often ranted about it, that I was not interested in ever seeing the Council or their paychecks again.

Bilba sighed, his shoulders dropping. "All that stuff went down with Gemini. Angels killing hundreds to rescue him. And in the past year, what has happened? Nothing. That's what. They haven't retracted anything they said about you guys and sure as heaven didn't apologize to you for what they did, did they?"

We shook our heads simultaneously.

"Not that I'd take a coin from them, of course," Bilba said with a sour expression before looking at us from the corner of his eyes. "When was the last time anyone on the Council reached out to check on us?"

Ralrek grunted. "Lucifer's Council is a little busy for that."

"Zeke? What about you? After all, you're the one who started this. The Council recruited you. Ralrek and I are just your support team, but you're the one they wanted in the first place and you have always had an interesting relationship with them. Have any of them come to you?"

I didn't have to think about it. "No."

Bilba was silent for a few short roller-coaster shuffles forward. A weight pressed heavily, I could tell.

"What is it?" I asked.

He opened his mouth before snapping it shut again and half-spinning to face the front of the line.

Life was better without the Council in it. I guess that comes from wasting away in a prison cell with Ralrek. Bilba would understand if he'd been sitting on that damp floor, chained to a wall, waiting to face fate. He was trying to; I knew that, but because he did not live through it, he would never fully understand what it was like.

"Aren't you guys ... don't you feel, I don't know ... rejected ... from time to time," he said. His voice was lacking any conviction, and I felt pained for him. His had been a unique experience to ours. And his sense of rejection was coming from some place deep, as deep or worse than the rejection being labeled Hell's Segregate used to have on me. Bilba's pain came in the shape of a middle-aged succubus who owned a flower shop in the Eighth Circle and forgot to love her son.

Mine was just a label that meant far less to me today than it did a year ago, thanks to an angel, the mortal enemy.

Man, I did not want to think about Cassie again.

"I mean, I think about it from time to time," Ralrek said, interrupting my thoughts of the cocoa haired angel, "but I'm not addicted to it. There's enough other stuff to deal with."

"I ... I've been having a hard time with finding work and without their assignments, my confidence is sort of shaken. I think that's, in part, why I wonder why the Council is shunning us? To me, what's more important?"

"Torlan," Ralrek said in a way that sounded like a slip.

"Who?" I said, turning fully on him. There was something in his voice and the way he bit the corner of his lip that made me smile. "A boyfriend? You hellhound."

Ralrek smirked as I punched him in the shoulder.

"How long?"

"A few weeks," Ralrek dipped his head toward his raised shoulder.

"And why haven't we met him yet?" I said, narrowing my eyes.

Weird how quickly things change. A year and a half ago, I wouldn't have cared who was involved in Ralrek's lonely life. Now, being the first to learn of his secret, things had changed drastically. Behind that off-putting tall and handsome exterior hid a nice demon who had a personality and was actually vulnerable.

"I'm not sure I'm ready for that," Ralrek said, his eyes flickering at Bilba. "But at least this one is an immortal creature."

Subtle clues rarely get my attention, but this time I noticed Bilba hadn't said anything. He stood in our small circle, unresponsive, his face unreadable. The awkwardness was palpable.

I coughed, drawing Ralrek's whitening face in my direction. "Well, when you are, I'll be excited to meet him."

"Thanks, Zeke," Ralrek said. "That means a lot."

Another cart rattled overhead, reminding me I was standing in line to be voluntarily strapped into a death trap. My rising panic must have been obvious because Ralrek laughed and Bilba snorted through his nose before covering it and trying to play it off like he hadn't. Nothing like having good friends.

Underneath the fading roar of the cart disappearing into the tunnel of light, came the chattering of excited demons all around me, sounding like a cluster of annoying fairies—sorry, they're annoying, the way they flit about, mess with you by putting bugs in your hair and flying away before you can swat them, and the such. The air of excitement changed in seconds, moving away from the light-hearted and carefree feeling to one edged with anxiety. More demons chattered, the noise grew to more than an irritant as they engaged in the mysterious conversation rippling down the line. Incubi slapped each other's shoulders and made dumb faces. Succubi put hands to mouths or rubbed their loved one's arms.

"What's going on?" Bilba said, facing forward and craning to see down the line. He had a better chance of doing that then I did. There were implings who were taller than my sixty-seven inches.

Ralrek stretched to look over the heads in the crowd.

This was more than fairies chattering. This was the intangible nervous excitement that raced through crowds whenever something was happening that fell outside the scope of daily life.

A lump formed in my throat as I risked stepping out of line to catch a clue. "Not sure, but be ready," I said, my hand slipping to Creed's knob as I extended my senses outward. In addition to now being super sensitive to noises and the visual bombardment of life in Hell, the past year, me and the magical halberd bounded more than ever before. Not only could I call it from greater distances, but Creed had somehow hooked me into my surroundings. Now, everything was brighter, louder, and more aromatic than ever before. It was a wonderful skill to have picked up and developed, at home, in the relative silence of my Old Towne apartment. But here, surrounded by thousands of Fivers—my Fifth Circle neighbors—it was a little much. Whatever energy surged through the crowd, it irritated my senses, sort of like the fizzle of a firework, just without the bang, boom, awww.

Suddenly, I wasn't as confident about my level of control, which rivaled adolescent implings and their nocturnal emissions when dreaming of pleasurable things.

"Is something happening, Zeke?" Ralrek moved closer to whisper. Proximity was another outcome of our shared challenge with the Council last year, reluctant as it still was. At least he appreciated my talents for a change.

I shook my head. "No one's conjuring."

"Then what's going on? Everyone is jittery. I'm jittery," Bilba asked, his eyes growing wider, the tips of his big ears turning pink.

"You're always jittery," Ralrek quipped, but his expression was lax, unfocused on picking on our friend and more on picking up clues to the pockets of conversation that were swelling amongst the waiting ride-goers.

I put my finger to my lips. "Listen, instead of blabbing over top of everyone and we might just learn."

Slow but undeterred, the ripple of excitement waved from

group to group, carrying the ominousness typical of big news. As the news traveled back, the roller coaster became less interesting.

"Humans," an old demon said, shaking his balding head.

"Overworld." A young succubus with a bad complexion cupped her hands around her mouth, shouting the message back, filling the role of the informed expert.

"I'm not shocked." This irritated response came from a short, stout mother who placed her hand on the top of the young red-headed impling clinging to her leg. "What do you expect from them?"

"Full-blown?" A thin incubus, brown skin cracking with age, grimaced.

"That's what they're saying," the know-it-all with the bad complexion nodded her head aggressively.

"When?" a succubus who appeared too young to be an adult but too old to be an impling held her hand to her mouth.

Word of whatever event everyone was talking about was getting closer, but I didn't feel like waiting. The group in front of us was making me nervous with their fidgeting to hear. Leaning closer to the incubus in front of me, I asked, "What's everyone talking about?"

"I don't know," he said with a sneer, pulling away from me. "Talk about minding your own business." He finished with a laugh to his friends, who looked at me as if I was the oddball.

Further ahead, someone shouted, "Oh, my Lucifer! Not again!"

"When will they learn? You'd think they'd be tired of fighting after the last one." The old, gray-haired demon shook his head again, like it was his own children making awful decisions.

"Wasn't the last one supposed to be the end of it?" another asked.

"The war to end all wars?" The gray-haired demon's wife laughed bitterly.

"Nah, there was another big one after that, remember?"

"Can't keep 'em straight. Dumb humans."

"Best hope we don't get involved," gray-hair said.

I couldn't take it anymore. Stepping out of line, ignoring Ralrek's tug on my sleeve and Bilba's questioning look, I walked a few groupings forward to where gray-hair was holding council.

"What's everyone talking about?" I said, interrupting the small group who looked me up and down in yo-yoing flicks of eyes. Patience was for those who had the privilege of peaceful lives.

Noone answered immediately.

"The humans," know-it-all said, leaning into the conversation.

I welcomed her desire to be the center of attention. "What about them?"

"Supposedly they've started another war," she replied in a prideful tone. Her eyes widened as if she expected me to understand some implied message.

The older male piped in. "Bet the Council will be convening to recruit soldiers."

"Soldiers?"

Know-it-all's eyes scrunched and her head jerked back. "Yes, soldiers," she cackled, like I was the idiot here. "Just like every time. To join the mortal armies?"

I knew that. Everyone did. Just a few decades ago we went through something similar when it seemed like the entire mortal realm wanted to destroy itself. When the dung hit the fan up there, we got called to arms. But I refused to intensify these localized conversations. When I didn't revel in her drama-weaving she turned her back. I returned to Bilba and Ralrek, neither of whom looked calm.

"War, Zeke," Bilba said. "Can you believe it?"

"How did you know?"

"We told him," the incubus who told me to bugger off said without making eye contact. "Wasn't as nosy as you. Seems like a nice lad."

Of course.

"They said there might be a draft. The old incubus up there said there's already talk of recruiting demons for the human armies," Ralrek said.

"I wonder what they pay," Bilba said.

I noticed he was wringing his hands. "The human army?"

He nodded. "Guys," he paused, looking around, "I'm short on coin. Like, bad. If the humans are at war and the Council needs volunteers ... well, would you volunteer if we could?"

"Volunteer? You're serious?" Ralrek said with a scoffing laugh, looking around at the groups in line around us as if he couldn't believe the question. His smile dropped when he faced Bilba again. "You are, aren't you?"

Bilba didn't look humored. He squared on me. "Zeke?"

My love and respect for him drove the truth; well, that and the fact we didn't have anything to worry about because we were speaking in the hypothetical. "You bet, bud. Plus, I could use the coin too."

"You're not getting enough hours at Dialphio's shop?" Ralrek asked. "You're always there, or at least, that's what you claim when we've invited you out to the clubs for some dancing."

I shook my head. Ralrek knew I hated clubs. And dancing. And dancing in clubs. But that wasn't it. "No, she's been great. But I'm still renting the Old Towne apartment and, with the hours I'm getting, I'm saving up to get my own place. I can't rent forever."

"Don't tell me you burned through everything the Council gave you?" Ralrek's eyes narrowed.

"First, don't forget, they didn't pay me for the Aries

"How did you know?"

"We told him," the incubus who told me to bugger off said without making eye contact. "Wasn't as nosy as you. Seems like a nice lad."

Of course.

"They said there might be a draft. The old incubus up there said there's already talk of recruiting demons for the human armies," Ralrek said.

"I wonder what they pay," Bilba said.

I noticed he was wringing his hands. "The human army?"

He nodded. "Guys," he paused, looking around, "I'm short on coin. Like, bad. If the humans are at war and the Council needs volunteers ... well, would you volunteer if we could?"

"Volunteer? You're serious?" Ralrek said with a scoffing laugh, looking around at the groups in line around us as if he couldn't believe the question. His smile dropped when he faced Bilba again. "You are, aren't you?"

Bilba didn't look humored. He squared on me. "Zeke?"

My love and respect for him drove the truth; well, that and the fact we didn't have anything to worry about because we were speaking in the hypothetical. "You bet, bud. Plus, I could use the coin too."

"You're not getting enough hours at Dialphio's shop?" Ralrek asked. "You're always there, or at least, that's what you claim when we've invited you out to the clubs for some dancing."

I shook my head. Ralrek knew I hated clubs. And dancing. And dancing in clubs. But that wasn't it. "No, she's been great. But I'm still renting the Old Towne apartment and, with the hours I'm getting, I'm saving up to get my own place. I can't rent forever."

"Don't tell me you burned through everything the Council gave you?" Ralrek's eyes narrowed.

"First, don't forget, they didn't pay me for the Aries

"The war to end all wars?" The gray-haired demon's wife laughed bitterly.

"Nah, there was another big one after that, remember?"

"Can't keep 'em straight. Dumb humans."

"Best hope we don't get involved," gray-hair said.

I couldn't take it anymore. Stepping out of line, ignoring Ralrek's tug on my sleeve and Bilba's questioning look, I walked a few groupings forward to where gray-hair was holding council.

"What's everyone talking about?" I said, interrupting the small group who looked me up and down in yo-yoing flicks of eyes. Patience was for those who had the privilege of peaceful lives.

Noone answered immediately.

"The humans," know-it-all said, leaning into the conversation.

I welcomed her desire to be the center of attention. "What about them?"

"Supposedly they've started another war," she replied in a prideful tone. Her eyes widened as if she expected me to understand some implied message.

The older male piped in. "Bet the Council will be convening to recruit soldiers."

"Soldiers?"

Know-it-all's eyes scrunched and her head jerked back. "Yes, soldiers," she cackled, like I was the idiot here. "Just like every time. To join the mortal armies?"

I knew that. Everyone did. Just a few decades ago we went through something similar when it seemed like the entire mortal realm wanted to destroy itself. When the dung hit the fan up there, we got called to arms. But I refused to intensify these localized conversations. When I didn't revel in her drama-weaving she turned her back. I returned to Bilba and Ralrek, neither of whom looked calm.

"War, Zeke," Bilba said. "Can you believe it?"

mission," I said with the wag of a finger. "And they don't 'give' us anything. We earn it."

Ralrek threw his head back. "Don't start. I know. I know. Yield. I yield already. That's not what I meant."

"Are you sure? A prison term might not have been enough for you to see the light. You're pretty thick sometimes," I said with a grin and wink.

"I'm confident you're not as dumb as I used to think you were." Ralrek shrugged. "If it wasn't for them giving us the assignments they have, I wouldn't have what I do. My situation isn't like yours. I don't have a family; well, not in the sense you both do. Your mother is an issue, Bilba, but at least you have your father. And Zeke, yours is a dick, but your mother is awesome. Until Torlan, the only hope I had for a different tomorrow came because of what the Council gave me."

"So he's got potential to be a serious thing?" Bilba asked.

"Yes, if I keep him around," Ralrek answered nonchalantly. "We aren't even close to thinking about that type of stuff yet. Heavens, we're not even exclusive yet."

I blew a huge exhale out, letting my lips flap as I looked up at the next coaster cart about to plummet toward the surface. "Well, it doesn't matter what any of us would do, because it's not going to happen. We don't even know if there is a war in the Overworld. It's all just hearsay from a bunch of carnival goers."

"Hey, I'm more than a 'goer,' I'm a carnival lover," Bilba protested good-naturedly. "And, why would so many demons be talking about it if it wasn't true?"

I gestured at know-it-all, who was still reveling in the Hellfire-light of attention. "Because demons feed off gossip." I put my hands up in playful surrender. "Look, let's just enjoy this death trap and get in enough rides so you break even. Tomorrow, we'll see what the news says. But tonight, let's have fun." I paused as another cart rocketed overhead, shooting into the open mouth of the tunnel at irresponsible speeds. I swallowed that stupid lump in my throat again. "As much as we can."

Watching the full cart of screamers disappear into that frightening white tunnel, I wondered if it was possible for any of us to do that now, for different reasons.